ALL THE WORLD'S A WONDER

Editor: Kelley Jo Burke
Cover art: Tania Wolk
Book and cover design: Tania Wolk, Third Wolf Studio
Printed and bound in Canada at Friesens, Altona, MB

The publisher gratefully acknowledges the support of Creative Saskatchewan, the Canada Council for the Arts and SK Arts.

Canada Council for the Arts
Conseil des Arts du Canada

Library and Archives Canada Cataloguing in Publication

Title: All the world's a wonder / Melia McClure.
Names: McClure, Melia, 1979- author.
Identifiers: Canadiana (print) 20220397295 | Canadiana (ebook) 20220397457
ISBN 9781989274798 (softcover)
ISBN 9781989274811 (HTML)
Classification: LCC PS8625.C5845 A75 2022 | DDC C813/.6—dc23

radiant press
Box 33128 Cathedral PO
Regina, SK S4T 7X2
info@radiantpress.ca
www.radiantpress.ca

If I love you, it must be because we shared, at some moment, the same imaginings, the same madness, the same stage.

Anaïs Nin

ALL THE WORLD'S A WONDER

MELIA McCLURE

ACT I
SCENE 1

Lights up. A hospital room with a window. The PLAYWRIGHT *sits in bed with a notebook open on her lap, writing. She stops, looks up, and mumbles, gesturing as though reciting lines. Then: a fever of scribbling. There is a knock at the door, but the woman keeps writing. The knock sounds again. The door opens. Enter the* DOCTOR.

DOCTOR

Good evening, dear. How are you feeling?

(The PLAYWRIGHT *is silent. Continues writing.*
He takes a step toward the bed.)

DOCTOR

I said: how are you feeling?

(She raises a hand: just a minute. He crosses his arms and stares at her.
She puts down her pen.)

PLAYWRIGHT

Don't call me dear. We're not married.
(smiles)
Yet.

DOCTOR

Very funny.

PLAYWRIGHT

Oh, come on, don't you have fantasies about your patients?

DOCTOR

No.

PLAYWRIGHT

I've read that psychiatrists are often disturbed individuals. They're just the silverbacks among crazy people.

DOCTOR

I'm boringly sane. And I don't work with crazy people. I work with people whose minds just need a little massage.

PLAYWRIGHT

Massage? So back to those fantasies you don't have. In my experience, male sexuality is pretty detached from the basic personality. And you look like a man to me. Therefore, I must surmise that at least occasionally you jerk off while thinking about a patient. I mean, we all need your *help* and all, and God knows that can be a turn-on.

DOCTOR

I see you're feeling better. What are you writing?

PLAYWRIGHT

I'm a playwright. It's safe to assume I'm writing a play.

DOCTOR

So you're back in fine form.

PLAYWRIGHT

Don't you see the glow upon my countenance? I could do a Got Milk? ad, for fuck's sake. Excuse my French. I tend to swear more when

I'm writing. I don't know why. Maybe part of my synaptic wiring wants to fuck when I'm being creative. I mean, say fuck.

(smiles)

I believe your kind calls that a Freudian slip.

(Beat)

DOCTOR

So what's your play about? I was reading about you. Your plays get good reviews. I've always admired people who can make stuff up.

PLAYWRIGHT

Anyone can make stuff up. It's getting paid for it that's the tricky part.

DOCTOR

You do get paid for it. That's pretty impressive.

PLAYWRIGHT

Thanks. My people keep your people in business.

DOCTOR

What do you mean?

PLAYWRIGHT

Artists. To create, one must first destroy. Shrinks get paid to sweep up the ashes. I get paid to be the phoenix.

DOCTOR

That sounds dramatic.

PLAYWRIGHT

Did I mention I'm a playwright? Drama is my stock-in-trade. You need more sleep.

DOCTOR

Excuse me?

PLAYWRIGHT

You're not sleeping. I can tell by your eyes. What's keeping you up at night?

DOCTOR

I'm supposed to ask the questions here.

PLAYWRIGHT

Where's the fun in that? I won't trust you if our intimacy is one-sided.

DOCTOR

Intimacy?

PLAYWRIGHT

Is there an echo in here? Yes, intimacy. A doctor-patient relationship is highly intimate. *(sighs)* I miss Dr. Cliff. He abandoned me.

DOCTOR

He didn't abandon you, he retired.

PLAYWRIGHT

Rule #1: Never let the truth stand in the way of a good story.

DOCTOR

Duly noted. So are you going to tell me what your play is about?

PLAYWRIGHT

That depends. Are you going to keep standing there? Awkward much? Pull up a chair.

(Beat)

DOCTOR

(sits) Okay. Fire away.

PLAYWRIGHT

An actress. It's set in the '20s. New York.

DOCTOR

So the play is about Maxine.

PLAYWRIGHT

Ah, you've read Cliff's notes.

DOCTOR

Yes. I know Maxine is one of your, uh, "muses"—

PLAYWRIGHT

She's been wanting to tell her story for ages. *Murders*. Well, actually, I wouldn't call them that. Tragic justice, more like. But on stage and off, timing is everything. I've put her off till now. But now the time is right.

DOCTOR

I don't have anything down about murders...

PLAYWRIGHT

Oh, sure you do.

DOCTOR

What? What are you implying?

PLAYWRIGHT

Ooh, touchy. Why would I be implying anything? We're just getting to know each other.

DOCTOR

Sorry, I didn't mean to snap at you.

PLAYWRIGHT

Don't let it happen again.

DOCTOR

Or what?

PLAYWRIGHT

Don't ask the question if you don't want the answer.

DOCTOR

Is that a threat? I can have you put back in the isolation room.

PLAYWRIGHT

Relax. Maybe you should pop a few of my pills, Doc. I'm feeling like a million bucks. You look like shit.

(Beat)

But I can make you feel better. I'll tell you about my play, and you tell me if you'd pay to see it.

Blackout

PLAYWRIGHT

MAXINE HAS BEEN BUGGING me for ages to write her story. But I didn't feel ready. Until now. You can't tell a story till you can taste the words. And even though it's her story, that doesn't mean she knows how to structure a play. It's still going to be a climb up a sheer cliff face, blindfolded and wearing stilettos, while characters shout barely audible instructions from the safety of terra firma.

Maxine's emails were getting downright abusive. Drama queen. I told her she was being a narcissist. She told me the narcissus is no less beautiful a flower for knowing it is so. Cheeky bitch.

Here's one of her latest emails:

from: maxinedoyle@playmail.com
to: rememberyourlines@playmail.com
date: September 9, 2013
subject: All my life's a play, and all the men and women merely players

Bonjour, my most divine Playwright,

You had better get writing. I want to know my story is on the stage. The repose of my soul depends upon it. God knows you will owe your career to me once my play is out there for all the world to see. You owe me your brilliance. I do not appreciate being put off. You're a writer, you should be able to write on command. I can act on command, though I admit I prefer to give the orders. I know you say that the world does not revolve around me, or some such nonsense, but the truth is that the world revolves around story, and I have a story to tell. I know how to pick my moments. I know when to buckle up my dancing shoes. I've never yet failed you. And so, my dear, you're not allowed to fail me. Far be it from me to say so, but I can ruin you if I so choose. Ruination is my stock-in-trade, as is success. I'm clever with sharp objects.

Oh, and by the by, here goes a non sequitur: I used your—what do you call it?—oh yes, your Visa card to purchase a few frocks. From my favourite vintage store, of course. I know you told me to go to that other shop, but I simply cannot abide what you say passes for a dress. Do be a doll and say you don't mind. I was feeling terribly blue and you drank all the scotch, naughty thing.

Love, Maxine

So you see, what choice do I have? My muse, the one showing up the most these days, is tightening the noose. I just pray she won't make me do something terrible. Other than racking up my credit cards. I hate being at the mercy of a capricious temperament like hers.

I'm so glad my last muses haven't emailed lately. I can't cope with a Greek chorus. Since I finished my last play, they seem to have skedaddled. Looking, no doubt, for another playwright to harass. Having muses is easier, I guess, than having husbands. Maybe I'm wrong about that, I've never been married. At some point muses disappear, to be replaced by others. Just like husbands. But people who have been married don't have successful plays to show for their trouble. So I am the lucky one.

Maxine has been with me a long time. Longer than the others. She drives me crazy on a regular basis, but I must admit that her ideas are brilliant enough to justify the pain she inflicts.

I get up from my computer, where I've been staring at the screen instead of spinning thoughts into gold, as I'd promised myself I would do, and go to the kitchen window. If I'm going to stare at a square, I would rather have one with a view. Far below me, cars beetle along in the twilight, soothing, dumb with purpose. A vast expanse of city will soon prick the fallen curtain, bleed starry light. Dorothy Parker once wrote, "...as only New Yorkers know, if you can get through the twilight, you'll live through the night." I'm not so sure. Maxine says you find out what a city is made of after dark. She says you find out what *people* are made of after dark. Spoken like a true creature of the stage. I hope she doesn't visit me tonight. I need my sleep.

A few nights ago my next-door neighbour complained about the noise. Maxine was here rehearsing *As You Like It*, and she decided her voice wasn't up to snuff and commenced operatic vocal exercises. (I told her to quit smoking. She told me to mind my potatoes. Just watch, I'll end up with muse-induced lung cancer.) The only reason I know about this is she emailed me, ranting about my offensive neighbour and his gall in disrupting her hallowed creative process. He just moved in, so I've never met him. If I run into him in the hall, I'll have to pretend I'm Maxine.

I wonder if Cosette is dropping by tonight. My health insurance pays her to check up on me, make sure I've got food and haven't done anything that places me beyond redemption. Sometimes she drops in unannounced on her days off, I'm assuming because she's charmed by my winning personality, and maybe also because I always keep champagne in the fridge in tribute to Sarah Bernhardt's alligator, Ali-Gaga, who died from drinking too much of it.

Cosette isn't French. Her mother was obsessed with *Les Mis*.

Maxine and Cosette get along famously. Probably because Cosette is a fabulous cook and willing to indulge Maxine, who considers herself an epicure. From what Cosette tells me, Maxine can be downright bossy in the kitchen, which doesn't surprise me, except that Maxine couldn't cook to stave off certain death. But she knows what she likes, oh my, does she ever. For an actress, she doesn't worry much about her weight. She says childhood deprivation has ensured a whippet body. And I think women of the stage, and especially ones from days of yore, don't go in for starvation aesthetics.

I turn from the window and check the time. Past five o'clock. The Green Hour is upon us and I'm missing out. I don't have absinthe; champagne will have to do.

On each of my kitchen cupboards and drawers I have signs pasted so I won't forget what's inside. My signs were created in the name of practicality, but even pragmatism (God, I despise that word), with a little paint, can be beautiful. My kitchen looks like a gallery exhibit: "Utensil Still Life: The Magic of the Mundane." I can't stand the mundane unless it's juiced with a little magic.

There is only one flute in my champagne cupboard. I can't think where the others have gone. Damn. My muses seem to remember everything, and I don't envy them that, except when the gaps in my head are getting in the way of, say, Happy Hour. Otherwise, forgetting is essential to surviving, and fictionalizing is essential to thriving. You see, I have it all worked out.

Well, I only need one flute at the moment. If Cosette shows up, she'll have to fend for herself. I pull the bottle out of the fridge and note the lack of food. I haven't the faintest clue when I last went grocery shopping. Maybe Cosette is on vacation? Can't recall. Maxine won't buy groceries. She'll go to a restaurant. That little cow spends my money like a sailor on shore leave. Don't tell her I called her a little cow. She would find a way to get back at me, and it wouldn't be pretty. Thank God my first five plays were hits. Otherwise I'd be, well, dead, I suppose. Of course, death could be darling, who the hell knows?

I pop and pour, realizing with the flush of the first sip that I've been weary. But no longer! As Sarah Bernhardt reminds us, "The main thing is willpower, sustained by an excellent champagne."

Back at the window the only face I see is the moon's, pockmarked and marmoreal, a god who once roughed it, whose beauty warns of tragedy. I toast the moon because there's nobody else here. And if my agent calls and asks if I'm drinking alone, I can say no with a lily-white conscience. Clearly I am untroubled by imbibing in solitude, but he seems to find me a sad case. Perhaps that's why he drinks most of the bottle whenever he's here—he thinks he's saving me from myself.

That man can drink all my champagne any day he wants. Indeed, he has saved me more times than I care to admit.

Half the bottle is gone and I can't think how that happened. Since the moon is my only companion, I cast blame skyward. The dearth of edibles in my fridge makes me wonder when I last ate. It can't have been recently, because I'm dizzy. I should call Cosette, ask if she would mind bringing me a nibble. Today is not an outside day. I'd rather stay in my own little orbit, like the moon.

I wander back to my computer. I have the opening pages of Maxine's play, or the play about Maxine, I should say, and I hope she'll be satisfied. She's a rather harsh critic. Granted, it *is* her story, and naturally she envisions herself playing herself, so she is picky as hell about getting the voice right. But I know her voice cold. Very few people can hear or see themselves with any accuracy. Nor do they want to.

Whenever she again chooses to grace me with her presence, the first thing she'll do is check to see if I've started the play. And then she'll send me an email lobbing opinion grenades through cyberspace, which is all anyone does anymore. God, actors. They always have notes. And always about making their own parts better.

I turn off the computer. The champagne has made me too dizzy to keep writing. And while I can't shut Maxine out, I'd like to pretend to for a little while. I miss the early days, when she first showed up, before she learned how to use the computer. We'd exchange handwritten notes. She has the most beautiful handwriting. True, she bossed me around and gave me grief even when she was using a pen, but she couldn't read letters from my other muses because I hid them. I didn't need them all talking to each other behind my back.

But now they all use email. Maxine reads everything in my account. She forced me to give up my password by threatening to withhold her most scintillating ideas. Whatever happened to privacy? Everyone can always get to you.

My last play nearly killed me, it had such a big cast. Though I did find Dr. Cliff's baffled face, during our psych consults, amusing. My relief at only dealing with Maxine at the moment knows no bounds. But then again, she's a full production stuffed into one drop-waist dress, so it would be silly to let my anxiety take a vacation. I doubt there is another playwright on the planet who lives the job as fully, and I am well aware of the bucket of catastrophe above my head, rocking on piano wire.

To the red velvet sofa, huge and enveloping, although it looks mortifyingly like something Hugh Hefner would wear. But I took one look at it, sitting in a used-furniture store window, and knew nothing really bad could happen to me there. Every playwright needs upholstered ramparts. Sometimes I sleep on it when I'm working late and decide the bedroom is too many steps away. It's the closest I get to camping. Lately I've been fighting a perverse notion to put a bunch of stuffed animals on it and play *Life of Pi*. Maxine hates it and has sent me many an email about tossing it. I'm afraid she'll take a knife to it one day and I'll return to find red wounds gaping with clouds of stuffing. (But she would be sorry if she did that. I would make her sorry.) Other muses have quite adored it, but Maxine fancies her tastes more elevated than most. She can be an annoying bitch, but annoying bitches sometimes say true things, the things other people wish they could say. In the case of my sofa, though, she is dead wrong.

As I lie here the ceiling starts to spin, a modern art I-paint-with-one-colour kaleidoscopic effect that pleases me. Outside, New York puts on a cacophonous show, three sirens signalling the climax of a dissonant sonata. How does anyone sleep in silence? Even when it's not an outside day, I still like to know the world is not yet killed.

Maxine likes to go out. But she complains bitterly about how the city has changed, about how uncouth New Yorkers are. *Of course it's changed,* I wrote in my last email to her. *It's not 1925 anymore.* I find it hard to believe New Yorkers were teeming with couth in any decade. Nostalgia is a disease for which there is no cure and Maxine, though she would be loath to admit suffering an affliction so common, has quite a case. The world grows ugly when forced to compete with the wistful backward glance.

I had a muse who was a Victorian man from London. He complained too, in many an outraged email, about New York: The food is grim, no proper cuppa, the women talk like men. He was a royal pain in the arse. He was only a minor character in my play, but he was a witness to the main events and the one who told me the story. That play may win a prize (Move over, Tracy Letts! Step aside, Amy Herzog!), so really, I owe him—Mr. Chipley—a thousand steak-and-kidney pies. I had to order in and eat a pile of those revolting concoctions to keep him satisfied while we were writing. Thank God when the muses are here I don't remember anything. As far as I'm concerned, no quease-inducing British food ever breached my lips.

My Victorian play turns on the pivot of murder. I seem to be a conduit of violent demise these days. Maybe that's why, more than ever, I've been clinging to my overstuffed sofa as though plush is the last defence against the predators that show up in my living room. Mr. Chipley hated the couch too. One of the few things he and Maxine would agree on.

Now I'm in the kitchen and I have no idea how I got here. I'm assuming I walked across the living room like a normal person, but I don't remember doing it. Maxine may have hidden food, and I intend to find it. I know, I know, I live in New York City, I could have anything delivered. But the only two people in the world I could stomach talking to right now are Cosette and Sam, my agent and inviolable centre, and I don't want to bother either of them because I suspect I do that too much. Today is not an outside day, and so I cannot talk to the delivery man who would bring the pizza if I ordered one. Don't ask me. You figure it out.

Cosette started a garden of herbs on my windowsill. She said it's impossible to starve if you have dill in the house. I'm sure I could prove her wrong. I pull a bit and chew, decide chlorophyll and bubbly could date but never marry.

Something looks different about this kitchen. After a moment, I see what it is: one of Modigliani's women is staring at me from atop a cabinet, leaning against a wall. I have three prints of Modi's women and Maxine and I keep moving them around the apartment, according to our conflicting whims. But I would never put his work way up there, where it's not likely to be noticed. That's a waste of nudity.

When I climb onto the counter and lift the painting down I find dinner: a tin of caviar and a box of unsalted crackers, with a note pinned to the tin that reads *If you can find me, you can eat me. Love, Maxine.* It's unclear whether the note is for me or for Maxine, since she likes to delight herself with letters and gifts from herself, but what is clear is that my muse has just averted a famine in the middle of Manhattan.

I stick the caviar in the freezer and set the oven timer for ten minutes. I'm not a caviar connoisseur like Maxine, and I'm famished, but I'm not so uncivilized as to eat room-temperature fish eggs. Instead I stuff four crackers in my mouth.

I wish Maxine were sitting here. She's lonely, though she would never admit it. But it's not as if we could converse with each other. I guess these days everyone emails more than they talk, so we're not much different from all the rest. I don't know whether that's depressing or reassuring. Probably the former, so I top up my flute.

With two minutes left on the timer, I pull the caviar out of the freezer and yank open the drawer that has my still life of spoons taped to it, and search for the little ceramic spoon set that Maxine insisted I buy.

from: maxinedoyle@playmail.com
to: rememberyourlines@playmail.com

date: January 1, 2011
subject: How to eat caviar

Darling,

I had to eat caviar with my fingers last night, and it is all your fault. Must I explain everything? You cannot handle caviar with a metal spoon as it ruins the taste. One may as well swallow a clot of tiny metallic bombs. You must buy ceramic spoons. I would do it myself but I am due at a rehearsal I'm holding for myself. And really, I don't care to shop for household sundries. You should get a woman in to help you, they're not expensive.

Happy New Year!

Love, Maxine

That was back when I was just getting to know her. Or rather, the people I know were just getting to know her. She showed up quite suddenly—they always do—when I went to see Sam about a production of one of my plays being mounted at a small theatre in London. He was mad because I was late and was probably pacing as he does when he's annoyed, and then Maxine made an entrance. They were both in a terrible state of confusion, he less so because he's met the other muses. Poor Maxine, as he told it, was like a hysterical bird, a spray of plumage and wounded sparrow eyes. He said the scene would have made a glorious opening to a play. Ah, that it would. She has been with me ever since, sometimes fading into the background for weeks at a time, surging to the fore when I cried out for a fresh editorial voice, or when she felt like buying a bunch of "glad rags" I don't need and issuing flowery handwritten complaints. (At the time, she was afraid of the computer). But now she is where she belongs, in the starring role, insisting that the stage is ready for her story. I wonder if, when I've finished writing her play, her house will go dark and the lights will come up on a new muse. I hope so. If no one shows up, it'll mean I've got writer's block, I suppose. Or I've been medicated into oblivion. Regardless, Maxine, for all her irritating, self-important histrionics, will be missed.

The spoons are in a little case lined with purple velvet. I found them and their plush home at a Jewish thrift shop the day after I got the caviar-complaint missive. It pays to keep my muses happy. Before Maxine, I'd never had a muse who was an actor. True to expectations, she is the most demanding of the lot. She also has the best ear for dialogue and knows as well as I know what will and will not work on stage. I've never written an autobiographical play with someone who sees herself starring in the production. Maxine is invested in a way that the other muses could not have been. This may seem, on the surface, a good thing, a recipe for a play that will keep me in bubbly and a New York dwelling. But I think a muse as imperious as Maxine could spell trouble. She has told me this will be her last star turn, and that she expects perfection. Sam told me she seems desperate, unsettlingly incandescent with some unspoken need. It scares me. She scares me. I have always had a knack for loving those of whom I am afraid. That tendency, like my plays, has rarely dropped the curtain on a happy ending.

Tonight has a happy ending, though, in the form of crackers and caviar. I move my feast to the sofa, along with the near-empty bottle. Maxine is going to show up soon, and I'm nervous about what she'll say. This afternoon I emailed her the first scene of the play. I hate people reading my work as I'm doing it, but she gave me no choice. I hope she doesn't trample all over it. The beginning of the process is delicate, easily murdered by relentless opinions. I know it's her story and all, but I wish she trusted me more.

For tonight, I'll celebrate the end of hunger, call it a grand finale, and let the curtain fall.

MAXINE

HOW I WISH she would get rid of this appalling sofa. Her taste in furniture is nothing to write home about, not that I anymore have a home to write to. Or ever did. She emailed me some silly bunk about feeling safe on this sofa, and I can't think why she feels this way. How can one feel safe when one's senses are assaulted by an overfed monstrosity of rouge velvet?

"*Ee*-mailed." What a strange word. I kept pronouncing it "*ehm*-ailed" until Sam corrected me. Such a darling man. She really should marry him, even though he's a fairy. (Oh dear, I'm not supposed to call him what he is. I can't recall why. My playwright has some frightfully odd ideas.) There are many examples of successful lavender marriages. If she doesn't marry Sam, I don't think she's got much hope. Perhaps it is better this way, though, her curled up on this homely sofa reciting dialogue to herself. I think she might have a difficult time explaining her tendencies to prospective suitors. But really, isn't that always the case? Does anyone really know who they trod the middle aisle with? God knows my arrangement was no testament to romantic bliss. But I aspired to be an actress more than I aspired to be happily coupled, so I suppose I can't really complain. Now what point was I trying to make? Oh yes, she is to stay single. At least as long as she is writing my play. I am in the director's chair now, and I prohibit all distractions. My, I quite fancy the view from here. I don't know why it didn't occur to me to direct anything until now. I rather like being the voice of God. Oh, that's right, Robert would have put a stop to such ambitions. What man wants to be in the shadow of God Herself?

Perhaps it is just as well. I like making faces. I was born to do it. I just pray I don't end up wearing them.

I really must get out of this oppressive apartment. I miss my own desperately. Here I am, back to sacrificing for my art. Well, I suppose it's not really so bad in this place, it's just not my style. Those little still-life paintings she makes: they are an attractive convenience, I'll give her that. They make it awfully easy to find things, even though there is no one to help me except that sweet Cosette every now and again. My playwright's not bad with a brush, I must say. My mother was a watercolourist and for some reason these paintings make me think of her, which is odd since there isn't a watercolour in the bunch. I haven't thought of her for a long time.

I am going in the bedroom now to change. I can't go out in these wretched clothes. The trousers—a woman in trousers, imagine!—are tight as the day is long, and this blouse looks like a camisole. Indeed, I think it *is* a camisole. New York seems to have been overtaken by people running around in their undergarments.

I bought myself a stunning walnut wardrobe. Well really, I bought it for us; but alas, she doesn't seem to want to use it. Fine with me, I prefer not to share. Anyway, she wasn't grateful, far from it. She sent me a nasty message in which she ranted about the price, and insisted it was crowding the bedroom. I very calmly told her that I wasn't about to hang my dresses in that explosion of ugliness she calls a closet, and that I was thinking, as always, of both of us. She is a good writer, but she has no sense of the art of dressing at all.

I strip off some of the ugly clothing in question and open my lovely wardrobe which, I neglected to mention, is inlaid with mother-of-pearl. It reminds me a little of the one I have in my own abode, probably a bad thing, come to think of it, as I am so homesick I could cry. But oh, what a charming collection of frocks herein! They cost a mint but I've told my playwright in no uncertain terms: if she wants my story, she must keep me suitably attired. I can't work while looking a freak.

I think it's warm outside. I have trouble keeping track of the weather. Or perhaps it is more accurate to say I have trouble keeping track of the season, the date on the calendar. I've learned how to use that thing she calls a television, and according to the rather dashing newsman I saw only moments before I started talking to you, it is a pleasant September day in New York City, the oppressive sultriness and lingering smell of fermenting trash mostly dissipated. I must say I haven't fallen in love with television; it gives me a headache and I can't find my favourite headache powder anywhere, not for any lack of searching druggists up and down Manhattan. Television seems full of strange people doing strange things while looking strange. I am all for surrealism, but I fail to see the point of most of what I have seen on that box. How I miss my Radiola Grand.

Don't tell her I said this: I am hoping against hope she listens to my instructions and writes at a galloping pace, because I am unhappy here and want to leave. No one can say I don't suffer for my art. True, I haven't the foggiest idea where I might go next. I no longer have a home, but that does not mean I can stay in this cramped apartment. There really isn't room for two. I am accustomed to having my own boudoir, my own vanity, my own everything. Some women aren't cut out to share. At least I am directing this play. A director, though, should be staying at The Plaza. Hell, even if I weren't directing, I am a damn good actress and good actresses should be treated with kid gloves. I haven't roughed it since I was a kid.

I am being dramatic, I know. This apartment isn't rough, it's just foreign; I don't recognize myself in anything. So I'll just pretend I'm playing a role. I am Maxine the Muse. This apartment is a stage, everything in it a prop. The faint sound of applause rings ever in my ears.

Now back to the weather, and hence, my choice of attire. Did I say it was warm? I have dreadful trouble keeping track of my line of thought. Robert blames the gin. I open the bedroom window and wave my arm outside. Yes, warm, and that scent is in the air, that sweetly burnt scent of coming autumn. A deepening that makes sadness seem delicious. What a lie. Even the seasons are out to get us. Robert says cynicism is unattractive in a woman. Robert is an idiot.

Oh Maxine, you are getting off topic. What was the topic? Oh yes, what to wear so I can break free of this stuffy apartment. Jewellery first, an oyster-fruit necklace and drop earrings, and then I choose a simple blue day dress which—wait for it—I shall top with a lightweight overcoat, black and white, Egyptian-themed with hieroglyphs 'round the cuffs and King Tut's head in regal splendour on the back, his eyes staring down anyone who walks behind me. I have learned the hard way: I need eyes on my back if I am to walk the streets of New York and survive. But now, thanks to my playwright—if I can direct her with an iron hand—my story will survive, and at a certain point that is all that really matters.

I look through her shoe collection to see if she has any I like better than mine. We wear the same size. She really should go shopping. Most of her shoes look like men's, or else like lethal weapons. I shall stay with my cunning little heels, thank you. Why am I feeling so anxious? I'm trembling like a goddamn leaf; it's pathetic. Oh. Of course. It's afternoon by that clock there beside the bed and I haven't had a gasper. Dressing was distracting me, but now I realize I feel like hell. I've got a headache, which probably means no java. It's a wonder I'm alive at all.

There is a full-length mirror I must avail myself of before I go in search of sustenance. It's a beauty, ornate, gilded, just like the glass I had in my lavish nest. I haunted quite a few shops before I found the right one. Prior to my appearance, there was no mirror in this bedroom. I protested and she sent me a silly message about not wanting to watch the deterioration. About her doctor having enough to contend with, without me purchasing a melancholia-inducing looking-glass. I do hope she sorts out her head troubles, poor dear. I simply couldn't do without a mirror of proper size. I might forget who I am.

My mirror reveals me wearing makeup, but I can't remember applying any. It's strangely done, unfashionable. I must not have been myself when I put it on. Fix it I must, but first, I may just faint if I don't have a gasper and quite possibly some food as well. I pray she didn't leave me with an empty apartment.

To the kitchen I cross, and it doesn't seem promising. There is a frighteningly shiny contraption she calls an "espresso machine," but I don't know how to use it, so java will have to wait. Beside it, an empty bottle of champagne is, I hope, evidence that she passed a productive night of Ibsen-like genius. I open the icebox to see if there is giggle water to spare. Alas, we shall have to replenish the essentials. Put that on your list, Maxine. Do I have a list? You bet I do. I shall organize my writer's life exactly as I want it. I am not giving up my story unless conditions are right.

Now: food. I'm a lousy cook, as Robert would attest. A girl can't be good at everything, and he didn't choose me for my apron strings. God, I figure, invented restaurants for a reason, and I'm it. But at this moment, I can't delay for the white-tablecloth treatment. Starvation and a lack of cigarettes is taking hold. It is possible I've hidden treats around this abode by which to delight myself and ensure my survival. I don't know whether I succeed at hiding anything on her, but I dislike sharing, so I'm willing to try. I have told her in no uncertain terms that she is only to use things of mine that I have expressly agreed to share, but you can't trust writers, they lie. Then again, actresses lie too. Only to capture the heart of the audience, of course.

The other trouble is, I have a demon of a time remembering where I've hidden things. You would think in such a little place there would be a dearth of hiding spots, but my creativity knows no bounds. I am a victim of my own ingenuity, really; my memory can't keep up. If my playwright would only keep the icebox filled, I wouldn't have to struggle so. Doesn't she pay people for that? Cosette, for example? Well, I can only but speak from my own experience: in the modern world of the middle '20s, good help is hard to come by. Perhaps for her as well. She and I, we are both alone in this world.

At least she hasn't moved Modi's paintings. Every time I get things set just as I wish them to be, she undoes all my work. Playwrights are used to being alone, doing whatever they want. Unlike thespians, who have to function in a company. I started at the bottom, you know; I learned to compromise. But I can't expect her to understand hardship—I must be gallant of spirit and fucking Christ-like, pardon my salty language. Where was I? Oh yes, the paintings. It's mostly her own artistic muckings she has scattered about this place, and they're not hideous, to give her her due. I love Modi's work, though. Such a tragic case. A poet friend of Robert's met him while wandering the Continent. Brought Robert three of the great man's paintings, which this stingy poet got by buying the artist steak tartare and crème brûlée in Montmartre. Said you could sense the doom clinging to Modi like a cloak, a tremulousness like a new lover, so cursed was he with genius. At the moment his genius may be hiding my caviar. I climb up beside the sink to reach my favourite nude on the cabinet above, the eyes of which are telling me there may be fish eggs behind the pubis. Why else would the painting be up there, unless it was due to one of my inspirations of obfuscation?

Nothing. Damn her. She ate one of my few happinesses in this life. Goddamn, I'm going to break my neck climbing all over the place. There must be more. I know there's more. I survived a girlhood of destitution; I know enough to hide food in more places than one. Let's see. Modi's other two women are safe on the walls. Where would she never look? Oh. My brain must be going soft as custard. The wardrobe she resents me buying—I bet she hasn't been in there of late.

The wind's kicked up. I left the bedroom window open and papers are flying off the night stand. They're not my play, so I can't say I much care about the mess. Indeed, I don't much care about anything at the moment—I feel faint. Ah yes, who doesn't want a wardrobe with a secret drawer? Herein lies a tin of caviar, a box of unsalted crackers, and a tin of roasted nuts. Some salmon mousse would be nice too, but one cannot always demand the earth. I've even included my ceramic spoon set—I bought two of them, but she doesn't know that yet. A feast in bed is precisely what I deserve. Don't ask why; I just do. And don't ask why I am living with a writer who rarely has any food in the house except when Cosette fills the larder, only to have it promptly emptied before I can get to it. I suspect Mr. Chipley is still hanging about now and again, he always was a robust eater. God, Maxine, you know how to pick 'em—playwrights, that is. She's got talent, is why. Talent excuses a fair number of faults, though not everything, as I have come to learn. I used to think it was only the artist who suffered, and maybe their spouse, but not the muse. No role is without its agonies, I suppose.

I always did like playing tragedies best. Comedy seems like monkeys dancing; desperation in drama is more attractive.

Half the box of crackers has disappeared. Fresh caviar is ever so much better than this tinned stuff, and I do not recommend consuming caviar at room temperature, but it was either warm eggs or falling to the floor in a dead faint. One must accept resuscitation in the form in which it comes.

There were no gaspers in the secret drawer. A flaw in my contingency plan, apparently. I'll have to fetch some on my sashay to Broadway. It's been a long time since I've had to run errands. This city has become so petrifying overnight that every outing presents a veritable gauntlet. But I am an actress, and thespians are children who can survive anything, and most already have.

Perhaps the rush of sustenance is turning my brain, or perhaps it is the warm breeze coming through the window and the sound of rustling papers, but I am struck by a feeling which might be happiness, and it is very disconcerting considering the circumstances. Sometimes that's all we have, isn't it? A feeling resembling happiness on a warm day in New York with the scent of autumn coming on. I should be in dress rehearsal now, about to open. I should be gracing the stage, alive, born anew every night, meeting myself as if for the first time. I shall have to settle for this apartment as my stage, and my playwright shall have to show myself to me.

The tins are empty, the crackers gone. A bit of water, and I will have the strength to face the day. But first I must just lie here for a moment, wrapped in a most luxurious furry blanket—I didn't buy this one, I must give her credit—and let the sun lie beside me. It's comforting, you know, a beautiful blanket, to one who was born on the wrong side of it.

Get up, Maxine, wallowing is bad for the complexion. Weak people wallow. Gaspers. Coffee. Broadway. In that order. Onward we go.

A used glass—not used by me—in the kitchen sink still holds an inch of champagne. How could I have missed this nearly dead soldier? I drink it, flat as it is, and feel more ready to face the world beyond these walls. I can't think where I put my keys, though, and this could be a problem. My damn playwright is always stealing my set.

I go back to the bedroom and crawl along the floor—looking at the world from a different height can yield up new vistas. Sure enough, I find her handbag under the bed. What a place for it! Perhaps she got half-seas over and had a cake-eater up here for a party and then some. If she was indeed fraternizing with a snuggle pup, she better damn well tell me about it. I like to know my onions, you know what I mean? Ah, she seems the type all work and no play, but you never can be sure.

What I am certain of is that now I got the green stuff, and a plastic card called Visa, you can use it everywhere, did you know that? Such a convenience. It's shocking how modern the world is getting. There are two sets of keys in her purse—I told you she steals mine incessantly. As if she could really keep me here like a prisoner. But usually she hides them somewhere other than her purse, which is not a hiding place at all. I think she's still trying to size me up. I like to imagine I'm more difficult to control than her other muses. I'm not some dumb Dora she can push around. Don't forget who holds the cards.

I transfer the goods, which include a tube of scarlet lipstick, into my little white beaded handbag. Now, as Robert would say in a vain attempt at youth, "Let's blouse!"

As I open the front door, excitement finds me. I am off to my beloved theatre, and everything will soon be right with the world.

But I open the door at the wrong moment. A man is coming out of the apartment across the way, and he glares at me. Glares daggers. Do you see what I mean about the couth in this city? Couth has gone the way of all flesh. He looks familiar, and I know I dislike him, but our history is sitting at the edge of my memory, teetering just out of sight. I have terrible gaps in my memory, but I never forget my lines. Scientists may puzzle over me when I am gone.

"You again," he says. "Next time I'll call the cops."

"Police? Why in heaven's name would you call the law? What's happened?"

"Are you fuckin' nuts? I told you: I'm not puttin' up with your racket no more. Some people gotta sleep."

He has a most unpleasant Bronx accent.

"Racket? Sir, I have no idea what you're on about. I too need my beauty rest."

"Fuck you. Don't play dumb with me. You kept me up half the night, all these voices and singin' and weird sounds. A real loud-ass party."

I'm hot all over, hot with rage, and then cold, two currents burning and icing my nerves, and my hands twitch, longing for something I once carried. Still, I am oh-so-dignified until I'm not.

"I am not in the habit of hosting parties at this address. I did all the time when I lived in my beloved nest, but now I'm strictly working. You must be hearing things. Perhaps you should seek a doctor's counsel."

His fat face is turning red in splotches, eyes popping strangulation-style. What the demon is his name? Something nondescript. Jack?

"Lady, yer the one needs a doctuh. What the hell you doin' in there? Whatevuh it is, keep it down or I'm callin' the noise police."

We've had this conversation before. Now it all steps into the limelight. He's the mac who pounded on the door last time I was rehearsing.

"I'm a stage actress. I perform at night. One becomes accustomed to keeping late hours. The muse doesn't live by the clock. Do you frequent the theatre?"

I already know the answer to that question. I can spot a rube a mile away.

"Look, I don't give a shit who you are. Just keep it down awready. A little consideration, that's all I'm askin'."

He says "axin'," which fills my snobbish self with glee. He doesn't scare me.

"I have great consideration for everyone, most of all for my art, which is a living, breathing being unto itself. Perhaps you'd like to see me perform one of Hamlet's soliloquies. Sarah Bernhardt played the role with great success."

He stares at me with his buggy eyes and shakes his head.

"There's room in the nuthouse. Fuckin' actors."

He turns and lumbers down the hall, doesn't look back. I want to scream obscenities, but—well, he frightens me just a bit, I'll admit it. He's built like a baby grand. I might be able to land one in the kisser, though only if he were lying on the floor semiconscious.

So I stand here shaking, taking big gulps of air and softly chanting "Fuck you, fuck you, fuck you."

Damned if I would ever let him see my Hamlet.

DOCTOR

MY HOOKER JUST LEFT and I'm looking for scotch to disinfect my mouth. I don't usually have those women in my home—I don't want them touching my stuff or stealing. I'd prefer to meet in a hotel. But I had an itch tonight and, well, Kasey-With-a-K—"*Enchantée*"—I am pleased to meet you too.

Where the hell did I put that bottle? Was trying for a dry spell. Don't know why. Maybe I could channel Hippocrates if I laid off the sauce. Not that I'm an alcoholic. I was just drinking alone more than psychiatrists deem wise.

Fuck psychiatry.

I'm agnostic, but if I weren't I guess this would be the time to pray not to end up like I heard my father did, drooling, mindless, a skin-and-bones obsolescence.

Fuck prayer, let's drink.

I fill the tumbler with four fingers of scotch—I have slim fingers.

The clock says 2 AM. I've got my bedroom window open. September warmth is gone, killed by a chill wind. I stand in the window and stare out at the lights, drinking, feeling like a Leonard Cohen poem. I should be snoring after sex, like most men, but sex with a hooker keeps me on edge. "Escort" is the more polite term. However, we're keeping this between us, and I hate euphemisms. Only the weak need to euphemize life. Shrinks are forced to speak in platitudes all day long to avoid upsetting the disassembly line of broken toys that streams past. If I am to survive I have to say it like it is whenever possible, which means whenever I'm not at work. No wonder I'm so goddamn tired all the time. I'm paid to make ineffectual conversation with hopeless cases. The meds are the only thing that make much of a dent in any of them. I can't be one of those shrinks who deal in hope—I've gotta call hopeless when I see it. And I see it all the time.

Just between you and me, I think psychiatry is kinda bullshit.

I know how to play the part, though, and I think I do a pretty decent job. I was in the drama club in high school. Girls like actors. And I figured *Death of a Salesman* was easier than making the football team. Girls like musicians even more, but I can't sing and my father had my drum set hauled away.

Still, I'm tops at pretending to heal the world. (As you may have already concluded, I am not Hippocrates.)

I do, however, have leftover Greek food in my fridge. It doesn't go with scotch, but Kasey-With-a-K worked up my appetite and I don't feel like ordering pizza and feeling badly for the windblown Mexican who delivers it. Middle-of-the-night loneliness shouldn't be made worse by nonessential food-ordering. Just a little tip from your friendly neighbourhood psychiatrist.

When I get to the fridge, my glass is empty. What the hell. Scotch goes well with the taste of a woman. Let's pour another couple of fingers, shall we? Savour the combination before I ruin it with leftover moussaka.

I eat Greek food once a month, a sad sort of ritual. Stuff my face with moussaka and reminisce about Mediterranean wanderings, after I dropped out of med school, a water-wrinkled copy of *The Colossus of Maroussi* in hand, trying to retrace Henry Miller's footsteps. *"Don't expect me to be sane anymore.... I feel murderous, suicidal."*

I had not yet met my Anais.

There is a certain light in Greece like no other. Now, all these years later, it mixes with the blinding light of nostalgia and the bronze liquid light I slide back and forth in my tumbler. Reminiscing is the most pathetic pastime known to man. If my younger self had known I would one day become a man who eats Greek food in the crevice of night because it tastes vaguely of happiness, I would have drowned myself in a blue lagoon. And I would never have seen her, the curve of that shoulder, the bare back traced with tan lines, the dark head that turned and knew which eyes were watching her. Freeze. Freeze it there. This is my nostalgia show, so I get to pause it wherever I want.

Time to break out the moussaka. The sex and scotch have me on a ledge. Good thing my job supplies me with free pills.

I'm not a depressive—I treat depressives. I fix broken toys or I have them locked away till they die. Very few must be kept in the closet. Most can be tinkered with and made to light up again, at least for a while.

There. Eggplant as good as new. Almost. A nice retsina would help cover the warmed-overness, but it's 3 AM and something's gotta give.

Anais could cook anything. A good talent for a woman to have. Every man ever born agrees with me. I never learned to cook because I'd rather a woman cook for me. Gender-neutral is gender-neutered. Another little tip from your friendly neighbourhood psychiatrist. You're welcome. I may not be your first choice for relationship advice, but I have a piece of paper that says I'm qualified, so how wrong can I be? I don't know if any of my advice has directly resulted in a happy marriage; unlike *eHarmony*, I don't keep track.

Good, I'm starting to get tired. Full, tipsy, the taste of Kasey long gone. I'm an insomniac. Alcohol works better than sleeping pills. Or maybe not better, I just trust it more. I don't want to pop Ambien and end up sleep-driving, or worse, committing a sleep-murder. I'd prefer to let scotch nurse me into a pleasant, non-murderous stupor.

I haven't always been this way. Only since Anais. Which is a pretty long time. A long time that seems like no time. Sometimes, time stands still. Time, time, time. I'm drunk now, that's why I'm talking shit. I like the word "time" on my tongue. I lied when I said I was tipsy. I've been drinking fast because I've gotta work tomorrow, so I'd like to get some shut-eye. I can't face the broken toys without curling into a ball for a couple of hours. Sleep the sleep of the dead. One more finger of scotch, and that's what I'm gonna do. One-and-a-half fingers. Two at the most. For purely medicinal reasons. So I can play my part. The part of the good doctor. I am sacrificing my health for the art of medicine. I don't hear anybody applauding. Fine, fine, I know—you think I'm a prick. You aren't entirely right. Don't tell me you sound like a prize when you're half in the bag.

I was sober when I met Anais. Sober, and not an insomniac. Not a lot of the things I am now. I can't say I was a better man, I'd just had less time to fuck things up. See, I can be honest. I won't subject you to a version of myself covered in moonglow. Though I specialize in moonglow. If I want, I can make people believe they are better than they are, which makes them believe I am better than I am. That's how I got a job as a psychiatrist. That's how I got everything.

I don't need moonglow for Anais. *"God bless the child that's got her own."*

Oh good. When I start quoting Billie Holiday, sleep isn't too far off.

I don't really drink so I can fall asleep. I drink so I won't have to see her face when I close my eyes. But maybe you've already got it figured. I don't know how smart you are. I'll soon find out. That's a talent of mine—figuring out what people know and what they want, and making it useful. It's really very easy, since most people don't know what they want and they're not even sure what they think they know. And most people don't know who they are, and they would really like you to tell them.

I'm an expert at telling them. My expertise bought me a view of Central Park, and I stare at it every fucking morning. A few leaves have changed colour, but the rest are holding their own. Until October eats their youth.

I want Anais to decay. As in get old. I want her to get old.

Life doesn't care what you want, deal with it.

Anais is always perfect. There's no tarnish; there's no crack. The lips still have the plump sheen of fruit skin. Her hair smells of figs.

When we met, her skin tasted of honey. She had bathed in it, honey and milk, that morning, pretending to be Cleopatra. *But Nefertiti is my favourite.* There were still sticky bits on her, stickiness warmed by her heat and the sun. On her neck, anyway. The other bits came later. Not much later.

One more finger. One more finger of scotch and I'll drink it in bed. Kasey-With-a-K and I didn't use the bed. I'm the only one who uses my bed.

But first I'll lean against this doorframe and swim with the lights beyond the window. I think someone spiked my drink. It's a starrier night than it should be. Yeah, I know there's nobody here. I guess I drank too much, too fast. Everything has gone a little Van Gogh on me. I mean the lights, they look like exploding stars. I'm not seeing giant sunflowers, though I'm sure I have a patient who has. Fuck, I was an idiot about the moussaka. Eggplant is doing the Electric Slide in my stomach. If it comes back up, I'm trusting you to keep that info to yourself. I don't want people thinking I'm the kind of drinker who doesn't know when to say when. It's not the alcohol that's yanking my guts; I might be getting an ulcer. I think I've held it together pretty damn well. But life doesn't care. It's going to eat me from the inside.

Alka-Seltzer, Pepto-Bismol, go. The floor seems closer than it did a few minutes ago. Jesus H. Christ, I'm gonna have a hangover. But I'm not thinking about Anais, I'm thinking about how not to puke, so I guess my plan is working. I'm ripping apart my bathroom cabinet and I can't find the Alka-Seltzer. Christ, I found scotch in my bathroom and now I can't find its angel of mercy. I'm not drunk enough to have lost my appreciation for irony.

The cold marble floor looks inviting. I'm sweating like a nauseous pig. I should take my shirt off and lie down. Lie down on the frigid floor. Oh, that feels better. A piece of glistening meat on a chilled marble slab. I don't lie on the bathroom floor that often. Or I didn't used to, it's just lately, lately I want to lie on it all the time, in the night, in the night when I feel—we used to cold-wet-pack crazy people. Coldness can have a calming effect. Freeze myself to sleep.

Anais was lying on the floor. Onion skin near her face—

Freeze. Freeze it there. That's not the nostalgia show I agreed to watch.

Shit. Scotch isn't working. Her face is hovering above me, not close enough to touch.

Change the channel. This is my house. It's my show. We're watching what I want to watch.

I watched her for a long time before I walked up to her, that first time. She was watching me watch her. Watch, watching, watcher. Watch, botch. I like to rhyme, helps me sleep. Sometimes. It used to. Counting sheep doesn't work. It's bullshit.

Her hair is like black glass. Black glass streaked with purple because why the hell not. I can't quite tell what colour her eyes are from here. Pretty soon I'm going to locate my balls and get closer. Soon, not yet. She isn't the sort of woman who has to smile to apologize for looking at you, and I like that about her. An even, open, you-move-'cause-I'm-not-going-to stare. Who doesn't want a stare like that?

It's like she's right here. I can almost touch her.

She was sitting at an outdoor café. Yeah, this story starts like that, deal with it. There was the Greek light and the whitewashed everything, deal with it. Hell, Henry Miller could have been sitting at the next table. He wasn't, he was dead, but he could've been. I had his book in my bag. I'd been reading it that morning in bed to keep from wondering what the fuck to do next. An existential wondering, not a tourist wondering.

Miller told me to get off my ass. *Stop wondering about existence, live it.* And there she was.

The back of her, anyway. Hair in a giant knot stuck through with six chopsticks, like some kind of weird topiary. Bare brown back. Arms covered in bangles that shot back the sun. *I like to have my own instrumental.*

I was staring at that back. I was across the narrow street leaning against a building staring at that back and my temples started to throb. She looked up from her notebook and put down her pen. Then she stood up, slow, like she was unfurling herself. Taller than I thought. Stared straight ahead, arching her back just a little. Stayed standing like that, back to me, for a full minute. Or that's how I remember it, and this is my nostalgia show, right?

When she turned around it was slow, like she never rushed anything, never made a move unless it was on her own time. She looked right at me, unblinking, unsmiling but amused; *you gonna come over here or not?* That's what I thought she meant, anyway, because I'm a man and that's what we like to imagine. We stood there for a long time locked in a staring contest, and then she shrugged and turned back around, sat down and picked up her pen. She wrote something and then stopped, turned her head to the right. I've always loved her profile. I could've crossed the street and said hello then, but I didn't want language to ruin our silent talk. I wanted to know the colour of her eyes—I'd find out soon enough. She started writing again. I knew she was writing something about me, and I wanted to know what it was.

There was a strange feeling in me, like I'd swallowed an egg and it was making its way at a glacial pace to my gut. I remember the scene as silent even though I know the noise of Greece was all around us. And it has a grainy quality, like a home movie, because it seems so long ago. Because it *was* so long ago. Freeze. A snapshot. I remember that scene as a polaroid, the melting light, the bare back, the pointed chin fluting up into a heart—and then the photo sparks and fire burns it all away.

Lying on the cold bathroom floor always sobers me up pretty damn quick. Defeats the purpose of the scotch, as my memory collage attests, but at least the moussaka has stayed put. I should get up, get into bed, but I'm wide awake.

I crossed the street, of course I did, and you already know that. I walked slow, we were doing everything slow then, until we did it fast. She knew I was coming and stood up, turned around. Dark-blue eyes in an olive face, strong bony nose, ample mouth. I stopped when I was close enough to touch her. Her mouth wasn't smiling, her eyes were. I blushed and hoped I just looked sunburnt. She didn't blink, as though every day she had staring contests with strangers and it was no big thing. I was used to women blinking—her eyes unnerved me.

"What are you writing?" I said. Just saying hello seemed stupid.

"Are you wondering if I'm writing about you?"

Scotch voice, single malt.

I wasn't sure whether to say yes or no so I shrugged. She kept looking at me, still not blinking, waiting.

"You must be writing about something more interesting than me," I said. "Besides, you don't know me."

"You don't know what I know. Maybe I'll read you some, if the mood strikes. Sit."

And, like a dog, I did.

She signalled a waiter and ordered retsina, speaking Greek. Retsina is like addictive furniture polish. Turned out she was addictive, too.

"I don't speak Greek," I said.

She laughed. It was the first time I'd seen her smile. A gap between her front teeth, webs of crinkles around her eyes.

"Obviously not. You're American."

Goddamn. We're so easy to sniff out.

"Please don't hold it against me. What about you?"

"My mother was Greek. I'm Canadian."

"You live here?"

"For now. You?"

"I don't know what I'm doing here. Wandering, I guess."

Anais leaned in close. I felt a bit dizzy and it wasn't the wine because I'd only taken one sip. Her neck was very long. *Like Nefertiti's. I could be an Egyptian queen.*

"Do you want to know what I wrote about you?"

I nodded. "It's the only thing I want."

She didn't move, didn't look at her notebook. I wanted to reach for her hand.

"'The man watching me is hiding.'"

I froze.

Anais smiled. "Guess it's lucky I found you, isn't it?"

Freeze. There. Pause it there. I'm still lying on the bathroom floor feeling like shit and I don't wanna tell this story tonight. Or this morning. What time is it? I need to get my ass in bed or I can't face the crazies.

Sex and scotch are unreliable. They can't be trusted. Amnesia is elusive. I should've learned this. Clearly I haven't.

I'm going to get up now. In a minute. Maybe two. Freeze. Here. Pause it here.

ACT I
SCENE 2

Lights up. Hospital room. The PLAYWRIGHT *and the* DOCTOR *are seated in facing chairs. She is dressed in a hospital gown and bathrobe.*

PLAYWRIGHT

Do you think it's possible to die of a broken heart?

DOCTOR

Uh... It's possible. Well, no. Maybe. No. I don't think a broken heart alone can kill you. Why?

PLAYWRIGHT

You're a lousy shrink.

DOCTOR

Excuse me?

PLAYWRIGHT

I thought you were supposed to understand what makes us tick.

DOCTOR

I do. Mostly. I don't claim to know everything—

PLAYWRIGHT

A broken heart is the number-one cause of death.

DOCTOR

So that's why you do things to put yourself in hospital. Who broke your heart?

PLAYWRIGHT

I'm more interested in who broke yours.

DOCTOR

My heart's fine, thanks.

PLAYWRIGHT

Yeah, right.

DOCTOR

Anyway. I look forward to meeting Maxine.

PLAYWRIGHT

She hates hospitals. Some of my other muses don't mind, but Maxine is phobic about them. So she may not show up. Dr. Cliff met her. That was in his office, though. If I like your office, she may decide to visit. If we make it that far.

DOCTOR

What do you mean, *if*?

PLAYWRIGHT

Well, we have to get married first, in a sense. I can't be your patient if I don't trust you, and I don't trust you. Remember intimacy? So we'll see if we fall in love. Though come to think of it, how often do married people trust each other? I'd say not very often. We've got an elaborate institution in which to showcase how much we suck at love.

DOCTOR

I wouldn't have pegged you for a cynic.

PLAYWRIGHT

Oh. What would you have pegged me for?

DOCTOR

Aren't acts of creation acts of optimism?

PLAYWRIGHT

Very insightful, Doctor. You're right. I believe in turning cynicism into beauty. In order to write plays, however, one must first see us for what we are. True optimists are those who keep their eyes peeled to humanity and carry on anyway.

DOCTOR

You don't talk like most patients.

PLAYWRIGHT

I'm not most patients. You're not most doctors either.

DOCTOR

What makes you say that?

PLAYWRIGHT

You're awfully defensive for someone who makes a living telling people how to get their shit together. I don't think you like this job. Something's getting you down, my friend.

DOCTOR

Forget about me. I'm not interesting.

PLAYWRIGHT

Oh, you're very interesting. Look, I'm not the average stupid person on Prozac. I'm smarter than you and we both know it. I'm not taking the meds, by the way.

DOCTOR

I'll ignore whatever you think about my intelligence. The meds can help you integrate.

PLAYWRIGHT

I don't want to integrate, I want to create. Integration is death to creation. Check my file. Dr. Cliff wrote that down. I need my muses and if they land me in hospital every once in a while, so be it. I don't see how my muses and I are different from every other family. My stays here are a necessary evil, like a colonoscopy. Family is a necessary evil, like a colonoscopy.

(The PLAYWRIGHT *stands, starts pacing the room.)*

God, it's hot in here. Aren't you sweating, I'm sweating. Don't ask me to give up my family, you wouldn't be that cruel. I'm doing okay. Better than okay. You've read my reviews, I'm often lauded. Most writers can't say that. Being lauded even occasionally is like winning the fucking lottery.

(She wanders to the small bedside table, looks fondly at a vase of gardenias.)

Thank God for these. I couldn't stand being here without flowers. Mr. Chipley sent them to me. Victorian men went in for chivalry. It's nice to know one. He disappeared after I finished his play. He has a way of showing up, though, when there's food in my fridge he likes. Or when I'm in need and I could use his strength. He hears my cries and I don't even have to use the phone.

DOCTOR

Mr. Chipley? Isn't he...? You mean you sent the flowers to yourself.

PLAYWRIGHT

No, Mr. Chipley gave them to me. Thoughtful, don't you think? You know who he is, you've read the file. He used me to tell a story. We're indebted to each other. I'd say that warrants flowers.

(Beat)

Sorry it smells like a funeral parlour in here. I find it comforting. Sarah Bernhardt slept in a coffin, you know. I understand the appeal of that. A bit utero, wouldn't you say?

(She moves to the window, presses her hands to the glass.)

Sunset soon. Will you watch it with me? Might make you feel better.

DOCTOR

I feel fine. You're the one I'm worried about. Why are you so interested in my life?

PLAYWRIGHT

I told you: I won't trust you if I don't know you. You think you have all the power here but you're wrong. Besides, I might put you in a play. You've got a story to tell.

DOCTOR

Oh? What kind of story?

PLAYWRIGHT

Greek tragedy.

(Beat)

DOCTOR

There's nothing tragic about me.

PLAYWRIGHT

Oh, we both know that's not true.

DOCTOR

I thought you wanted to watch the sunset.

PLAYWRIGHT

Fuck the sunset. I want to watch you.

(She stands right in front of him, close enough to touch.)

DOCTOR

I can leave if you're going to waste my time.

PLAYWRIGHT

Of course you can leave. I'm not holding you prisoner.

(Beat)

Much to my disappointment.

DOCTOR

I'm not holding you prisoner either.

PLAYWRIGHT

No, of course not. I'm just here for my annual rest cure. I'm very Victorian that way: I have TB and you're my Italy! It's all so gloriously romantic. Which of my muses would you like to meet? They can't all travel with me. Some are otherwise engaged. Some leave me, never to be heard from again. It's horrible. How many times can one person be left in a lifetime?

(Beat)

Tell me, Doc. You're the expert. How do we go on?

DOCTOR

I thought you were going to tell me about the play you're writing.

PLAYWRIGHT

Maybe I am.

Blackout

PLAYWRIGHT

I AM ON MY RED SOFA when I awaken, spooning a pillow. Crashing headache, nausea, and I can't blame Maxine. Now commences a whole other kind of Green Hour. Is there somewhere I'm supposed to be? I can't remember.

None of the blinds are shut and sunlight is mocking my sorry state. Maxine would be mocking me too, if she were bearing witness. Her tolerance for alcohol is well beyond mine, all the practice she's had with gin. You'd think, since she's my muse, that some parts of her would rub off on me. God, does my pounding head ever wish that were so. I don't know what time it is and since that information won't add happiness to my life, I'll just lie here and pretend I'm still asleep and hope no one notices. Maxine seems to have stayed away last night—I don't sense her presence here. There's no point in her showing up if I'm only semiconscious. That might be the real reason I drank too much: to keep Madam Thespian at bay so she doesn't inflict too much damage, such as pissing off the noise police. Her play will be a spectacle to remember, so long as I am not destroyed by the process.

Get up, get up, get up, get up, get up. My morning chant. Is it still morning? Doubtful. I'd like to say I spring up to face the day with bravery. I won't lie to you, though. My intersection with life requires an ongoing pep talk. My muses are braver than I.

Okay, I'm going to pretend to be asleep for just a little longer and then I'll check for messages in case I've missed something extraordinary, like a Pulitzer was tossed at me while I slumbered. Oh wait, it's not Pulitzer season. And maybe I don't deserve one. So what? A writer cannot help but hope awards will grow in her garden overnight, like mushrooms, a delicious morning surprise to nourish her through the gauntlet of revisions.

So much for a morning spent penning dialogue for Maxine. She'll have my head if I fall behind schedule. I'll explain to her that I've been busy injecting the unconscious into my creative process.

Staring at the ceiling or a wall or the ground is an important part of creating anything. People don't understand this. Thus it's better I live alone, for several reasons, actually. One must stare at something flat, something blank, something that could become anything. You must look at nothing to see everything. If you think that sounds grandiose, I don't want to talk to you. Staring at the ceiling is like sleeping with my eyes open. I'm more likely to remember my dreams.

Okay, I'm up. Well, I'm not up in a vertical sense, but I'm reaching for my phone. Does anyone love me? Possibly. There's a message and scads of missed calls.

Sam's voice is my favourite way to start the day, when he's giving voice to good news, that is. My agent has brought me back to life many times, and today is no exception.

"A good theatre in Sydney wants to mount a production of *Obelisk*; it's your lucky day. So I hope you're still alive. I couldn't get hold of you yesterday. Call me," says Sam via my voicemail. *Obelisk* is my second play, set in Ancient Egypt. A rather surprising cash cow. Sex and violence make everything modern. There is no such thing as cutting-edge in art. Same edge, different handle.

And just like that, it's an outside day.

Getting off the couch is so much more pleasant when there's a royalty cheque on the way. Somebody downstairs buzzes me in agreement. I somehow get myself to the buzzer. I'm lightheaded.

"Hello," says a frog who doesn't sound like me at all.

"Oh good, you're alive," says Sam. "Let me in."

He sounds a touch annoyed. It scares him when he can't get hold of me. I used to apologize.

"What time is it?" I say, opening the door before he knocks.

He wraps me in a crushing hug. "Noon. Thank God."

"Thank God it's noon?"

"No, thank God you're here."

"I'm often here. There haven't been many outside days lately. You know I can't negotiate that with myself."

"Maxine likes to go out. I hate it when I can't reach you. Panic city, pet."

He still has me in a death grip so I talk into his chest.

"Maybe she'll email me about where she went. She keeps forgetting to take my phone. Or she leaves it behind on purpose. It freaks her out."

"Have you eaten anything?"

"Today?"

"No, last year."

"I just woke up. I drank too much. And I have a feeling rations are scarce. Chipley probably ate everything. Sometimes treats can be found in the oddest places, though. It's a nice metaphor for life."

Sam sighs, as he often does in my presence. It used to annoy me; now I take it as a proclamation of love. The ability to fill another with panic at the thought of your absence is a treasure people kill for.

He lets go of me and marches to the fridge.

"Jesus Christ. It's not a pretty picture, kids. Why hasn't Cosette brought you any food?"

"She's on vacation, I remembered last night. I told her I could manage, and I have."

"So what have you been eating?"

"I have vague memories of caviar. I starve in style."

A sharp exhalation, like he's been stabbed.

"Get dressed, let's do lunch. We're celebrating."

"The sale in Sydney?"

"No, precious pet. That we keep each other alive."

"I'm always happy to celebrate that. I probably look a mess but you're used to it. What day is it? I've been eating fine. It was only recently I ran low. I think."

"It's Friday. Time to play hooky."

I catch a glimpse of myself in the hall mirror. I have yet to determine which hour is my finest. This certainly isn't it. As usual I'm playing second fiddle to my hair, which is headlining as Medusa on fire. My gaunt face is getting longer by the day. I'm not exactly pretty, but I've always hoped for a certain bohemian gravitas. At the moment I'm nailing consumptive, you can forget about boho charisma.

"Can you hang tight while I jump in the shower?"

"I thought you were rockin' the bath these days."

"Maxine takes baths. She bought all this perfumey oil. Her play better make money 'cause she's spending mine like it's going out of style."

Sam stands in the bathroom doorway while I squeeze toothpaste.

"Stand aside. Remember, I must walk while I brush."

"Darling, everyone else in the world brushes their teeth at the sink."

"I pity them. I'm not an OCD person, this is my only ritual. It helps me think. Plus, this way I brush my teeth for longer. Haven't you seen how nice they are?"

Sam smiles at me in a way that makes me wish he were straight. "You have the nicest teeth of any playwright I know."

"That's not a compliment. Most playwrights don't have health insurance."

Commence walking and brushing. It's an effective antidote to nausea. Good thing I haven't eaten much or it all would have come back up. I am willing to suffer more for champagne than for a lover. Don't want to know what that says about me.

"You moved Modi's women."

"Waxmeen id," I say with a mouth full of toothbrush.

"You sure put up with a lot from her."

"Bwilan teeter duh cuh eep."

"What?"

I move to the kitchen sink and spit. This session of walking and brushing will have to be cut short.

"Brilliant theatre doesn't come cheap. And for the record I'm not calling myself brilliant, I'm quoting the *New York Times*. Anyway, what the hell am I supposed to do? 'Fuck the playwright' seems to be the muses' motto. I just wish I could be in on all the fun they have. I mean firsthand. It's nice that they write to me. I just wish... We'll always be separated from each other."

"We're all separated from each other, pet."

"If you care about my mental health, don't say things like that."

"I've always told you the truth, why stop now? Anyway, you're a saint and Maxine should know it."

"Maxine thinks she's the one who's angelic and long-suffering. She's expecting Saint Peter to drive her through the pearly gates in a 1925 Renault 6."

Sam laughs his deep laugh that fills every hole and crevice, every dark place, and I'm no longer weak or hungry and I remember it is possible to live on laughter alone.

I didn't show up for our first meeting. My muse did, and she scared the shit out of him. Sam had called me after he saw my fourth one-act, staged way the hell off Broadway by a group of NYU grads I'd met before my muses forced me to drop out of playwriting school. Somebody's uncle knew him, told him he had to see my work. That uncle, whose name I don't even recall, in a mere moment redeemed any bad karma he may have been dragging around from past lives.

How many years ago was that? Ten? Thirteen? Fifteen? I can't keep track of time or how old I am. I'm not being coy, I really can't. From what she's told me of her story, I'm guessing Maxine is still in her salad days. She refuses to tell me her age and I don't blame her. The 1920s buried women with rapacious prematurity, and the only safe age for an actress is not too many years after first blood. Though stage is more forgiving than film. Maxine, however, is too good a liar not to use her proclivity for doing tortuous and pretty things to the truth to her advantage.

"I'm a theatre agent. I was at your play last night, and I love your work. Would you be interested in meeting?" This was Sam, that first phone call.

Thump. That was me, begging a wall to keep me from fainting.

Thump, ahek-ahek. That was me, regurgitating my heart.

"Hello? Are you still there?"

Don't hang up, don't hang up, I have vocal cords, I don't remember where I put them.

And so we agreed to meet and my whole life was going to change and I was going to attend our meeting being cool and professional, reveal a quirk or two for charm without pretension, and dazzle him with my artistic virtuosity.

My then-muse had other ideas.

I woke up that morning feeling very much myself. I woke up early because the earlier I wake up the more important I feel, even if I don't have to be anywhere, just the idea that the world couldn't twirl another moment without me having my eyes open. On this magical morning, I did have somewhere to be, oh did I ever, and I was feeling so important that I was fairly paralyzed by the importance of myself. Until, sitting there in the bed propped up against my throne of three pillows, just plain paralysis won out over nascent self-esteem. After five minutes of deep breathing interspersed with intervals of hyper-ventilation, like breath anaerobics, I reached for my notebook and pen and told myself to pull it to-fucking-gether. In those days I was still writing with pen and paper, which seems like an affectation now; it wasn't, I just couldn't type. My first full-length play stared back at me without blinking. A piece of writing can win any staring contest, any day. The words looked different with an agent in the spotlight. I put the pages to my face like I was sniffing for something. Maybe royalties had a scent.

It was a storm-kicked morning in November. I enjoy writing under a noisy sky—it's like someone out in the ether is applauding my subversive life-and-death struggle. Plus, I don't trust quiet clouds, I like a heaven that puts its cards on the table. The room kept lighting up and I could see my silhouette—which, really, is the best version of me—in the mirror opposite the bed—which, by the way, is bad feng shui, I didn't know any better at the time—and I wondered if it was the silhouette of a successful playwright. It was, as it turned out. Just not the silhouette, not exactly, that showed up to my first meeting with Sam.

My parents had died the year before, Jackson Pollock-style, on a skateable stretch of road one wintry night in upstate New York. I'd like to be able to say I miss them. I don't. I'll stop short of saying I'm glad they're dead. Their estate wasn't huge but it was enough that I could do nothing but playwriting for a while, until I either became successful at it or wilted outside a Bronx soup kitchen. Feigning gratitude might cast us all in a more flattering light but I can't do it, because I think they owed me. My characters don't get to stand in flattering light so why should my mother and father? Anyone who says that parent-child love is unconditional is an idiot.

"Are you suitably shampooed? For pity's sake." This is Sam, calling through the bathroom door. Like most born New Yorkers, patience is not his middle name.

I am surprised to find myself in my naked body under a spray of too-hot water. My autopilot is a point of pride and the pivot upon which my survival jerkily turns.

"How long have I been in here?" I call back.

"Twenty-two minutes. I don't dine with prunes."

"I wasn't walking around naked, was I?"

"You put Modi's women to shame, my darling."

That's a lie. I have a wispy body and thus a brand of sex appeal that requires a discerning palate. Sam has borne witness to my wispiness on myriad occasions, and he's still as gay as he ever was.

The morning I met with Sam, I was working on a scene in the play I was writing about the love affair between a circus acrobat and a man who may have Asperger's. The man's name is Wellington, called Welly. The acrobat is Sever, as in sever all ties. Someone with a name like that isn't destined to have a happy love life. Write what you know, isn't that what they say? Besides, who wants to watch a play about a happy affair? It isn't that happiness is boring; it's quite fascinating, actually. It's just that it tends to inspire hatred and you're better to win sympathy from an audience and leave them feeling not as bad off. Both Welly and Sever were serving as muses, showing up regularly and making me crazy by arguing about how their story should be written. Everyone's a critic and muses are the absolute worst of all. Sever kept bashing up the walls and furniture by practising acrobatics in the living room. Welly would scar the walls on occasion because he'd bash them with his head if he got mad. Two concussions he gave me. I damn well deserve the awards that play won. Acclaim and free cake are balm to an awful lot.

In the predawn darkness on the morning I met Sam, I was going over the notes they'd left me. That was a mistake. I shouldn't have tried to write. It's just that I was nervous about the meeting and thought if I sorted through the filaments of direction my muses had left in their bad handwriting (Welly writes like a doctor and Sever on a severe slant like the words are mid-backflip.) and spun a scene, I could walk into Sam's office feeling successful and in control. My muses don't visit every day but writing makes them more likely to show up, since they insist on meddling in everything I put down on paper or up on screen.

Sever's notes read:

The first time I had sex with Welly was totally awkward. It was his first time, well, practically his first time, I don't count a brothel in Chinatown as a good education. I thought I could teach him a thing or two. I mean, I'm an acrobat, for Chrissake. He got offended and we had a big fight and he slammed his head into the wall. So I won the first round by technical knockout and all I had to do was yell. Kidding. It was hell. Make sure you bring in the tenderness at the end. Because it was there. Man, was it ever. Tenderness is so much sweeter when someone is bleeding.

Welly's notes read:

Sever is a very beautiful woman. The kind of beauty that makes its audience feel flushed. I don't blush but if I did I would when I look at her. I went to her apartment to fix her computer. I'm her computer guy. I can fix anything and build anything. So I fixed her computer while she stood on her head. She can bend into any shape. Standing on your head can nourish your brain. Then we were in her bed. I am missing some steps but I'm telling you the important part. At first, I didn't understand. I find it hard to understand her face. Everyone's face. If we are supposed to read faces, then why do we have voices? Why aren't we all deaf? Don't you ever think of that? But I don't like being told what to do. I can fix anything and build anything, so I'm the boss. I got mad and she got mad and there were crashing sounds. In the end, we were so happy. I put my hands on her face. I think I can read faces better when I touch them.

It takes a particular brand of masochism to write a he-said-she-said play. Men and women ain't never gonna agree on anything and stage directions don't change that fact. Or maybe it isn't masochism since I don't have a choice about who shows up to tell me their story. Sadists. I'm at the whim of sadists who spend my money and make holes in my wall and show up to meetings with agents who want to change my life.

So I wrote Sever and Welly's sex/fight/sex/tenderness scene by candlelight, thinking that writing would not only strangle and bury my nervousness about meeting Sam but would also keep my muses off my back. Candles are preferable to turning on a bulb. When writing, invite the shadows to come out and play.

That scene stayed in the play because it was damn good, if I do say so myself. Sam loves it, even though he met the characters before he read the script, an experience which was no doubt startling.

When I finished writing, I only had a stub of candle left and the storm had stopped. I was still myself. I was still myself when I got on the subway to Sam's office and when I rode the elevator, making faces in the mirrored wall, to his floor. When I stepped out of the elevator, I realized my knees were weak. I was way more nervous meeting an agent than I was the first time I had sex, which I guess proves I'm more a writer than a lover. The office was exactly as

I'd pictured a New York agency to be: sleek, modern, with photos of Broadway productions and famous people dining at Sardi's all over the walls interspersed with abstract art, and fronted by a hippie-chic, irksomely pretty receptionist named Phaedra.

"Hi, you must be here to see Sam," she said in a sparkling voice. "I saw your play, it's spectacular."

Oh, how I loved that place already.

"Thanks. I'm working on a full-length one now."

"Can't wait. Come on in and meet Sam."

And that's all I remember of my first meeting at the agency.

–

THIS IS SAM'S VERSION:

She strode in and sat down. Phaedra bustled out and shut the door. The person I hoped would be my newest client was looking at me with strange amber eyes. Not strange: hard, tough, ready for a pre-emptive strike. For pity's sake, I rep enough high-maintenance writers, I'd hoped she'd be sweet and malleable.

"I'm delighted to meet you. Your one-act is the best new work I've seen this year," I said, smiling past her unsettling expression.

"My one-act? I just call it an act. I can do a solo gig or with a partner or a group or whatever. But listen, the circus I been with has been workin' us into the ground. So I'm only gonna consider this if you're offering me a decent contract." She said all this in a pebbled voice different from the one I'd spoken to on the phone. Then her small face softened for a moment. "Thanks, by the way. I've worked really hard on that act. You were there the other night, weren't you? I saw you in the front row."

Obviously, Phaedra had let the wrong person into my office. But no, I knew what the playwright looked like and this was her. I didn't know what to say so I came out with "What's your name again?"

"Sever," she said. "People don't usually forget it."

I always know what to say, kids, and I fucking hate it when I don't.

"Sever? Uh...isn't that your character, the acrobat? Of course I read the scenes you sent me from your first full-length; they're fabulous. But I don't represent actors, just writers. I didn't know you, uh, were an actor."

She laughed, the first time I'd seen her smile.

"An actor? Well, I've never thought of myself as an actor, just an acrobat, but I guess everyone in the circus is an actor. Thanks for noticing."

Her smile was the sort that crinkles the eyes.

"I still wanna decent contract," she said, her face darkening again. "Flattery will get you nowhere."

ItwasoneofthosesurrealNewYorkmomentswhereyouthink:Should I call Bellevue? Should I call the cops? Should I play along?

It wasn't a pretty picture, kids. But I was between boyfriends and it had been a boring Tuesday till she walked in. I thought: What the hell. "What the hell" is always the right decision.

"I don't believe in flattery, pet. And it goes without saying that every good performer deserves a contract worthy of her talent. That's why God created me."

"Can we keep rehearsal to eight hours a day? Enough time off for injuries?"

"You're an artist, not a workhorse. My job is to fight for your rights. You create, I fight, we both dine out. It's a rather divine little arrangement."

Of course, I didn't know if I wanted to represent a complete nut-job, even if she was a promising writer. Or maybe this was some kind of bizarre game she was playing. Whatever this was, it was bound to be more trouble than I needed.

Her smile was crinkling her eyes again. She seemed to be liking me. Trouble can be fun.

"If I could take a copy of the contract home and show it to Welly... You know, he's better at facts and figures and contracts and stuff in black and white."

"Welly?"

"My friend, uh, computer guy friend, boyfriend."

"Uh...yes, I've read the scenes, the scenes of the two of you. It's great stuff. Really inspired writing. You've got a pretty staggering talent."

"The scenes? Oh right, the play, of course. We want our story told. And we're helping tell it, naturally we would, I mean, we lived it and we're still living it, but I can't really take credit for the writing. I went hunting for the best playwright for the job and I found her. We're lucky. I conducted a hell of a search and then: there she was."

I wasn't sure whether to laugh or cry or back away slowly. Call for Phaedra and get her to ring for the men with butterfly nets? Tell the skinny amber-eyed piece in front of me who claims her name is Sever and she works in a circus that I've changed my mind about repping her? Keep watching the show?

I'm a sucker for good theatre.

"Well, uh, she's a very lucky playwright to have been, uh, found by you."

"I tell her all the time. She gets annoyed by that, you know how writers are, they like to think they come up with all the original ideas."

"So...you have regular conversations with her?"

"We write letters, you know, because of the distance. I give her notes on our play. Obviously, I want to make sure the story is told just right. Welly and I both give her notes. Our versions don't always agree. You know, you get the man's version and then you get the truth."

I liked her, this woman who said her name was Sever. Disturbed people are not always dangerous. Eccentricity pays my mortgage.

She sprang up in one fluid motion and stood at my window before I could blink. This playwright, or whoever she was, moved like a dancer, or a circus acrobat.

Her back was turned. I waited for her to speak.

The dramatic pause seemed long. My office is in Union Square, with a view of the W Hotel. Maybe she was meditating on the giant

W like I do, as if it's some signpost of urban Zen. You know, pet, so long as the giant W stands, the apocalypse has not yet taken us. I guess I should have been freaked out by her at that point, and I was. Well, kids, I wanted to know what would happen next. The best writers make us want to know what will happen next.

"Does your computer need fixing?" she said, only her voice was not the voice I had heard on the phone, nor was it Sever's. It was deeper, young and masculine and not unfriendly. She didn't turn around.

"My computer? Uh, no, my computer's fine. Why do you ask?"

"I am a computer specialist. I am a specialist with many specialties, in truth. I can fix anything, build anything. What do you need me to fix for you today? I enjoy this view very much. W is my favourite letter."

I took a swig of cold coffee and shook my head. "Why is W your favourite letter?"

"W for Welly. W is my favourite letter because I am called Welly and Welly starts with the letter W. My full name is Wellington but I don't like that name. What is your favourite letter?"

"Um...I like to stare at that big W out there. It chills me out. So I guess I like W too. My name is Sam, so I think S is a nice letter."

She turned around. She was different, arms crossed, slightly hunched, blocky and ungraceful.

"Chills you out? It makes you cold? I also enjoy S. S is for Sever, the woman I love."

"Oh yes, Sever, she was here just a minute ago."

"Dammit, I missed her. Dammit and dammit and dammit. Do you know where she went?"

"I wish I did. Sorry, can't help you. How did you two meet?"

"Fixing her computer. That's a nice way for a man and a woman to drop in love."

"You mean fall in love?"

"I was teaching her about hardware, and she showed me a backflip. Her name should be Grace. To sever means to cut, but all her movements flow together in one silk ribbon."

She/he continued to stand, leaning against the window frame. The light from outside hit his/her wildfire hair, a psychedelic halo.

"I, uh, I agree. You love her, it's clear as day. Are you also helping the playwright turn your story into a play?"

"Yes, I am. I can't let our playwright only listen to Sever's side of the story. That would not be fair." She/he paused for a long moment. The air felt heavy, like grief had entered the room, but the expression on his/her face didn't change. "It's a sad story."

"Tell me about it."

The eyes seemed to take unnaturally few blinks.

"It is hard for me to understand what other people feel. I cannot read faces. Sometimes I am not sure what I feel either."

"Maybe that's a tad true for everyone. If I had known what my last boyfriend was feeling, I would've tossed him to the curb much sooner."

"Tossed him to the curb? But that would hurt."

"Exactly."

Welly looked horrified.

"No, no, I don't mean literally tossing him to the curb. I mean metaphorically, as in telling him to fuck off and die. Not literally die, I mean as in goodbye, don't call me anymore."

"Don't call you anymore?"

"My ex-boyfriend. He's not allowed to call me. But you can call me."

Did I really want Welly calling me? Why did I say that?

"Are you going to give Sever a good contract? Her last circus tried to backflip her to death. She wants me to look over her contract because I am good at that. I don't get emotional, so I make sensible decisions. I know what is best for her."

"You love her a lot. But I thought you said your story—the story about the two of you—is sad."

"It is. We're both dead. We still love each other and we're helping our playwright give our story to the audience. Those last two things I said are not sad."

"You're dead? But..."

Don't ever think a Manhattan office makes you safe from surrealism. It can come for you anytime.

"May I see the contract? I will take it home with me and look it over with utmost care. Then I will tell Sever if I think she should sign it."

"Home? But where do you live if you're dead?"

Welly's expression didn't change yet I could feel myself turn red, as if he'd told me I'd asked a stupid question.

"I visit the playwright's apartment. It is necessary that I do so during the creative process. One day I will have to leave forever. Not until the play is done."

I didn't know what else to do, kids. I liked Sever and Welly and didn't want the men with butterfly nets to tie them up. So I handed Welly my agency's contract, the one I give to all new clients.

Welly flipped through it and nodded. "I thank you for your time. Please treat Sever well. She is very special to me."

And with that, Welly made his exit.

Three hours later, I got a tearful phone call from the playwright. She'd come to with the contract in hand and had figured out what'd happened. She said she could explain. I said she didn't have to. I'd reread the scenes she'd sent me, and I wanted to see her work brought to life. Every writer needs muses, and hers know what they want. How can that be terrible?

We became friends.

—

WHAT IS THAT AWFUL BANGING? I'm reminded that I am still standing under a jet of lukewarm water. It is so easy not to know where I am at any given moment. Since life is more surprising to me than it is to other people, I like to think I am more alive.

"Did you drown? I'm starving out here, pet. I want to lunch before cocktail hour."

It's Sam, a high timbre of bitchiness in his voice. Right, lunch. How long have I been standing like a motionless drowned rat, forgetting to use soap? No wonder the water is nearly cold.

"Thirty seconds and I'm dragging you out," Sam calls, opening the door. I quite enjoy his bitchy act, worlds away from real anger. He forgives me everything.

I turn off the water. "Okay, done. You should have dragged me out ages ago. I got distracted. Running water is catnip to the reverie-prone."

I wrap a towel around myself while Sam stands in the doorway with his arms crossed.

"You know full well I'm the very soul of patience. I always refrain from dragging you, usually against my better judgment."

He still has the bitchy tone but it's the love kind, the one with retractable claws. Sam has a rosy face and plump cheeks, a Santa Claus-ular cherried nose. Blue eyes that look kind even when they're trying not to. Every time I see him I fight the longing to squeeze his sweet face and run my fingers over his John Waters moustache, my favourite talisman.

But today I just uncross his arms and root my face in his chest. "Just for a minute," I garble, breathing in a mélange of cologne and Tide. "I know you're hungry. I'm hungry, too."

Platonic marriages are the best.

ACT I
SCENE 3

Lights up. Night in the hospital. The PLAYWRIGHT *is sitting on the floor, leaning against her bed. The room is lit only by a bedside lamp. Enter a* NURSE *with a small paper cup of pills.*

PLAYWRIGHT

I'd ask you what time it is, but it doesn't matter.

NURSE

It's meds time.

PLAYWRIGHT

Doc says I don't have to take it.

NURSE

I doubt that. Why are you sitting on the floor?

PLAYWRIGHT

I'm connecting lotus pose to my hospital-gown fundament. You know, you're too pretty to work in a place like this. Especially at night. You should be on a date.

NURSE

It's Thursday.

PLAYWRIGHT

So? People go on dates on Thursdays. Love pays the calendar no heed.

NURSE

(offering pills)
Here, take these. They'll help you sleep.

PLAYWRIGHT

You're new.

NURSE

I just started last month. But we've met before.

PLAYWRIGHT

And what's a nice girl like you doing in a place like this?

NURSE

Trying to help you. And paying off my student loans.

PLAYWRIGHT

And how's that working out so far?

(The NURSE sits beside the PLAYWRIGHT.)

NURSE

I'm making a dent. The helping-you part? I don't know, you tell me.

PLAYWRIGHT

I'm here for my annual constitutional. Right on schedule. It means as soon as I can get the hell out of here, my play will be done. Within a few days, anyway.

NURSE

I'm not sure I follow. I don't know any writers.

PLAYWRIGHT

Consider yourself lucky. F. Scott Fitzgerald wrote, "A writer's temperament is continually making him do things he can never repair."

NURSE

You need to take your meds if you want to get out of here.

PLAYWRIGHT

It's the climax of a play that always kills me. As soon as I get to the climax, I fuck something up and then I come here for a rest of sorts. All that's left is the denouement, and that's easy. Maxine must be happy.

NURSE

Maxine?

PLAYWRIGHT

My muse. She's helping me write my latest play. It's her story.

NURSE

Oh. Well, good luck with it. Sorry, I'm not really a theatre buff. I'm more into movies. But it must be amazing for you to see your work on Broadway.

PLAYWRIGHT

Almost makes the nuthouse worth it.

NURSE

I bet you've never really done anything you couldn't repair. I mean, you come here and, well, get repaired.

PLAYWRIGHT

My muses have. Done things they couldn't repair. Bad things. And there's still time for me.

(Beat)

You're so young. Young and pretty. Do you want a little piece of advice from someone who knows a lot about people?

NURSE

Okay. Shoot.

PLAYWRIGHT

Don't sleep with the Doctor. He's dangerous.

(off the NURSE'S look)

Maybe. I'll keep you posted.

Blackout

MAXINE

I AM IN A COFFEEHOUSE on Broadway and I hate it. Nothing is as it should be. The props are wrong, the players are wrong, the music is wrong. The world has gone mad with its staging and I am powerless to stop it. The set is frightfully ugly, all Bakelite and shiny enough to damage one's sight. Most of the players stare at the glowing rectangle they've set up in front of them; they don't talk to each other. Every time I come to the theatre district, I expect it to look as it should; every time I am ruined to find it does not. There are few things worse than finding your home has betrayed you by becoming something else.

All of the coffees have odd names. The boy behind the counter is sporting pink hair. I can't think of any reasonable explanation for this.

"What can I get for you?" he says without smiling.

A brown wig, I think, which I would plop on your frightful pink head.

"I would like an espresso, please." I developed a taste for it when Robert took me to dine in Little Italy. Such an adventure. I had never eaten Italian food before, and I had never eaten anything while in the presence of a charming mandolin player.

"Short or tall?"

"I beg your pardon."

"What size do you want?"

"I would like two shots, please. *Doppio,* in Italian. I learned that in Little Italy."

"Good for you," he says dismissively.

"It was truly good, indeed. It was my very first time eating pizza."

He looks at me like I have six eyes and a full beard. I can't think why. I hand him the dough I took from my playwright's purse. I'm helping her succeed; it's only fair she pays my expenses. Good grief, this place charges the earth.

"I like your outfit. Very 1920s." He still isn't smiling. You can't get good help anymore.

"Why, thank you. I like to stay current."

He gives me an odd look, and I start to wonder if I have indeed sprouted extra pairs of eyes. "You have to wait over there. It'll be ready in a minute."

It would be civilized if a waiter would bring it to my table, but I refrain from asking because the pink man is already talking to someone else. How I wish I were dining at Henri on East Fifty-Second Street, savouring a bit of Paris in New York. Robert's excellent taste in cuisine made me quite Continental in no time. I cannot abide *escargot,* though. A snail is a snail is a snail. Or, would that I were supping at The Alps on Sixth Avenue; s'always the bee's knees, that spot. Actually, for real comfort, I'd give a limb to be *toute seule* at that cozy place run by charming Mr. Sardi and his adorable wife, the one right next to The Little Theatre on West Forty-Fourth Street. Quite suddenly, I feel like crying. Darling, I am mistress of the tearful scene. Alas, in this sorry java joint, I doubt anyone would look up from their glowing rectangles.

When I at last have my espresso, handed to me by a girl with *green* hair and terrifying silver rings on her face, I make my way to the only empty table, an unsteady thing with splotches of stickiness on its surface. I want to go to my old theatre, but I'm pure useless without java and, a little later, a bit of giggle water. One cannot grace a theatre unless one has unfolded one's wings with the appropriate aids.

One of my aids is my diary, which I am reconstructing for my playwright. I want her to have it, something in my own words, to keep long after I can no longer return. Silly, isn't it? We need somebody to shelter our story, to nurse it like an infant, to usher its coming-out in the world. I'm not sure if I want immortality or sympathy or both. I'm an actress—of course I want both. I haven't been through hell just to scatter and disappear like a bit of ash. If you ain't tough to kill, you ain't fit for the stage. It was impossible to keep hold of my original diary, of course, but I still remember my lines and thus I shall write them again. I am the only actress I have ever met who has never forgotten her lines, not ever; even long after the final curtain I can recite from beginning to end. Not an inconsiderable talent and I shan't let it go to waste, not now when the final curtain is soon to drop and never rise again. Well, actually, by commissioning my playwright I am making sure it will rise and rise and go on rising, I just may not be here to bear witness. I cannot but help wanting to go on starring in show after show, even if I am somewhere else, twinkling in some other heaven.

My favourite coffeehouse is gone, along with everything else I held dear. I've searched and searched, though I don't know why, it was ridiculous really, if it isn't where it was then walking up and down Broadway isn't likely to change that. "Luca's," that was the name, run by Luca, an immigrant from Naples, and I sat in a corner of it on my first day in New York, crying into a cup of plain black java. One's first friend in New York is usually a place, not a person. You take ownership of it, make it yours, because if it belongs to you then you belong to it and, just like that, you are no longer alone.

I had broken the heel of my shoe that day, right before I sought refuge in a dark corner of Luca's, which made being alone and penniless in New York all the worse. My tears weren't simply a trap I laid to ensnare a sympathetic soul, though I confess I was hoping for pity, from God if no one else. It was quiet in the coffeehouse; it often was in the early days. Perhaps my tears were louder than I intended. After a while, I felt someone holding my hand.

"Why you cry uh, bella? Huh? Why you cry uh?"

A short, swarthy baby grand of a man too old to have fought in Europe was sitting beside me, eyes melting with pity in just the right way, the way I wished my father's had done. It was very bold of him to hold my hand like that, but you know what Italians are like. I never imagined someone would touch me on my first day in New York City. His skin was warm and I wanted someone to notice me so I didn't pull my hand away. I couldn't think what to say so I just squeezed his fingers and kept blubbering.

"Whatsa your name, bella?"

"Maxine," I managed. "My shoe's broken."

He looked down at my feet, then up at me and smiled.

"My name is Luca. This my shop. And it's your lucky day. I can make coffee and I can fix shoes. Let me see."

He reached down and took my broken shoe off my foot. The heel hung by a thin strip of leather.

"Wait here, bella. Don't cry no more."

Luca took my shoe and disappeared into the back of his shop. I dabbed at my face with a lace handkerchief, one of two things my father had given me of my mother's. In a few minutes he returned, holding up my shoe like he'd won a prize.

"See? I fix for you. Beautiful shoe for beautiful girl."

He proceeded to bow and drop to one knee, like a knight-errant, and return my shoe to my foot.

"Now: no more cry?"

I shook my head. "No, no more cry. Thank you. I'm an actress, I cry a lot."

Luca's eyes lit up. "Actress? Movie star?"

"No, stage. I'm a stage actress. Trying to be."

"I should have known. You have the eyes. I sang a little opera, in my country. But now, my life is coffee. I miss singing, I miss people look at me. People are gonna look at you."

"I hope so."

"No!" Luca grabbed my hand and squeezed so hard it hurt. "You no hope. You know! In your heart, you know."

I nodded. "In my heart, I know."

"Ah bella, when the stage is calling to you, you must answer. Answer, or you will die."

It is terribly hard to argue with a kneeling opera singer.

"Yes, I will die. Die if I don't answer. Will you come to see me on the stage?"

"Front row. If I can pay ticket, front row." He smiled and squeezed my hand, more gently this time.

"Thank you, Luca. You've saved me. And my shoe."

"You are welcome, bella. Remember what I say to you. You answer."

Chivalry is found in the most unexpected places.

The day of the broken shoe was the first blush of spring 1925, and I went to see Luca every week thereafter. My lucky charm. A week after we met, I landed a part at the Bijou Theatre. Before I turned up in New York I'd been touring with a little rep company upstate, starring in every show, but I was nobody in the city and my father had only given me enough money to last three months, and an admonishment not to get knocked up. Robert was producing the play at the Bijou and we started fucking right after I was cast. I'd say my career in New York started with a bang. A month after the fucking began, he set me up in my charming nest of an apartment. My boarding house had bedbugs, and who wants to live in a boarding house?

—

I STARE INTO MY ESPRESSO. I cannot abide this horrid place, this shiny cold coffeehouse with no warm chivalrous Italian to recommend it. On the way here I bought a charming leather-bound notebook in which to recreate my diary. The price of things is truly obscene. I started keeping a diary as soon as I landed in New York, and I got it for a few coins. This leather thing demanded I plunk down a fistful of Abe's Cabes. Can you imagine? How scandalous! I did it because it's terribly pretty and I hate being deprived of the terribly pretty, but really, the expense. But it's my playwright's money and I'm giving her a hit play. Now that I am a muse I seem so full of good sense, which is quite refreshing. Actors are never full of good sense; if they were, they wouldn't be actors. If they were, I wouldn't have a tragic story. So there: good sense is the enemy of high art. I should write this down for the benefit of my playwright. I charge for my story, but sundry bits of advice she can have for free.

I recall the exact date of my first diary entry and what the entry said. Remember: I've never forgotten my lines.

March 22, 1925

Welcome to New York City, Maxine Doyle. We are simply tickled pink to have you.

How I wish someone would say those words!

But no, I am alone in a boarding house whose bloom has faded, and were it not for the rent I lately handed the moustached landlady, she would not be pleased to have me. Soon that will all change. Hell, I intend to make this city damn happy to have me or die trying!

Miss Hannigan used to say I use too many exclamation points in my writing, but this is my diary and no one else's, so I will use as many as I damn well please!!! Sometimes an exclamation point and a nice smile are all a girl has. In my case, I also have my consummate thespianism. That sounds like a disease. Father says I caught the bug and now I'm doomed to misery. I quite enjoy being miserable on stage; it makes all the offstage misery worthwhile. I am talented at tears, and I think finding a way to get paid for something you do anyhow is the mark of an intelligent person. My tears will prove my fortune. Broadway, here I come!

It's cold in my room. Luckily for me, I find the view of Washington Arch quite warming. Grandness always warms me up, I find. One look at that arch and I am convinced I shall never be cold again. How I wish I had money for a nicer room. Papa gave me his gambling winnings, not with a blessing, but because "I have nothing better to do with my ill-gotten gains." I know I am lucky to be here at all.

There is a nice man in this house, Mr. Thirlwell, a writer. He was finishing breakfast when I arrived and invited me to sit with him. He is a novelist and a playwright. One of his novels was published last year, but not one of his plays has yet been produced. ("This year, Maxine, my words shall grace the stage. And so shall you!") He said he would delight in writing a part for me. What a stroke of prodigious luck! I feel I am really setting off on the right foot.

I am an actress in New York City, just think of it! True, I have not yet been employed by any theatres in this sprawling town—darling, that is but a minor detail!

I shall desist from the flagrant use of exclamation points now, Miss Hannigan. She never did want us girls to have any fun.

I will close with this: I am here, I am ready, my life may now begin—and my dear Sarah Bernhardt, my muse, my guiding light, I shall commence following in your hallowed footsteps post-haste.

–

I WAS A STUPID GIRL then. How I wish for that day. Youth before the milk is spilled has such a glow about it. How I wish for a moment so full and tender with possibility. How I wish Luca were here to hold my hand in that bold and tender way of his. I miss how stupid I used to be. Life is easier when you're too dumb to know you're done for. When you believe the mantle of destiny is upon you and the wings of fate are lifting you above all that is bloody and sad. How could I not miss my fleecy-soft dumbness? I don't miss Robert, though. Not a whit.

April 30, 1925

A month and more has passed since I arrived and last I wrote, and I have scarce been able to breathe since then. This is only the slightest of exaggerations. Two momentous things have become true since I last visited with myself on these pages: I am a working stage actress in New York City, and I have fallen in love.

I believe I am in too much shock to make use of an exclamation point.

The day after I arrived, I put on my red shoes and tucked my gumption under my dress and went up to the Bijou Theatre to show them what I'm about. When it was my turn, I marched on stage—or tried to march, but my knees were shaking and a thousand butterflies were emerging from the chrysalis of my stomach—and gave them my best Ophelia and my best Puck. As I spoke the words, I felt as though I were flying. When I was through, a man stepped forward, Robert Sullivan, the producer, and said, "My dear, we don't do Shakespeare, but that was delightful. Welcome to the company."

And that, ladies and gentlemen, is how I came to be a working stage actress in New York City. My Shakespearean wings lifted me above the crowd. True, I now have a nonspeaking walk-on role in a comedy called *The Squab Farm*, but still, I have made a start. And what a start it is! Mr. Sullivan ("Please call me Robert, darling, everyone does.") insisted upon taking me to lunch afterward, to celebrate my hire. My first time drinking good champagne! ("We must christen you, darling, with a nice bottle.") I was nervous, him being a producer and terrifically handsome and all, and he kept insisting I drink more, so I had a snootful and ended up a bit canned. Not falling-down drunk, God help me, just a bit rosy and giggly, which Robert seemed to enjoy.

"You've shaken me with your talent and beauty, Maxine Doyle. This is only the start. I know the role of Gladys Sinclair is beneath your ability, but please, bear with me. I envision great things for you, for us, and when we are finished with this trifle at the Bijou I will set us up in a bigger marquee."

Then he touched my hand. Less than two days in New York and two men had touched my hand!

"You really are something of a find, princess, and I shall see to it that your talents are not wasted on this town."

How could I not be in love? I came here to shed all the rural upstate dust and I've done it in short order. I suppose it is unbecoming to seem too impressed with oneself, but since this is my diary there is no need to hide just how terribly impressed I am. Well done, Maxine! Not only am I in love with Robert, he is in love with me, which is the truly impressive part. At least, he says all the things one is supposed to say when one is in love. And insisted I move into an apartment he keeps as a "spare," of all things, when the bed bugs hit (and bit), which was just last week. These living arrangements may be a touch hasty. But the truth is, I am still afraid of the dark. I can't bear to be alone in another boarding house. I am used to being alone as Papa was never great company, but if I have the choice of living in the sumptuous abode of a man who makes me feel safe and calls me darling and princess, do I really need to dither long? Robert has all sorts of plans for my career. He wields quite a stick in New York City, it seems. His family is in mining in Colorado. I don't know the details, save that it appears they are not poor. So I have gone from Washington Square to Central Park in a tick. Splendid, Maxine! Well done, old girl! Robert says I have an old soul, that I have wisdom beyond my years. I didn't think wisdom was something men noticed in a woman. That's another thing: I guess I am officially a woman now! What a thought! There have been so many firsts in such a short spell, I am well and truly dizzy with it all. Pain falls away as the wings of fate carry me high above the bad and the ugly.

I wonder what Mother would think of me now. I suppose she hasn't thought of me at all since she ran off. Imagine if she knew I managed to snag both a part on the New York stage and the heart of a Broadway producer, all in a day's work. Then she'd surely claim me as her daughter.

I wrote to Papa, letting him think I am settled at the boarding house. Why upset the apple cart, and a fairly unpleasant apple cart at that?

Oh, Robert is calling through the bathroom door. I'm writing this in the tub. It's difficult to find privacy with a man around. Robert is devilishly attached to me.

God knows what I will have to report when next we meet!

–

THAT STUPID GIRL makes me cry, and I want to murder her for it. I mean, really: how could I have been so goddamn dumb? Ah, well. The young are always sure they can swim before they've been baptized in a swamp.

I feel too ill to continue. I want my playwright to know everything, but I can't do it all in a day. That might kill me, and then who will tell my story? I look up from my new/old diary only to be saturated with a fresh torrent of nausea at the sight of a woman in a very short blouse, her gourmand's belly rolling for the world to see. This town and all its denizens really have gone to hell in a handcart. I am a stranger in the city I once loved.

ACT I
SCENE 4

Lights up. The PLAYWRIGHT is asleep. Bedside lamp is on. The DOCTOR enters, stops when he sees her sleeping. He stands and watches. Moments pass. She opens her eyes and sits up.

PLAYWRIGHT

How long you been standing there?

DOCTOR

Not long.

PLAYWRIGHT

Right.

DOCTOR

We have our session. I didn't think you'd be asleep. It's two in the afternoon.

PLAYWRIGHT

I'm in a hospital. Isn't naptime kind of a thing here?

DOCTOR

Touché.

PLAYWRIGHT

So: what do you want to talk about?

DOCTOR

How are you feeling?

PLAYWRIGHT

My stitches itch. But I don't have gangrene or sepsis, so I'm basically quite fabulous. Except this green getup does nothing for my complexion.

DOCTOR

You're lucky you missed your heart.

PLAYWRIGHT

Am I? It would've been much more dramatic if I'd hit it. One must think of the play of life. We all want a grand climax, don't we, Doctor?

DOCTOR

You really want your grand climax to be stabbing yourself in the heart?

PLAYWRIGHT

Do sit down.

(pats the bed)

I'm sorry, I'd offer you bubbly but you keep the cupboards downright dismal. And you seem like a scotch drinker.

DOCTOR

(sits on a chair)

I'll sit here.

PLAYWRIGHT

Tell me about her.

DOCTOR

About who?

PLAYWRIGHT

The one you can never forget.

(Beat)

DOCTOR

I don't know what you mean.

PLAYWRIGHT

Oh, I think you do. You want me to be honest with you, right? You keep blathering about trust. It works both ways. I've explained this. Maybe I know more about you than you think.

DOCTOR

I'm not here to play games.

PLAYWRIGHT

Neither am I. You think this is fun for me? Is that what you think? I want to know why you look at me the way you look at me. I want to know why you're afraid of me. It isn't 'cause I'm taking a rest cure at the Loony Riviera. Shrinks aren't afraid of crazy. Or so they like to believe. You know I know something about you. So tell me about what I know. Let's be close, you and me.

Blackout

DOCTOR

I AM IN BED WITH ANAIS in her tiny house in Greece. In my mind, that is. Prozac can't touch that house in Greece or anything in it. It's in my head to stay. Maybe all the things I do to forget, all the liquid amnesia, can't get past the me who stands at the door to that house, protecting her. I am protecting her from myself. Isn't that what every lover should do?

The sounds of Greece, of the sea, are on us through the open window. The air leaves the damp footprints of a midnight rain. Beneath her hair I am safe, and if I can stay there, I will stay happy. *Nobody stays happy. It is the possibility of becoming happy that keeps us alive.* Anais hasn't stirred and I like the warmth of her against me, her face deep in my side as though breathing is needless. *If you need to come up for air, it's not real love.* She uses the word love a lot. It is a word I can't recall ever saying out loud. During a week mostly spent fucking someone who is more a stranger than not, the idea of love never occurs to me. Now I wish it had. I wonder whether love come late is better than no love at all. I am not a romantic so for me, unless I'm at the bottom of a bottle, lovelessness trumps loss.

That morning, I traced her hip with a finger and wondered what to do next. I could hear Anais's goats bleating softly in the yard, and I wished they could give me some advice. They appeared, from everything I'd seen about them, to have life figured out. I was copying them, keeping my plans to fucking and eating. Perhaps I was at my best then, my peak, imitating goats. Who I had been, who I was, didn't matter to me or to her or to the animals roused by a laceration of light on the horizon.

I wish that was the end of the story. Me inside her inside that bed inside that house inside that country called Greece. Life doesn't stop when you want it to. Instead it keeps fucking you long after you've fallen out of love.

"Stop thinking," says Anais, and I jump, startled. She is the first woman I have known who tells me to stop my mind, instead of demanding to know what's in it. My relief is immense.

"I wasn't."

"Liar. Good morning, my love." She does what she has done every morning for the past seven days. She closes my eyes with her fingers and kisses each eyelid.

I keep my eyes closed and touch her face. Face Braille, she calls it. "You barely know me," I say.

"That will come," she replies, a hand on my cock.

"It already has," I answer, and we both dissolve into the hysterical laughter that bonds strangers who have been inside each other.

Then Anais is on me, absorbing me in a single sharp gasp. I did stop thinking then, her face floating above me, a single dark-blue eye, a point of light.

"Now," she says when she has rolled off and curled against me, our puddles seeping through the crumbling mattress. "Now I want to know more than just your name."

"Why?" I ask. "You're the one who keeps telling me to stop thinking. Shouldn't that apply to you too?"

"It's the seven-day rule. After a week, I need more than your name. I need a story."

"I can give you a story."

"Not *a* story, *your* story."

I wished the goats could do the talking. Post-orgasmic torpor does not lend itself to storytelling.

"You have no questions about me?" Anais said, speaking into my shoulder while braiding a lock of her hair. "I'm not just some woman you're fucking. I hardly ever bring a man here. Certainly not an American."

She laughed hard, like that was the funniest joke she'd heard in ages. It had been a while since I'd found a giggle I wanted to hear more of.

"Into every life an American must fall."

We both jumped into laughter, a safe language for those who may not share a common tongue. Anais was still giggling when she began braiding a lock of my hair, longer back then, an ode to the times and my aimless Grecian wanderings. I pulled my head away but she hung on.

"Ouch!"

"Stay still. I've always wanted a Ken doll with real hair."

"That's what I am to you? A Ken doll?"

"So far. Until you tell me more about you. But I loved all of my dolls very much."

"Pigtails don't suit me."

"I'll decide what suits you."

"Have you always been this bossy?"

"Yes. Besides, I'm older than you."

"You don't know that."

"No, but I'm guessing. A woman's intuition."

"I think we know all we need to know about each other. Let's keep things simple."

"Oh, you're one of those."

"One of what?"

"The cowardly ones."

"I'm not—"

"How long you planning on staying?"

"I—"

"Because if you want to stay in my house, you're gonna have to tell me who you are and why you're here. And don't just say it's because you enjoy fucking me. There's no need to state the obvious."

I pushed her hands away from my hair and sat up. Morning light was hitting her full in the face, a face too strong to be pretty, a fat, wet lower lip and man's thick eyebrows mocking prettiness, a bony profile carving into the day. The sexiest women are never the prettiest. Anais has a fierce beauty. Devour it or be devoured.

"What do you want to know?"

"Start talking. I'll tell you when to stop."

I rubbed my face with my hands and reached for the water jug. There was an actual ceramic water jug on the bedside table, like we were in Victorian times or some other distant era. Her tiny whitewashed house was like a Greek postcard, a paean to Mediterranean rustic. She too seemed to have stepped out of another time, belonging to a bit of history just beyond my reach. But I was reaching anyway. Or maybe I'm just looking at her through the magical eyes that time and pain make. She was different, at any rate, from the young American women I had known. Husky-voiced, self-possessed, unafraid, with an obvious love of her body I had never encountered. She didn't shave her armpits, something I had never seen up close and thought I would find kind of, well, gross, but I was wrong. There was nothing on her body I didn't want to touch. Nothing I didn't want to possess, inhabit, know again for the first time. It was better, I thought, if I didn't know anything about her story. But I wanted to know everything about her skin. She had bite marks on her breasts and shoulder where I'd dug my teeth into a sticky honeyed patch of flesh. Anais didn't seem to mind. *I like a story on my skin*. I wanted a record of everywhere I'd been. Or maybe I wanted to consume her before she consumed me. Men can be intuitive too. What use prophecy? None. There are bite marks on both of us to prove it.

When she brought me home from the café that first day, she insisted I carry her through the front door.

"We're not married," I said. The idea seemed a lot weirder than licking honey off a stranger's neck.

"No shit," she replied, an impatient heat rising. "But you're a man, this is a door, and we're about to fuck." Then her face softened and she smiled. "This might be my only chance. Nobody's ever carried me anywhere."

And nobody had ever asked me to carry them anywhere. For some reason, in the moment, it seemed like the best thing that had ever happened.

That little blue door in that little white house. Her large heavy-lidded eyes fixed on me, blinking slowly in the shadowed planes of her face. The sun almost down, almost, not quite, a last bleed of heat on the water. We had spent the evening in each other's necks and faces, coming up for breath rarely and ouzo more often. I remember the café and I remember her door. I don't remember riding on her Vespa for what must have been a drunkenly zigzagging journey from one to the other.

I had arrived from Athens three days earlier. Corfu. The name appealed, and I wanted to be somewhere I could walk instead of run. Athens made me nervous. Of course it wasn't the city that scared me. At any rate, I was strung out on nerves when I showed up on Corfu, promising myself I wouldn't talk to anyone.

And then there was Anais, and here was my tongue on her skin.

"Well?" she said, pushing open her front door.

For a second I pictured throwing her over my shoulder like firemen do but thought that probably wasn't what she had in mind. So I scooped her up, straining a bit under the weight of her solid body, and carried her into the house. If there is a God, which there isn't, he must have laughed at me for those few moments I spent stumbling across a threshold with a woman in my arms believing everything might turn out all right.

That was the first time I heard Anais laugh, a whisky laugh pealing upward into a surprising bell tone, surprising because its beginnings were low and deep. I'd never thought to like a woman's laugh for its own sake before, only to notice whether what I was doing was working.

"All the way to the bed, turn right," she said, still laughing. I was trying not to take a header in the dark.

When I placed her on the bedspread—printed with Greek Orthodox crosses, I discovered in the morning—she pulled me down on top of her and then I pulled her down on top of me and we kept doing that and not much else and now it's seven days later and she is sitting up in bed demanding to know who I am.

People would be so much happier if they asked each other no questions. Nobody really wants the truth, anyway. Why would I ruin her with mine?

She takes the cup out of my hand and drinks, still watching me.

"More," she says, handing it back to me.

The room is still cool and a shiver passes over me. I like to think I'm a good storyteller, but this audience is hard to peg. In a manner of speaking.

"So what are you doing here? In Greece, not in me. Let's start with that."

"I'm a doctor. But I needed a break, so I decided to wander someplace warm."

Anais raises an eyebrow. "A doctor? A cut-me-open kind of doctor?"

"No, a head doctor. A shrink. I can almost read your mind."

She seems amused. "Oh please. Shrinks aren't telepathic. You seem kind of young to be messing with someone's head."

"I have a talent for it."

"I'll bet you do."

Her eyebrows are raised, a disturbing look of disbelief on her face.

"Why are you looking at me like that?"

"Where do you live?"

"Chicago. But who knows, maybe I'll stay here for a while."

"Why come all the way to Greece for a break?"

"I was reading *The Colossus of Maroussi*. Henry seemed to think Greece was a good idea. Who was I to argue?"

"That seems awfully romantic for a psychiatrist."

"I'm not your typical shrink."

"I guess not."

I reach for her hoping she will shut up now.

"Wait. Still too many mysteries in this bed. Don't you want to know anything about me?"

I suppress a sigh and my desire.

"Of course I do." That was both true and untrue.

"Okay." She seems relieved, as though my willingness to listen to her recite facts about herself means that seven days of screwing me hasn't been a mistake. Maybe I sound like an asshole, but the idea of love was far from my mind.

Anais curls against my chest in the classic talk-and-cuddle position. I love the smell of her hair and the feel of her skin and think I should probably get the hell out of here.

"This was my aunt's place. She left it to me and my brothers in her will. I don't really know why, she only came to Canada twice to visit. But she didn't have any kids, and she was very attached to this house. Wanted to keep it in the family. So I decided living in it for a while was better than braving another Toronto winter and throwing pots."

"Throwing pots?"

"I'm a potter. You know, I make clay pots. Get my hands dirty and bake the dirt in an oven for nice people to put in their kitchens. I'm functionally artistic."

"Good with your hands."

She lifts her head and puts both hands on my face. Those eyes that look like they know too much about you.

"Exactly."

"So how long you staying?"

"Till the money runs out."

"Yeah, me too."

For a second I think about telling her my real story, just to hear it out loud. But I stop myself, because stupidity is never the answer.

"I'm going to write in my diary, go swimming, drink, and cook. I think it's enough of a plan."

"It's enough for me."

"Something always happens while you're minding your own business. I never thought I'd have a shrink in my bed."

"I guess you're just lucky." I kiss her, because I feel like saying I'm sorry. I have never told anyone I'm sorry before, and I don't start then. That comes later, spoken into the dark, when Anais is gone.

"I'm not finished asking questions," she says between kisses. "You got any brothers and sisters? Parents?"

"No," I answer into her mouth, my hand moving up her thigh. "A father."

"I...have...two..."

"Parents?"

"Brothers..."

Later I would learn she'd been orphaned by a car crash, raised by relatives. But at that moment I didn't care. A hard cock has no conscience.

I listen for the tiny sigh that means she won't talk anymore. She is more than willing to be distracted and I am a master of distraction. It may be my only talent.

The goats are bleating louder in the yard and the room is starting to heat from various sources. Sex and murder aren't so different. Both consume. How hard you squeeze the throat. Greek crosses. Sharp edges. Soft flesh. Low voice. Her voice higher now, reaching up. A tear in the pillow. Feathers flying up, falling down. Everywhere, feathers. In her hair, in mine. Her nails in my arms. My hand on her face. My hand on her throat.

I hope I die here.

–

I ROLL OFF THE GIRL. We are panting, or I am, I must be getting old. We're on my living room floor, on the Nepalese rug, no doubt woven by underfed children. I can't look at her. She's blonde. I wanted one with black hair but forgot to specify. New York shoves three sirens in my ears. There were no sirens on Corfu.

"Do you want me to stay?" the girl asks. What was her name? Who the fuck cares. "I've got another hour."

I look down at the glistening remains of myself then out at the night.

"No, thanks. Money's on the table."

"Okay." She pulls on her dress.

"Do you need food?" I ask, maybe thinking of the hungry Nepalese kids who wove my rug.

"I'm fine. I had dinner. Well, see you."

She goes and I turn out the lamp and sit back down on the floor in the dark.

ACT I
SCENE 5

Lights up. The DOCTOR *sits on the floor of his office, drinking scotch. A siren sounds in the distance. He refills his glass, downs it. Enter the* PLAYWRIGHT. *The* DOCTOR *jumps to his feet, takes a step back. She closes the door.*

DOCTOR

What are you doing? You can't be here.

PLAYWRIGHT

That's odd. Because I *am* here.

DOCTOR

I mean it, you need to leave. Go back to your room. I'll have a nurse bring you a sedative.

PLAYWRIGHT

It's still early. I thought you wanted me to interact with people.

DOCTOR

Not in my office. How did you find me?

PLAYWRIGHT

(looking around)

Nice place you got here.

(looking at the bottle of scotch on the floor)

It's a little early for highballs, wouldn't you say?

(sits on his desk)

What's troubling you, Doctor?

DOCTOR

I'll walk you back to your room now. Or I'll call security.

(She hops off his desk and wanders over to a wall of framed diplomas.)

PLAYWRIGHT

Emory University, huh? I don't picture you in the South.

DOCTOR

Why not?

PLAYWRIGHT

You seem cold.

DOCTOR

I'm not.

PLAYWRIGHT

We'll see.

DOCTOR

Okay, we're done here. Let's go.

PLAYWRIGHT

You're drunk.

DOCTOR

No, I'm not. I had one drink. And I shouldn't have. But let's just—

PLAYWRIGHT

(looking at him more closely)

You are. You're drunk.

(In one quick motion, she grabs the bottle off the floor.)

DOCTOR

Give me that!

(He grabs for the bottle but she leaps away and runs behind the desk.)

PLAYWRIGHT

It's empty.

DOCTOR

I didn't drink—

(Beat)

I did not drink it all today. I almost never drink at work. This is a very rare—

PLAYWRIGHT

Bullshit. Liar-pants-on-fire. Don't treat me like I'm stupid or I'll put you in one of my plays.

DOCTOR

Your plays?

PLAYWRIGHT

Writing someone up is the best revenge. Immortalizing all their flaws on the stage.

DOCTOR

Revenge? But there's no need—

PLAYWRIGHT

Relax. I wouldn't do that to you. I just want you to level with me, is all. So you like to drink at work. Why should I tell anyone? Have you got any white powder?

DOCTOR

White powder? No, I—

PLAYWRIGHT

Save that for home? You strike me as a multitalented kind of addict. I doubt alcohol is your only vice.

DOCTOR

I am not an addict. Give me the bottle.

(Beat)

Give me the fucking bottle.

PLAYWRIGHT

I've been bored, lying in that bed. I need a little exercise.

(He runs toward her, lunging for the bottle. She eludes his grasp, darts to a sofa on the other side of the office. He comes after her and she evades him. They are running in a jagged circle. She leaps onto his desk, still holding the bottle.)

DOCTOR

Get the fuck off my desk and give me the bottle!

PLAYWRIGHT

Ssshhh! Do you want the whole hospital to hear? I'd keep my voice down if I were you.

DOCTOR

Why? You think anyone's going to take your word over mine!

PLAYWRIGHT

Yeah, I do! Do you want me to scream? Because I will fucking scream this place down. Stop chasing me. We've both had our exercise.

(Beat)

Wasn't it fun? I just feel sorry for you.

DOCTOR

I don't want your pity.

PLAYWRIGHT

You want somebody's pity. No—mercy. You want somebody's mercy. A woman's. Female mercy is always the best.

DOCTOR

Oh, for fuck's sake. What do you want? Why do you care who I am? What the fuck does it matter?

PLAYWRIGHT

Of course it matters. I want to help you.

DOCTOR

You're my patient. I'm supposed to be helping you.

PLAYWRIGHT

Maybe I don't need help. I'm a successful playwright with no major addictions. I'd call that a mental-health success story.

DOCTOR

You turn into other people.

PLAYWRIGHT

Who doesn't? I tell stories. Every storyteller needs a muse, or many.

DOCTOR

You stabbed yourself.

PLAYWRIGHT

We're getting off topic. Anyway, I admit the stabbing was not my finest hour, but it really, in actual fact, wasn't *my* hour at all. It was Maxine's. And now that it's over I can finish her play. As soon as I get the hell out of here. But I'd like to help you before I go. You poor unfortunate soul.

DOCTOR

This is fucking surreal. And ridiculous.

PLAYWRIGHT

The surreal is often ridiculous. And the ridiculous is often surreal.

DOCTOR

And how would you propose to help me? Assuming I actually need help, which I don't.

PLAYWRIGHT

She wants you to know she forgives you.

(The DOCTOR *grabs the* PLAYWRIGHT *and slams her against a wall.)*

Blackout

PLAYWRIGHT

SARAH BERNHARDT and Eleonora Duse were arguing in my dream last night. Whenever they show up and fight about who's a better actress, it's a sign my play is going well. Maxine will be pleased. There's no cause for her to murder me yet.

Sam is lying beside me. We always share the bed when he stays over. He lets me put my feet against his leg when they get cold. Saintliness is a collection of small tender things.

It's early and he's asleep. I'm so glad I'm still here. When we went to sleep I had no idea, of course, if I would be here in the morning. Sam has only woken up next to Maxine once. He said she seemed rather horrified to find him in her bed, and then demanded he make breakfast and pour the giggle water.

I've told Maxine explicitly that she is to be nice to Sam at all times, but God knows I can't control her. Though if I haven't scared him off yet, I'm not likely to. And he doesn't just stay because I make him money. That could be the biggest miracle of my life.

It's always a comfort to wake up to someone who snores. At least then you know they're not dead.

My last boyfriend snored. My only boyfriend. My only love. People with muses shouldn't have boyfriends. I learned that the hard way. Or I knew it already, really, but what the hell. He lied about his snoring, I lied about the people who inhabit my body from time to time.

Seems like a fair trade to me. Love is a series of small lies, convincingly told. People don't seem to stick around when the jig is up.

I look over at Sam, his belly rising and falling, a small dome backlit by the light conquering the Indian shawl covering the window, and know I should feel lucky that one man in the world met me and my cast of characters and chose to stay. And I do. But I'm greedy. I want more.

The only lover I've ever had disappeared. Well, that's not true, that first part is a lie. I've had lots of lovers; I just don't remember most of them. They came and went like the night. But I loved only one, and he stayed for longer before disappearing. I like to imagine he loved me too. Imagination can be more helpful than truth.

He had red hair, almost as red as mine. I've always thought people who look like brother and sister shouldn't have sex. I made an exception for him. Henry. Henry with his crooked smile. Henry with his pale hairless belly, the skin almost shimmery, like a fish. In bed, I used to trace the geometry of his body, drawing lines from one freckle to another to make shapes. Isosceles triangle. Cube. Parallelogram. And Henry would trace lines on me, following the blue veins running beneath my Saran Wrap skin. It was the first time I was ever good at math.

He came to fix my computer, that's how we met. He isn't like Welly, if that's what you're thinking. Welly is a completely different person.

Henry is a violinist. A Canadian in New York without papers, busking in the subway and fixing computers on the side. He was carrying his violin case when he showed up at my door. I had a bump on my forehead from bashing it against the wall. My first reaction upon discovering that I might have erased my third act. I was writing a play about two people trapped in hell, a love story. It got great reviews.

I answered the door holding a package of frozen peas to my noggin. Henry cocked his head to the side, his expression Tarzan-ing between alarm and a fit of laughter.

"Are you all right?"

"If a person has frozen vegetables stuck to their brow, it's safe to assume they're not all right. Come in."

"Do you mind if I put this here?" he said, setting his violin case down.

"Do anything you want, just please, save my play."

I started to cry. Henry didn't recoil and look paralyzed, the way most men do in the face of female ocular leakage.

"Don't worry," he said. "I'm good at finding lost things."

I led him to my fount of anguish, the laptop sitting menacingly in the middle of the living room floor surrounded by notes my then-muse had shredded the night before, alphabet-tinged snowflakes.

While he got to work I slumped against a wall, letting water from the melting peas run down my face.

"I'm sure I backed up the file. I don't know what happened. I don't know what happened. I don't know what happened. Unless they didn't like it. Maybe they didn't like it. Oh my God. Maybe they erased it."

"Who?"

"My characters. Well, fuck them, anyway. I wonder what they didn't like."

I let the bag of peas fall to the floor.

Henry stopped working and stared at me. "That lump on your head looks bad. What happened? Do you have any more frozen vegetables?"

"Broccoli. But I don't need broccoli, I need my third act. Please."

"Okay, love. Hang on."

Nobody had ever called me love. An aural life preserver if ever I heard one.

While I sat on the floor with my arms, legs, fingers, toes, and possibly eyes crossed, Henry worked his magic. Or what I was hoping against hope, crossing against cross would be his magic.

"I think I found it," he said, after what seemed many lifetimes. "This it?"

I don't remember getting from the floor to Henry, or clinging to his arm—though he later claimed I did—I just remember seeing my third act smiling at me, resurrected from the dead.

"Oh, I've missed you!" That was me, talking to my third act.

"If God exists, you might be It!" That was me, talking to Henry.

"Thank you. I wish women would say that to me more often."

A fit of hysterical laughter seized me, because hysterical laughter is the best antidote to hysterical tears, as I've had copious occasions to learn. It's also infectious, so soon we were both bent double, spluttering and gasping, trying and failing to speak. Insanity loves company. I'd been holed up writing for three weeks and hadn't seen anybody except Cosette, who'd brought the frozen peas like she had a premonition I would need them. I hate peas.

"Do you like champagne?" I asked, when I could speak.

"Of course. What's not to like?" Henry replied, looking at me like he was trying to gauge what planet I had parachuted in from.

"My thoughts exactly. Then you must have some. It's the least I could do for a man who just saved my life."

"It's only noon."

"It's five o'clock in London. And one of my plays is being staged in the West End, so I'm there, for all intents and purposes. Or a piece of me is. Thus, Happy Hour is upon us. You don't have anywhere you need to be, do you? Your violin case makes you look mighty important."

"I was going to busk in the subway, but Happy Hour sounds better. Pour away."

"I was hoping you'd say that. Look, I'm very calm and very sane now that you've saved my third act from certain oblivion. I couldn't let you leave thinking I'm a lunatic."

"I don't think you're a lunatic."

As the vise of hysteria released, I saw Henry's face for the first time. A full mouth, crooked when he smiled. Eyes lit with a strange amber light. A scar, a single knife stroke, through one eyebrow. Freckles advertising his paleness. And the hair, not Medusa-wild like mine, but fiery and standing on end like an electrified brush.

I don't want you to go. Pour the champagne, hurry up.

Henry smiled that crooked smile. "Sorry, I haven't seen any of your plays. I'd like to, I'm sure they're amazing."

"I like to think so too, for all the hell they cause me, including physical injury. But most of the time I'm consumed by self-doubt and feelings of failure, like any self-respecting writer." My head was throbbing.

He followed me to the kitchen. His eyes moved over all my hand-painted signs illustrating the contents of each drawer and cupboard.

"I'm practicing my still-life skills, and the paintings help me find stuff."

"Oh. I should do that, it's a smart idea. You're a good painter."

"Thanks. It's the most practical thing I've ever done."

The cork popped. That really is the most relaxing sound in the universe.

"Damn. They're never where they're supposed to be," I said, staring into the flute cupboard. "Somebody must have moved them. I know it wasn't me."

"Did you have a party?"

"No. I've had...houseguests. They're gone now, thank God. I don't always like sharing my space, but I don't have a choice."

"Why don't you have a choice?"

I stopped searching and looked at him. My saviour really did have eyes the colour of honey.

"It's a long story."

"I love long stories. You're a playwright, you must tell good ones."

"Oh, I have help."

"You mean an editor?"

"Lots of them."

"But you're the one who has to come up with the ideas and do the actual writing."

"Inspiration can be found in unexpected places."

"Well, I'm honoured to meet a playwright. You're my first," Henry said, his lopsided smile feeding a deep dimple. I imagined sticking my finger in it.

"Thanks. Hang around New York long enough and you'll meet plenty of neurotic writers. This city isn't big enough to hold all the self-doubt."

Henry laughed. "I'm a neurotic musician, we'll get along fine. And we have the ginger connection." He gestured to his hair.

Then he just sat and sipped, slow and easy, not seeming the slightest bit awkward about sitting on a life raft-sized couch with a woman sporting a giant goose egg who minutes earlier had been clutching herself and churning the waters of hysteria. Henry always says yes to life, and I love that about him.

"That looks bad. The lump. You really smacked yourself."

"I know. Sorry you're looking at two heads instead of one."

"Well, one's a little prettier but I'm sure the other has its charms."

Wow. It'd been ages since anyone called me pretty. I didn't know what to say. A charming redhead on my sofa. What are the odds?

"Anyway," Henry continued, "I'm all for collecting surreal moments."

"Is this the weirdest New York experience you've had so far?"

"Not any weirder than playing Bach in a subway station. Two women and one guy have flashed me in the past week. And then they gave me money. You seem lucid for a crazy writer."

"I try."

Say something interesting. You write dialogue for a living, for Chrissake.

"Your eyes look like goldenrod honey."

Holy fuck. That was the best I could come up with? My muses always have better personalities than me. It's a real piss-off.

"I mean, it's just...your eyes... I was raised upstate and my father kept bees."

Henry smiled, tilting his head like he could understand me better on an angle. "I can honestly say nobody has ever said that to me before. Are goldenrod-honey eyes a good thing?"

I nodded, feeling heat flood my goose egg. Thank God I write better than I talk.

"I'm glad," he said. "Thanks for noticing."

"Forget I said anything. And please don't tell anyone I was acting crazy. Or that I opened the door with a bag of peas stuck to my head."

"I won't tell anyone."

"Thanks."

"I'm actually really good at it," he said.

"What?"

Henry touched my face. "Keeping secrets."

–

AN HOUR LATER, Henry was standing on my bed naked playing his violin, because sometimes Bach and sex are easier than conversation. He played as if for Carnegie Hall, unperturbed by nakedness. My own aggressively ectomorphic brand of birthday suit was obscured by a strategically placed pillow. There was no need to hide, though, at least not that part of me. Henry had already traced my collarbone and ribs and said, "Pieces of ivory." So I pushed the pillow aside and the fiddling mass of freckles above me smiled. That's how I like to remember Henry: naked and smiling, with a bow in his hand.

ACT I
SCENE 6

Lights up. The DOCTOR'S *office. The* DOCTOR *has the* PLAYWRIGHT *pinned against the wall.*

PLAYWRIGHT

You don't want to do this. Not again.

(Beat)

DOCTOR

(releases her, backs away)

I—I'm sorry. I didn't mean... It's just... How did you—

PLAYWRIGHT

I won't tell anyone. Your secret's safe with me.

DOCTOR

I'm not usually— I don't know what happened.

PLAYWRIGHT

I do. I'm good at knowing what happened. That's how I write my plays. My characters tell me what happened.

DOCTOR

I'm not a character in a fucking play.

PLAYWRIGHT

We're all characters in a play. And we all get a turn being the bad guy.

Blackout

MAXINE

June 1, 1925

ROBERT IS MARRIED. I didn't know that when he insisted I move into his apartment. I am an idiot. I shall admit it on these pages and nowhere else. A man who keeps a "spare" apartment is a man who has a mistress, or is looking for one. I am growing up fast.

Now: think of every expletive you've ever heard, and picture all of them coming out of my mouth in one undammed river of invective and, oh my, was that a Tiffany vase that went flying past his head? I'd never heard of Tiffany vases. What's so special about them? They break like any other.

–

THEY BREAK *like any other.* Yeah, that was the first entry I wrote after I started growing up fast. It was high time, I guess. I thought I was pretty damn grown-up when I got to New York City, what with no mother and all. But I hadn't seen nothin' yet.

I'm sitting in the bar at The Plaza. They let you drink bubbly right out in the open; not all change is bad, I'm sure you'd agree. I need to be somewhere that looks vaguely familiar. Yet I'm not sure that vague familiarity is better than complete transformation or absence. Something that both is and is not what you loved might be more terrifying than outright destruction.

I spent a night at The Plaza with Robert two days after we met. I figured I might learn something and boy, I wasn't disappointed. So that's what all the fuss is about. As soon as he got me into our room, he ripped off my blouse.

"Hey!" I cried. "That's new! And it's my best one!"

I don't know why I didn't think to be afraid. I guess he seemed too sophisticated to be dangerous. After spending years with my father's drunken rages, I thought of dangerous men as ones with dirty fingernails, a two-day shadow, and whisky on their breath. Ones who liked to hunt deer while on the giggle water.

"Forget it, princess," Robert said into my mouth. "I'll buy you plenty more."

The late afternoon sun shot through the curtains and hit the chandelier overhead, which fired buckshot light all over the room. The lights made me dizzy but I kept my eyes open even as Robert devoured my mouth, because I wanted to know what he looked like with his eyes closed. He was twice my age and had creases 'round his lids. They made me feel like I was stronger than him. Damn, what a heady feeling.

I had no memory of anyone seeing me in the altogether. You'd think I would've been shy or something, but I wasn't. Modesty is for amateurs. Besides, Robert is an old cake-eater and he knows what to do with his hands. And so, it turns out, do I. It's always a delight to discover a new talent. Robert and I got a bit giddy with our talents and maybe a little zozzled, and I was naive enough to believe a man's lust meant everything was copacetic. A man's desire does give a woman power, after all, no doubt about it. It's just that desire isn't a fixed constellation like I used to imagine love might be, and sometimes you gotta kill to stay on top when your star begins to fall.

But back then, in that suite at The Plaza Hotel, I was happy to be naked and wanted and dizzy with the shattered light of the swankiest chandelier I'd ever seen. It was a big step up from letting a boy from Latin class put his hands on me out behind my father's woodshed. Robert's touch wiped me clean of all the rustic dirt I'd grown up in. Hell, with him inside me, I was practically a swell now. The pain of his plunges seemed heroic. I distracted myself with the softness of the softest sheets I'd ever had the fortune to recline upon, and with staring at the lines around Robert's eyes, which were still closed. This is easy, I thought, if the audience isn't even looking. But damned if I became an actress so I could be ignored. So I yanked on a fistful of his hair and that got his attention right quick, and it also got his hands around my throat, but I was only frightened for a moment and then it was over. Hell, being a swell and a Broadway star didn't seem like it was going to be much harder than the rough-and-tumble I was raised with. If only love were as easy as pulling a man's hair.

Robert rolled off, got up and rummaged through his jacket for gaspers. He sparked one for himself and one for me.

"I don't smoke."

He stuck the cigarette in my mouth.

"It's easy to learn, darling."

I took a puff and coughed. Sex is forever linked with hair-pulling, strangulation and the first foul taste of tobacco. Maybe love is, too.

Robert sat on the edge of the bed smoking and touching my face.

"You got a nice puss. You're a real doll."

"You're not so bad yourself." My voice sounded different, and I figured the sticky blood between my legs must have something to do with it.

"I can see you going real far, baby. I mean, you got talent, and with a face like yours."

God in heaven, I think I heard bells at that moment and I got shivery all over. Sometimes all that keeps us going in life is a belief in some great destiny, and when you land on destiny's doorstep and knock and the door flies open, well, that might be better than love itself, though don't count me an authority.

I sat up and took a drag of my ciggy. I hacked a bit, but not too much, and then I said in my new deeper voice, “I'm made for Broadway.”

Robert blew a smoke ring, a trick I would learn in a jiffy.

“My dear,” he said softly, “you most certainly are.”

–

“WOULD YOU like another?”

I look up, half expecting to see Robert standing in front of me. It's my waiter, come to collect my empty glass.

“Yes, please, why not. I always drink champagne before noon on Fridays.”

“It's Thursday.”

“Close enough.”

I pull out my notebook, the one I am rewriting my diary in. The original was destroyed in my fireplace, have I told you that? All burned up, along with some duds. Anyway, when sitting in a joint alone, I like to appear to be doing something important, otherwise I look like a disappointed wallflower jilted by her date, or a high-class whore. I would rather the latter, if such a choice need be made.

Does it seem stupid, writing anew an old diary that got burned up? I want my playwright to understand me. And it makes me feel better. Funny, isn't it, how we never stop wanting to be understood. I didn't mean giggle-funny. Well, you know what I mean.

June 5, 1925

Robert replaced the Tiffany vase and bought an extra one for insurance. I guess he's anticipating I might have cause to break another. He seems to have a practical head on his shoulders, and I like that about him.

“Baby,” he said, “I know I didn't tell you about my wife, but how could I? I'm crazy in love with you. I take care of her and that's it. We haven't liked each other for years.”

“So what am I, then? A concubine? I read a penny dreadful that had a concubine in it, and nothing worked out real good for her."

He grabbed my face and pulled it close to his. I struggled but he wouldn't let go.

"You're my love, that's what you are. My love."

My knees got weak, and his tongue got mine. I should probably feel bad about what little fight I put up, but what the hell. I love his hands and damn if I ain't more spice than sugar.

Robert has already cast me in another play, and this time I've got a speaking role. I can feel the limelight on the sizzle. All the characters I pretended to be while Papa drank and raged and broke the house are going to give me a happy ending.

We ended up on the floor, Robert with his eyes closed and his hands around my throat, me with my eyes on the two new Tiffany vases, wondering which one would break first.

–

I LOOK UP FROM WRITING when my waiter sets down another glass.

"The Divine Sarah drank half a bottle with every meal. I don't think I'm being excessive."

He furrows his brow, but it doesn't make him look distinguished, just confused. "The Divine Sarah? Was she a drag queen?"

"A what queen?"

"A man who dresses like a woman. I'm sorry, I don't know who you're talking about."

"Actually, she was a woman who dressed like a man, when she played Hamlet, anyway. Sarah Bernhardt, the actress, The Divine Sarah."

"Oh, sorry, never heard of her. Are you an actor?"

"An actress, dear man, I'm an actress. Men are actors."

"Oh, uh, I thought actor was the politically correct term."

"A true thespian is never political. The revelation of human nature is our only cause."

"Uh...right. Are you acting in anything I've heard of? Any TV shows?"

"TV shows? I don't know what you mean. I'm a stage actress. Keep your eye on Broadway, there will soon be a play opening about my life."

"You'll be playing yourself?"

"Not exactly."

"You look kind of young to have a play written about you."

"My dear, that is the nicest thing anyone has said to me all day."

He frowns again, like he doesn't know what else to say. "Enjoy the champagne" is what he comes out with.

Monsieur Waiter stalks off. It occurs to me that he didn't ask my name or the title of the play, so I suppose we can count him out of our audience number. Murder and mayhem are not for everyone.

July 26, 1925

Ronny and Benny were here until a moment ago. They brought two cases of bootleg, so Robert and I are set for a short while. Speakeasies are fun and all, but one must have one's own supply. Robert pays Stan, the elevator operator, some extra dough to let the boys up without asking questions. Robert always gets what he wants. Including me.

What a delight to have music! Robert bought me a Radiola Grand. Guess how much it cost, precisely? Three hundred and fifty clams. I'd never seen so much money. I'm sure he saw my saucer eyes.

"Sure, it's an orchid, but what's a pretty dame without pretty music?" he said as he handed over the cabbage. I feel I am living in a dream, and I hope I die before I wake.

My favorite song *du jour* (I'm ashamed of how little schoolgirl French I've retained. I dare say the language of love is a far more hotsy-totsy tongue than *la langue anglaise*.) is "Down Hearted Blues," as sung by Bessie Smith. Strange that such a blue song would captivate me when I am so wondrously happy.

Robert's fingernails are always clean. A funny thing to love about a man, perhaps. Clean fingernails make me feel safe.

Shall I have a drop of giggle water before Robert arrives? He always visits on Sundays because his fish-eating wife spends the entire day at church. Religion can be charitable in unexpected ways.

Am I very bad, do you think? Should I be sorry? Robert says don't ask the question if you don't want the answer. He has been very lonely, I believe. His wife is cold. A cold wife, I imagine, could drive a man to do all sorts of drastic things. I confess I quite adore being one of his drastic things. If ever a choice must be made, better to burn out in a flash than die of boredom. Life is a play, after all, and who wants to watch a boring play?

Speaking of which, I have news of my speaking role. Oh, wait, let me pour that drop and splash around a bit while I write. Splashing and writing help distract me from this cruel swelter. God, New York City in the deep of summer smells like a trash heap.

I'm back, glass in hand. Golly, it has been too, too long since I've written. So very much has happened. Now about my speaking role—I don't have one. Robert decided to give that play the hook when the temperamental leading man up and quit. I begged him to recast the role. He wouldn't hear of it. The man is nothing if not uncompromising. You might think I should sound more devastated, but—BUT—I do indeed have a job. Soon I'll be a Ziegfeld girl at the New Amsterdam, parading up and down flights of stairs for seventy-five dollars a week. Robert pulled the strings for me—I'm to replace a girl who's in the family way. He arranged a meeting with Mr. Flo Ziegfeld Jr. himself, who is as charming and imposing as I imagined him to be. Mr. Ziegfeld gave me the once-over and proclaimed me "as lovely as can be." I didn't get to show him my acting talent, but a girl has to start somewhere. And really, this somewhere is pretty damn far up the ladder. Mr. Ziegfeld makes stars as fast as the heavens. I may be winking from the sky in no time.

The show just opened. I'll get to strut my stuff all through the summer. It's an enormous stroke of luck, really it is. Though I should have liked to have got in on my own merits. It's damn hard in this town. That I got a walk-on part at my first audition is nothing less than the Eighth Wonder of the World. I would like to hold out for serious stage plays, not cheapen myself by parading around dressed as a bird. And since I've let Robert install me here on West Fifty-Seventh Street, perhaps it is silly to bother wanting my own seventy-five dollars a week. But I do. I came to New York to be an actress, not a concubine.

"Of course the Follies'd snatch you up. Look at that porcelain puss. But that's not acting, it's being a mannequin for pennies. I only pulled the strings to shut you up. I should never have wilted." Robert ran a hand through his hair. It's grey, his hair. He's not bald, at least.

"I want to be on the stage. This is my first year in New York and I don't want to stay in the shadows waiting for my big break."

"You're not in the shadows, you're living a damned lucky life. That walk-on I cast you for? Tallulah Bankhead played that part, her first time out back in '18. And now look at her, London loves her. Look at this apartment. How many actresses live in a place like so from day one in this crazy circus town? Huh? Answer me!"

His face was turning red then, and I backed away. I pulled my new kimono tight around me. Silk, with butterflies.

I didn't know what to say, so I said nothing. No, that isn't true. I knew what to say, I was just too scared to say it.

I fled into the bedroom, Robert in hot pursuit. He's got a temper like Papa, and longer arms. Lucky I'm a damn fast runner with a talent for giving men the slip. That's my father's legacy and I'm not sure whether to thank him or curse him.

I launched myself onto the bed and rolled off, quick as a cat. Robert stood in the doorway, flushed and glaring.

"My old lady does whatever the hell I say," he spat, a vein in his temple doing a spastic dance.

"I ain't your old lady. If she's what you want, then go home. I'll find someplace else to live."

"Don't say ain't, you sound like a damn rube."

"Ain't. Ain't ain't ain't ain't ain't ain't—"

In a flash he grabbed me by the shoulders, threw me against the wall. He was breathing hard. I held his eyes—I can beat anybody in a staring contest. My heart was coming out of my chest like a fist.

"Damn you little—"

And damn if he didn't stick his tongue down my throat. Deep down, he's a soft touch. Weak in the knees, at least for me. Being in love is the most wonderful, useful thing that has ever happened to me.

I think I'll have a little drink to that.

Giggle juice makes such a pleasant splash. Robert is late, but I don't mind. I am happy writing and sipping and looking around at my little piece of heaven on West Fifty-Seventh Street. The walls of the smoking room—I have a smoking room!—are the most exquisite shade of turquoise, as though I am living in a tropical sea. As of three days ago, I have the most glorious silver evening gown to complement my walls. Or rather, the walls complement me, a lithe slip of metallic against the blue blueness and green greenness. Last night I stood all alone in my dress, sipping away, feeling quite the bee's knees. I was part of the décor come to life. Never in my wildest imaginings.

And then I was frightened, so terribly, terribly frightened. Because I heard Papa's voice, as I often do when I am alone. I thought of his last words, the last words he spoke to me before I left him forever.

"You're just another dumb Dora with stars in her eyes. An actress? You think you're tough enough for the world, all five feet two, eyes of blue. But remember: the world eats the pretty ones for breakfast."

ACT II
SCENE I

Lights up. The PLAYWRIGHT *lying on bed. Enter the* NURSE, *a cup of pills in hand. The* PLAYWRIGHT'S *eyes pop open. Bolts upright. The* NURSE *jumps.*

PLAYWRIGHT

Good evening.

NURSE

You scared me. I thought you were sleeping.

PLAYWRIGHT

Where's Doc?

NURSE

He went home early. Wasn't feeling well.

PLAYWRIGHT

I have that effect on men. And here I thought we had a nice chat.

NURSE

I'm sure you did have a nice chat. He's not sick because of you. He's getting the flu.

PLAYWRIGHT

The flu is not what's wrong with that man.

NURSE

What makes you think there's something wrong with him?

PLAYWRIGHT

Like I said, we had a nice chat.

NURSE

He's a very caring doctor.

PLAYWRIGHT

Caring? We'll see about that. I'm still testing him.

NURSE

Oh. Well, I hope he passes. Now: it's time for your medication.

PLAYWRIGHT

The red, the white, and the blue. Patriotism is the last refuge of Big Pharma.

NURSE

So said a great man.

PLAYWRIGHT

Well done, you know your Samuel Johnson.

NURSE

I studied literature before I switched to nursing.

PLAYWRIGHT

Maybe I should've become a nurse. I'd be more adept at self-medicating. But that's the thing: I don't want to be medicated.

I need my muses to tell their stories. Why would I want to silence their voices? It's dangerous to handcuff the creative process. Creativity means destroying your way to giving birth. If you can't give birth, then you destroy for nothing.

NURSE

But why does creativity have to be destructive?

PLAYWRIGHT

Why does childbirth hurt? Why is my hair red? Why do people kill the ones they love?

NURSE

I guess I'm better at administering meds than rhetorical argument. Here, take these.

(The PLAYWRIGHT takes pills.)

PLAYWRIGHT

God, if only writing a play were as easy as swallowing a pill.

NURSE

Writing has always been really hard for me.

PLAYWRIGHT

Me too. If it weren't so damn hard for me, I wouldn't be good at it.

NURSE

That doesn't make any sense.

PLAYWRIGHT

Writers are just people who find writing damn hard and can't let it go.

NURSE

That sounds masochistic.

PLAYWRIGHT

And Bingo was his name-o. But I can't complain. My masochism draws an audience. People pay to see it. And this makes me the luckiest person alive.

NURSE

You seem happy tonight.

PLAYWRIGHT

I *am* happy. The players are right where they need to be. All of them.

NURSE

Are your stitches itchy?

PLAYWRIGHT

Like a thousand mosquitoes converging on my chest. Maxine owes me. You'd think she could have mimed it instead of being so goddamn realistic.

NURSE

Yes, well, I hope something like this never happens again. The wound is healing well.

PLAYWRIGHT

But I'll have a scar.

NURSE

Scars give us character.

PLAYWRIGHT

I got my character from my character. How poetic.

(NURSE exits. As soon as she is gone, the PLAYWRIGHT jumps out of bed and peels the fitted sheet off the mattress, removing the set of clothing hidden beneath. She dresses in a hurry. Looks for shoes—there are none. Puts on slippers. As lights begin to fade, she moves to the door. A spotlight hits her as she turns back to the empty hospital room.)

PLAYWRIGHT

Showtime.

Blackout

DOCTOR

I BOUGHT A CASE OF WINE and a bottle of scotch on my way home from the hospital. They're wrong about mixing alcohol and antidepressants—doesn't bother me at all.

I told everyone I'm getting the flu. I do feel shitty, so it could be true. A lie should always be textured with the truth. All good storytellers know this.

So, for medicinal purposes, I'm halfway through a bottle of Malbec and halfway through a block of Manchego. Next up is a nice Barbera and a chunk of Taleggio. And the scotch is waiting there, so patiently, ready to knock me out when the dark is deep and sleep is absent. A shrink's salary allows for stylish self-destruction.

A patient had cornered me in my office only once before today. A schizophrenic named Rodney who'd unwound a paper clip and was wielding it like a knife. I wasn't scared then, wild-eyed though he was. My right hook is pretty good, and he was skinny from consuming cigarettes and not much else for two months before he landed at my broken-toy factory. I yelled for security and Rodney was hauled away, leaving a trail of invective and spittle.

I didn't yell for security today. She scares me more than Rodney ever did, but I didn't want to be rescued. Rescued from what? The woman's hair weighs more than the rest of her. It's her eyes that freak me out, permanently wet like the eyes of Anais, and what she thinks she knows. She thinks she knows things about me. She doesn't know anything. That's impossible. And creepy as hell.

Anais had that look. It jabs a pin in your spine so you can't move, so you have to watch her watching you.

"Why are you looking at me like that?" I would say.

"Like what?"

"Like you know things."

"I *do* know things. I'm clairvoyant. Sometimes I have prophetic dreams. Just like my grandmother."

She had been raised, after her parents died, by her father's mother. Magda read tea leaves, palms and tarot cards in the back of a European food shop. *She was a brilliant reader. I'm not gifted like her. But I have some of her instincts.* In '56, Anais's grandmother fled Hungary with her two teenage children, and her tarot cards sewn into the lining of her coat. *She had to hawk all her jewellery. It was the cards that were really important to her.* She died three months before Anais came to Greece, leaving her granddaughter with an order to sleep with the tarot, and a fondness for raw kohlrabi.

"Clairvoyant?" I say on the eighth day of cohabitation, an eyebrow raised. "You mean like ESP? I don't believe in that stuff."

Anais looks at me with faint amusement. "You're arrogant," she says. "That'll be your downfall."

On the eighth day of cohabitation, at noon, we are dressed for the first time in a sweetly long time and sitting at her splintery wooden kitchen table smearing Tirokafteri cheese on bread. We are on our second bottle of wine, part of a large stash bought from the obese lady down the road who runs an olive-oil-and-wine stand. Anais can hold her liquor. So far, every damn thing about her makes this house a paradise in which to hide.

"I'm happy right now," she says. "I guess that's why I'm letting you stay."

"Happiness is everything. I should know, I'm a shrink."

"I don't know if I believe you're a shrink. My ESP tells me different."

"Then what am I?"

"I don't know, but I'm going to find out."

"Do you always get what you want?"

"Yeah. Except for my parents dying, I didn't want that. Since then, I make sure I get what I want."

"You loved them a lot."

"Yes. Didn't you love your mother?"

"I don't know."

"What do you mean you don't know? Aren't we supposed to love our parents?"

"Doesn't mean we always do."

"Don't you know what you feel?"

"She was cold. I don't know that she loved me either."

"Oh. Sorry. How did she die?"

"Liver cancer. She drank. My dad never remarried. He keeps a stable of women. Actually, I'm pretty sure he did that before my mother died, maybe that's why she drank. He's a bit of a cold fish too."

I don't feel anything as I speak. Her dark-blue eyes, in contrast, get even wetter, and she bites her lip. We are nearing the bottom of the second bottle. Her heavy eyelids give her a look like she's always nearing the bottom of a second bottle. A weird inebriate beauty.

"Well, that sucks," she says, squeezing my hand hard. "Eat some more cheese. Cheese makes everything better."

"This makes everything better."

"What?"

"Being here. With you. Thank you for letting me carry you through your door."

"No regrets so far."

"Let's keep it that way." I tuck a lock of hair behind her ear.

"Yeah. Let's."

"I guess everything changes."

"Don't I know it. My parents were killed by a Buick with faulty brakes."

"Let's pretend nothing'll change."

"We've only been sleeping together for eight days. We're both pretending. This is the best part. But wait till I break out the tarot. Then I'll get the truth about you."

"The tarot? What are you going to do?"

"Read you."

"Read me? I don't know what that means."

"You'll find out."

"What if I don't want to?"

"Then you can't stay here."

"You'll kick me out if I don't let you do voodoo?"

"It's not voodoo. You'll see."

She stares at me while she licks cheese off her fingers.

"How badly do you want to stay in this house?"

"How badly do you want me to stay?"

Anais smiles. "I'll live if you go. I'm sure you find that hard to believe."

"I don't believe it at all."

She grabs my face with both hands and bites my lip. "You," she says, drawing back, "are an arrogant prick."

I smile and put a hand up her dress. Can't argue with that.

"Now." Anais pulls away. "Before I finish biting you, let's check on the goats."

We head out into the heat, the sun and the gamey smell of animals mixing with the hot swill of wine in my head. Anais adores the goats. They're not hers. They belong to the sprawling farm that adjoins her small yard, seem to prefer hanging out near her cottage. She has named each of them.

"Daphne, my love," she says, chucking a fat goat under the chin.

I tune out while she talks to the goats and stare at the landscape. The forts of the Old Town of Corfu are visible in the near distance. Between us, the olive groves of our neighbour lean lushly toward the Ionian Sea, a deep bruise healing into a yellowish shore. Maybe I read that line somewhere. I used to like poetry. Those days are long gone. When I first arrived in Corfu Town I considered jumping into that deep bruise, keeping my head under long enough to find out if drowning is truly euphoric. That's what I was thinking about when I met Anais. The truth is, I'm too much a self-serving bastard to end it all. But it was a nice thought while it lasted. Nice in the way that a penance offers believers a sense of redemption. I'm not a believer, though, so why do I need redemption?

Because as I sat in a café on the Liston the night before I met Anais, drinking ouzo and watching tourists laugh in the lantern light, I noticed all the stars were watching me. There are more stars in Greece than at home. Or so it seems. All that sugar up there, watching me and making sure I didn't forget what I'd done. I waited for them to rupture me with their light. I was drunk, true, so I started thinking maybe the sea would take what the sky doesn't want. But I just kept drinking ouzo instead.

And now I'm here fucking a woman who tastes of honey so maybe the stars don't hate me after all.

I was right to leave Athens. Hell, was I ever. Noisy, dirty, oily-skinned Athens. The walls closing in on me. I can breathe on Corfu. There is green. There is life.

I was right to follow Henry Miller to Greece. Could have gone anywhere, money hot in my hand. But if he found his colossus here, who am I to argue? He's the only bit of English lit that stuck. Not sure why. He makes the primitive, the brutal, poetic. Maybe that's what I'm hoping for. My brutality as poetry.

Fuck, this wine has gone to my head. My head as a Petrokoritho grape, exploding in the August sun. I'm liquored among goats. Who says life isn't full of surprises?

Anais is crouched between two goats, cupping their faces in each hand and making kissing sounds. I wander into the olive grove of the adjacent farm. It makes a slight sound, barely audible, an in-breath of salty air. Or maybe it's just the wine in my ears. The Grecian landscape seems talkative in a way no American patch of ground ever has. There's an ancient pulse beating under my feet. The sea heaves and twists around the island like it wants to take back this quaint bit of firma that escaped its grasp.

If I could stay here with Anais. If I could. If. Last night she made a Greek dinner. *My mother was a fucking phenomenal cook. That's what I remember most about her. After she died, I mostly ate my grandmother's Hungarian food. I missed the Greek taste. But I bet I'm a better cook now than my mum. Watch me cook a Greek feast that'll knock your pants off. Wait a minute, your pants* are *off. Get dressed for God's sake. No more until dessert!*

I think it's funny that she says "mum." Apparently it's a Canadian weirdism. I told her the correct term is "mom," heavy on the nasal "ah." She says the American accent is atrocious. *But you have a nice voice, I'll give you that.*

I sat at her rustic kitchen table watching her chop and drinking Tsitsibira. *You can't leave Corfu without drinking Tsitsibira. It's literally the most refreshing thing in the world. Literally.* She was right—lemon, ginger, sugar, and water somehow add up to something Corfiots justifiably adore. If it made you drunk, it would be even better.

Anais is a whirling dervish in the kitchen. I had never actually watched somebody cook before. That might seem odd, having made it this far without seeing anyone whip out a knife and change earth into dinner. But my mother is long dead and didn't cook anyway, and my father didn't notice I was there. I never bothered to watch what our cook did in the kitchen. And then I mostly ate in restaurants. Food was survival. Until I saw Anais making it. Then it seemed like more.

"It's very important to keep your knives sharp," she said while slicing into the belly of an eggplant. "A dull knife is a dull dinner."

"Was that what your mother used to say?"

She smiled and wiped sweat from the fine hairs at the corners of her mouth. "You got it."

"I'm all for sharp knives."

"You said you've never cooked anything."

"I'm a guy. We like our weapons."

She rolled her eyes. "I'm not a guy, but I like my weapons too. Just remember that before you piss off the cook."

"Is that a threat?"

"It's a guarantee."

She stopped slicing and arched a heavy brow. I arched back and we stared until she burst out laughing.

"I always win staring contests," she said. "I let you win because cooking puts me in a generous mood."

"What are you making? Besides eggplant."

"I'm not making eggplant, my love. I'm making moussaka. Which you will soon kiss my feet for."

"I already kiss your feet."

"No, you don't. You suck my toes, that's different."

"Oh. I didn't realize one outranks the other."

"How much you have to learn of the ways of the world."

"Teach me."

"I am. You'll never forget me, she who enlightened you."

"You're probably right about that."

"I'm right about everything. You'll see."

"I won't argue with a woman holding a knife."

"Hmm...you're smarter than that towhead of yours might suggest."

I dyed my hair blond in Athens. She thinks it's natural. Which is the idea.

"I guess I'm the exception to the blond rule. I must be the exception to more than one rule."

"Oh? Why do you say that?"

"Because I'm in a gorgeous woman's kitchen watching her make moussaka. That doesn't happen to just any schmuck. I'm assuming you don't make moussaka for every guy you meet in a café."

"True. The only man I've cooked for since I moved here is Stefanos, the farmer next door, and his wife Vassy was with him. You're the only man I've bought groceries with."

We had ridden into Corfu Town on her Vespa to buy the mess of ingredients now spread in front of her.

"Taste this," she said, pushing a bit of cheese in my mouth. "Kefalograviera. Transcendent, isn't it? It's essential to the moussaka. American cheese is revolting."

"I didn't know cheese could be transcendent."

"Then you don't know anything."

"You're right," I said, suddenly sad. "I don't know anything."

"What's wrong? Here," she said, filling goblets. "Wine heals. You should never cook without drinking. Another of my mother's culinary rules."

I loved watching her peel potatoes. One perfect spiral. Another. And another.

When the moussaka was done and glistening in the centre of the table, Anais said, "Just let me stare at it for a minute."

Silence in the hot kitchen.

When she looked at me she had tears in her eyes. "Reminds me of my mother. I like to look at it when it's whole, before we cut it in pieces."

I squeezed her hand. I was tipsy by then and didn't know what to say. Not that I necessarily know what to say when I'm sober.

"Okay," she said. "Enough of that. Eat."

I never thought dinner could make me feel anything other than full. Potatoes, eggplant, cheese, lamb, cinnamon, cream. Under her alchemy they became something else, something I was still thinking about the next morning, today, when I woke up and reached for her hand and wished I could go on holding it. On and on.

The sun beats down on the olive grove and I stop walking and crouch in the dirt. I wonder how much longer I can stay here before something happens to fuck it up. I'm familiar with the law of inevitability, which says that something always happens after a while to fuck things up. I got a fake passport before I left the States. I'll burn it and get another fake if I go back. But why go back?

I can hear Anais still talking to the goats. Her voice is loud and strong and sure of itself. There's no reason to leave. Yet. No reason. Inevitability finds you, you don't need to find it. I pick a crushed olive off the ground, squeeze it between thumb and forefinger. Don't smash what hasn't yet fallen. Only stupid men do that. I'm a bad man, not a stupid man. Of badness and stupidity, I've always considered stupidity the worse sin. Now I'm not sure. Life leaves room for doubt. So much fucking room.

The sun is shining. The olive grove is sighing. So I should shut my fucking mind down and quit worrying. Well, of course I worry. But the cops in Corfu Town don't seem like a threatening bunch. They're too busy drinking ouzo and kumquat liqueur to care about serious cop business. And I'm fucking an amazing cook who talks sweetly to goats. It's just that I'm still shaking off the mess I left behind. And all my life I've worried whenever things were too good. I haven't been with Anais, or on Corfu, for anywhere close to a month. Not enough time for the law of inevitability to grab me by the throat.

"Where are you?" Anais calls.

For a moment I consider not answering. I like being in the olive grove. I like being alone.

"Are you hiding?" She's moving closer to the edge of the grove.

I like this role. Reinvention is a drug. It gets me way high.

"Hello... Are you alive? Where did you go? I finished talking to the goats. Daphne's crazy about me. Let's hide out in bed. The sun's making me drunk."

I drop the crushed olive and walk toward her voice. When I emerge from the grove I hold out my arms. Anais runs into them.

"I thought I'd lost you. What were you doing?"

"Thinking. And sweating. Fuck, it's hot."

"One word: tsitsibira. Actually, let's go swimming, drown our heat sorrows in the sea. I need to baptize you."

"Baptize?"

"I'm reading your cards later. First, I need to baptize you in the waters of Greece. The tarot cards. It's time to find out who you really are."

—

THE MANCHEGO AND TALEGGIO are gone. I've made a good dent in the wine. It's a little past midnight. I can't sleep—it's useless to try till I'm drunker—so I pour a scotch and stare out at the dark mass of Central Park. The moon is low, fallen. A tree may snag it, yank it to the dirt, flood the earth.

I think it's time to leave this town. I've been here quite a few years. A long time, for me. Don't know if I want to play the doctor role anymore. I'm surprisingly good at it. If penance helps, then shrink is a good role to play. But I don't believe in absolution. Or redemption. The brittle fantasies of those who strangle themselves with the stupidity of faith.

The moon drops lower. The scotch is working. Soon I can sleep. Without dreams, I hope.

Where would I go? If not New York, then where?

In New York, one can be both important and anonymous. An excellent and necessary combination.

This is the end of the line. I have no other lines. There is nothing left to say. There is nowhere else to go.

I'm drunk.

Sleep?

Maybe.

Ouch! Fuck. Fuck and fuck. That table wasn't there a few minutes ago. I fucking hate it when my furniture moves around. Never consults me first. I've always hated that table. Tomorrow, trash.

Damn, I think my toe's broken.

What's that sound? There's a sound. Like knocking. It *is* knocking. On my door? Is someone at my door? At this hour? I'm not answering. It's getting louder. Louder. Louder. Now it's pounding. What the fuck? I'm gonna fucking punch—

She's staring at me. I rip open the door, and she's staring at me.

The playwright's staring at me.

ACT II
SCENE 2

Lights up on the DOCTOR'S *apartment. He opens his door to the* PLAYWRIGHT. *Beat. She enters.*

PLAYWRIGHT

Do you have any champagne? I'm parched.

(The Doctor remains at the door.)

PLAYWRIGHT

Are you going to stand there all night? The flummoxed look doesn't become you. Besides, you're letting in a draft.

DOCTOR

How the hell did you get here?

PLAYWRIGHT

I took a cab. I stole a bit of money from the nurses' lounge, but I promise I'll put it back. I couldn't find my purse.

DOCTOR

Forget the money. You're not supposed to leave the hospital. How do you know where I live?

PLAYWRIGHT

My dear, give me a little credit, please. You're drunk.

DOCTOR

I'm not drunk—

PLAYWRIGHT

Yes, you are. Now: are you going to close the door? Or do you want your neighbours to hear our conversation?

(The DOCTOR *shuts door.)*

DOCTOR

What is it you want? You do realize I'm going to call the hospital and have you readmitted?

PLAYWRIGHT

No, I don't think you will.

(glancing at the empty wine bottles and half-empty scotch bottle on the living room table)

Having a party, are we?

DOCTOR

I, uh, had friends over.

PLAYWRIGHT

No, you didn't. Besides, I thought you had the flu. Don't worry, I won't tell anyone. But you should really see a shrink about your problem.

DOCTOR

If you're trying to provoke me again, it's not working.

PLAYWRIGHT

I'm not trying to do anything. Do you mind if I sit?

DOCTOR

Be my guest.

PLAYWRIGHT

So why aren't you reaching for the phone?

DOCTOR

I guess I'm curious.

PLAYWRIGHT

Curiosity can be deadly.

(Beat)

My wound's healed. There's nothing more you can do for me. Nothing more needs to be done. You should drink some water; your head is spinning.

DOCTOR

How do you know what my head is—never mind. Do you want a drink?

PLAYWRIGHT

I don't know, did you leave anything drinkable?

DOCTOR

Water. I have water.

PLAYWRIGHT

Sounds good.

(looking around)

You have a beautiful apartment.

(The DOCTOR gets water.)

DOCTOR

Thanks. Doctors usually do. I assume successful playwrights do as well.

PLAYWRIGHT

Not as nice as this. Besides, luxury isn't really my thing. It's Maxine's thing. My muses don't always get what they want. Actually, given many of them have tragic lives, they often don't get what they want. Which is good, or I'd have nothing to write about. Why are you limping?

DOCTOR

I, uh, banged my toe. It'll be fine in a minute. Look, it's really late and you're not supposed to be here. What do you want?

PLAYWRIGHT

My next muse has come to me. Her name is Anais and she wants me to write her story.

(Beat)

I want you to tell me who you really are.

Blackout

PLAYWRIGHT

THREE DAYS AFTER Henry fixed my computer, neither of us had breathed outside my apartment. I felt high, a lucid high like when you fly in a dream and hope to die before you wake. No muses had dropped by, thank God or whoever.

Tonight there's a chill wind, a foreboding autumnal message tacked up by the few sharp hard stars that pierce New York's polluting glare. I'm reading the notes Maxine emailed about the latest scene. She can be such a critical bitch. Everyone thinks they know their own story best, but few do. Everyone thinks they know themselves best, but few do. They need a playwright's fiction to find the truth.

I'm going to write her story my way, come what may. I've stood in my living room and said similar words while writing other plays, and trouble has always followed. Trouble that sometimes involved blood, or a hospital, or both. Fuck it. If a writer doesn't come to blows with her muse, it'll be a hell of a boring play.

Blood aside, it's time for Happy Hour, because on some plane of existence Sarah Bernhardt's drinking, so why shouldn't I?

Fuck Maxine. She's gone and dried me out. And left a note in the fridge.

My dearest dear Playwright,
I am running to rehearsal but before I go, I feel moved to inform you that your fridge is now bereft. Please remedy this debacle before we both fall to pieces.

With love,
Maxine

My muses use me and I use them too. Maybe that's what love is. It's the only kind of marriage I'm going to get. Well, that's not true. I have Sam. I wish having muses and a gay husband were enough to make me forget Henry. They're not. Who cast me in this fucking play, anyway?

Just yesterday I scribbled Maxine a note which read:

Dear Maxine,
If you don't clean up your spendthrift ways, we'll be bankrupt before your play premieres. In which case we'll have no one to blame but you. And in which case, you'll be lucky if you get cider.

Why do I bother?

Okay, it hasn't been an outside day in some time. But hell if Maxine is going to have all the fun. I look down. Right, get off the gargantuan sofa and get dressed. I'm wearing plaid pyjama pants and no top. Can't recall taking it off or why. No wonder I'm shivering. When Henry was here, I didn't shiver. The absence of goosebumps was proof of love. He found my habit of unconscious clothing removal endearing.

On the third day of me connecting Henry's freckles to make isosceles triangles, he says he better go busk to make some money. He's renting an apartment in Alphabet City.

"I'll pay your rent this month," I say. "Stay."

Henry looks at me, agog.

"Agog," I say.

"What?" Now he looks agog and perplexed.

"You look agog. I love that word. Any occasion to use it is a happy occasion."

"You're not paying my rent, don't be insane. Why would you do that? Why would I let you do that?"

"You saved my third act. You saved my life. It's the least I can do.

I'm going to win the Pulitzer thanks to you, remember?"

"That's not the point."

"What *is* the point?"

"You just met me."

"I know. And? I'm still waiting for your point."

Henry laughs and shakes his head. "I don't know what to say. You're kinda freaking me out."

"In a good way?"

We are in my bed. It is winter, the day surrendering early, flying a white flag of waning light. I've written nothing these past three days, and wordlessness has never smiled so much. This is dangerous, this happiness. And new. No muses have come to call. I haven't switched. Haven't missed a moment of Henry and his fish-skin belly and freckle-fingered Bach. Can't last long, I know. So why let him leave? Why not hang on till a muse shows up? He'll be gone when I get back. A muse can push him out the door. It sure as hell isn't going to be me.

Henry sits up and starts braiding my hair. I've never known a straight man who could braid hair. The rules are different for musicians. Or that's what he tells me, anyway.

"Yes, in a good way. But you're still freaking me out. I'm assuming you don't offer to pay the rent of every man who walks through your door."

I punch him and he stops braiding.

"Ow."

I punch him again because it felt pretty good the first time.

"Ow. Are you going to keep doing that?"

"Possibly. Depends what comes out of your mouth next."

He takes my fist in his hand, kisses each knuckle. "You're a pistol."

"Yeah, I am." I trace the scar that slashes his eyebrow. "I have to be. Don't forget it."

"Okay, tell you what. I'm gonna stay tonight. And then tomorrow I'm gonna play Ravel in the subway and fix a few computers. And then I'm gonna come back. And you're not paying my rent, but thank you. This skinny Canadian won't take money from a lady. But he definitely wants to see said lady again. He also has to water his plants, lest they die and he feel like a terrible person."

I am afraid to let him go because I don't know who will answer my door when he comes back. *If* he comes back. If it's one of my muses, they won't know who he is. When I switch back, I won't know he's been here unless I get an email from a muse demanding to know who the flame-haired violinist is.

All stupid and pointless worry. If I switch right now, I'll freak him out and he'll be out the door before I return. I mean, wouldn't you be? I know if I were in bed with someone and she turned to me and with a brand-new baritone British voice said, "Who are you and what the hell are you doing between my sheets? You're wicked cute, though, my lad, do stay," which is what Fred will say if he shows up—Fred is gay and in his fifties and has a ginger fixation—I'd hightail it before you could say Jack Robinson. Fred should be leaving soon for good; I've almost finished my play about his life as a drag queen in '60s London.

That's the thing: it doesn't matter who shows up, they'll make Henry disappear. I've never had more than a passing lover; some, I'm sure, came and went and I have no memory of them. Others I do remember. They thought I was on drugs. When you're an artist, blaming addiction for strange, undesirable behaviour is fairly socially acceptable. (See: Modigliani.) I guess I'm still hoping, like a nutcase, that a man will stay long enough to make some memories, enough memories to count on my fingers. All my fingers. And maybe even some of my toes.

I won't say any of this to Henry, of course. Why traumatize a man who has spent the better part of three days inside you?

"I hope you'll come back."

"You don't have to hope it, it's a certainty."

"If you do, and I seem different when I answer the door, will you still come in and wait for me to seem like myself? Or, if you don't want to, could you leave a note telling me you were here?"

"Why would I need—?"

I put my hands over his mouth.

"You'll see. It's all part of writing my plays. My characters...visit. I don't need to say any more until they do."

Henry removes my hands from his mouth and squeezes them. "Okay," he says softly, at peace with demanding no further explanation. "But I'm not going anywhere tonight."

Those three days, and many of the days that came after—Henry kneeling on my bed playing Ravel, his hands a blur of freckles—I felt rooted in my skin. A strange feeling. My muses left me alone. Fred left me alone, even though his play wasn't quite finished. He didn't email me. Sam did, wondering if I was still alive. I told him yes, I was indeed alive in a most sparkling fashion, because Henry had resuscitated my computer and all had become right with the world. I imagine Sam shuddered when he read my note, my elation being a reliable harbinger of tragedy. But tragedy, I told him later, much later, while curled in a ball on the floor, is the costume I'm stuck with.

On that third night, we, Henry and I, surfaced long enough to gorge ourselves on the organic, gluten-free, biodynamic hipster Indian meals Cosette had left outside the door when I refused to answer.

"Were you expecting someone?" asks Henry when Cosette knocks.

"Yes. It's just my...housekeeper. She brings me food. She'll leave it at the door if I don't open."

"Why don't you want to answer?"

"Because your skin is warm."

"Good reason. You have a housekeeper who brings you food? That's impressive."

"Not really. It's just necessary."

"Now that I think about it, I've seen your name in the theatre section of the *New York Times*. Your last play got a great review. Damn, I'm sleeping with a genius."

"One day you'll change your mind about that. But before you

do, are you hungry? I have a feeling there's chicken tikka masala just begging us to invite it into our lives."

"I'll set the table. Thanks to your lovely still-life paintings, I won't have to ask where anything is."

"That's exactly why I painted them. See, I've been preparing for you for years."

Henry laughs and tries to run a hand through my hair. It gets stuck in the Medusa whorls.

"I guess we should get dressed."

"Nah. Won't be the first time I've wandered into the hallway naked."

"It isn't?"

"No. Back in a sec."

I peel myself from Henry's warm damp flesh. I'm too spindly to be parading in front of anyone naked, but it's too late for modesty.

I open the front door and inhale a volcano of coriander and garam masala. My neighbour—or some guy, it could be anyone—is letting himself into the apartment next door. He turns and seems startled to see a naked woman clutching a bag of Indian dinner. My guess is he hasn't lived in New York very long.

Henry, naked, is setting the table like he's lived here his whole life and opening the last bottle of champagne. Soon we are licking our fingers, this time for culinary reasons. Henry has a real love of food which delights me and makes me want to eat and eat. The Indian spices make our pale skin flush. I don't remember food ever tasting this good. Coriander and sex are a marvellous combination.

I don't want to ask him a lot of questions. I don't want to know his middle name. I don't want to know if he grew up with a Portuguese water dog, or how long his last girlfriend stuck around, or maybe she's still around. I don't want to know about who he loves, or if he's ever spent three days holed up in the apartment of a woman who was a stranger until he fixed her computer. I suspect he's younger than me, but I don't want to know about that either. The less I know, the less I'll have to let go—

"I used to have a Portuguese water dog," he says.

Oh. Too much information.

He looks suddenly sad. "I miss him. Did you grow up with dogs? You seem like a cat person."

"Umm...my parents didn't really have time for animals. Except for my dad's bees. They barely had time for a kid. Why do I seem like a cat person?"

"I guess I just assumed all writers were cat people. You know, secretive and reclusive."

"I've never lived with animals. Well...I keep my own kind of zoo. Cages and cages of characters. Every once in a while, there's a public viewing."

Henry laughs. "Apparently, the public approves."

"So far the zookeeper is the only one who's been maimed."

He doesn't disagree with me, doesn't insist I look all in one piece. "Maimed can be beautiful," he says, touching my face.

"If you're not coming back, I don't want to know anything about you."

Henry tilts his head in that way I'm growing quickly, unnervingly attached to, and smiles. "It was too much, right, mentioning my Portuguese water dog? I knew it was too much. Damn, I've freaked her out already."

I drop my face in my hands and contort into spasms of laughter. Grief and hysteria are my specialties.

When I look up my face is hot and red as the siren that chides by, warning of too much happiness. Henry tears a piece of naan and offers it, gently, like I'm a skittish animal.

"You've got nothing to be afraid of," he says, pressing the naan, still warm, against my lower lip.

I accept it, and one of his fingers. "I've got everything to be afraid of. But if you love animals, then maybe you'll love this zoo. None of my characters will hurt you. At least not fatally."

"I'll take my chances."

"New York's made you immune to weird?"

"I'm naked, eating chicken tikka masala with a brilliant playwright, who is also naked. New York's welcomed me with open arms."

I start to laugh and he does too, high and low, contrapuntal chaos competing with the two melody-killing sirens that wail by. And winning.

–

TWO SIRENS BRING ME out of my memories of Henry. Now three. Now four. The apocalypse could strike New York and it would just seem like an average day. I try to remember the last man I slept with before Henry. Can't. Maxine had a one-time dalliance with a waiter at The Plaza in an attempt to recreate a Plaza fling she had in 1926. She emailed me afterward, informing me in explicit detail why the Jazz Age guy was a far superior sheik with whom to screw her sorrows away. Christ. I hope no one recognized me. And I wish I knew as much about my own flings as I do about Maxine's or any of my other muses'.

Henry is the only one I remember with perfect clarity. The only one who wasn't a fling. The only one I wish I could forget.

I'm on the street in front of The Plaza and have no recollection of getting here. I have no desire to go in—it's Maxine's place. Besides, I don't want to be accosted by her fling. The chill air has deepened, dropped down into base notes of frost and mouldering leaves courtesy of Central Park. I breathe through my mouth so I can taste the autumn. Even New York fumes can't kill the insistence of fall. Death likes to assert its smoky flavour.

I start walking, no idea where to. I should phone Sam, see what's up. But I don't feel like talking.

"You're cold," says Henry's voice in my head. "Go here. It's as good a place to drink alone as any."

Enter The Ritz-Carlton. I don't think I've ever been in here. Why would I? It's not somewhere Henry would've come either. Wood-panelled Americana populated by bored-looking tourists and stuffily suited businessmen.

"Warm is better than cold," says Henry's voice in my head. "They serve Dom. Be happy."

Easy for him to say.

–

WE FINISH EATING INDIAN FOOD on our third night together and then he says he has to go.

"I've gotta busk a little. Rent's due in a week."

"I told you I would—"

He puts a finger to my mouth.

"Hush. Bach and Ravel are depending on me to keep their music alive. And I'm depending on me to keep myself alive. And un-evicted."

Henry kisses my hands, pulls them to the hollow of his throat.

"Just one more," I say.

"One more what?"

"Night. Then you can walk away."

"I'll only walk away if I can come back."

"You can only come back if you stay tonight."

"Well, if those are your terms, what choice do I have? Let's go back to bed."

Let's go back to bed. One of the best five-word combinations in the English language.

"I did have a cat, when I was a kid. Not my own cat, it was a neighbour's cat, but it would come around and I'd feed it."

"Do you miss it?"

"Yes. It's the only thing from my childhood I miss."

"Oh. Sorry. I'm one of those irritating people who had a happy childhood."

"I'll try not to hold it against you."

"What made you want to be a playwright?"

"I don't have a choice. My muses show up and I have to do what they say or they'll kill me."

Henry laughs. "Murder by muse?"

I'm not smiling. "Yes."

He tilts his head and takes my hand. "You seem really serious about this."

"I am. You mean no one has ever threatened to kill you if you don't play the violin?"

"No. Well, there was a drunk guy in the subway... And I guess I've threatened to kill myself if I don't play the violin as well as Bach demands."

"Suicide is the least of my worries." I squeeze his hand hard. "Thank you for staying. You make me feel like myself."

Henry squeezes back. He doesn't know what to say. I climb on his lap. Behind him the moon rises from his fiery hair, a corona of bone.

"Take me to bed," I say.

ACT II
SCENE 3

Lights up. DOCTOR *and* PLAYWRIGHT *in living room. He grabs his phone. She keeps a safe distance.*

PLAYWRIGHT

Anais *emailed* me. You know how she is: a woman happy in her own skin. Didn't want to jump in mine. Thought that would be rude. She's not like the others.

(Beat)

Your name came up. She told me a few things about you. And if you're thinking about killing me—which you're not, you don't need any more anvils on your conscience—I would forget it. Sam knows I'm here. And I am not planning to out you, I would never do that. It isn't my place. The artist doesn't judge the muse, or the muse's lover. I won't use your real name. Anyway, if I don't tell her story, she'll be the one to kill me. Anais told me to go hard on you, shatter that brittle shell of yours—

(He puts down the phone.)

DOCTOR

Wait. How... How do you know her name?

PLAYWRIGHT

I told you: she emailed me. I'm allowed to check email at the hospital, you know. I have to, to communicate with Maxine. I'll be writing the denouement of her play pretty soon. The climax of a muse's story always lands me in the asylum. Being committed is actually a sign my creative process is right on track. I'm sure I've mentioned this. Anyway, I'm getting distracted. What was I saying? Oh right: Anais. I like her. She's got spirit.

(Beat)

DOCTOR

You can't— I don't— This is crazy. You need to leave. Get out. Get the fuck out!

(The PLAYWRIGHT sits.)

PLAYWRIGHT

Don't you want to know what she said?

DOCTOR

You don't know what you're talking about. You're not talking about anything. I never knew a woman named—

(Beat)

I never knew a woman by that name.

PLAYWRIGHT

You can't say it, can you?

DOCTOR

Your meds, they're not working. They need to be adjusted, that's all. I'll deal with this tomorrow, once you're back in the hospital.

PLAYWRIGHT

In Greece. You knew Anais in Greece. That's what she emailed me about. You were a handsome lost soul. Still are. That's what she told me.

Blackout

MAXINE

from: maxinedoyle@playmail.com
to: rememberyourlines@playmail.com
date: September 30, 2011
subject: diary entries

My most precious Playwright,

Please find enclosed some more diary entries. I am in a charitable mood this day, and I thought it would serve our most noble cause if I fed my sacred story into your contraption. I do not trust you not to misplace my notebook. That said, I am a terrible typist and it has taken me forever and a day to transcribe these entries onto this infernal machine. Good thing, then, that forever is what I have. One of the lovely things about being in my position is that one never fears running out of time. Anyway, I'm quite proud of myself, really I am. The typing, I mean. Aren't you? Yes, of course you are, it goes without saying. My sights were always set far beyond the swampy waters of the secretarial pool, but it is not too late to expand my repertoire of skills and feel quite the bee's knees for doing so. As you've noticed, these past few months I have left you far more handwritten notes; the—what do you call it, oh yes, like in a cinema—screen of this blasted thing hurts my eyes. I've come to the conclusion, however, that you pay more professional heed to correspondence issued in this manner, and so I've attempted to make my artist happy. Never say that as a muse I am ungenerous. That would be patently untrue.

It is a beautiful day in New York City, and I feel alive. This time of year makes me think of the apples I grew up with. Papa's cider. Which makes me think of his pipe, deep and mellow, smoky chocolate and vanilla, a chiffon drape all about the room. Papa was happiest when smoking his pipe; it had a calming effect on him. Damned if I didn't bless that pipe whenever I remembered to pray. A sweet apple, a cuddle of smoke: those evenings, those few calm evenings, were all I knew of happiness. The tongue, the nose: the forever homes of memory. I never missed my father after I hightailed it to Manhattan. I missed his pipe. It was the best part of him.

I don't know why you spend so much time in this apartment when all of Manhattan swirls beyond these walls. I mean, although it is downright ugly, I will allow that I have grown occasionally fond of your red sofa—it is the largest piece of furniture I have ever laid eyes on, and I admit it provides a better sense of protection than the average male of the species—but I have never been reclusive. I don't understand the concept. I want people to see me. The sidewalk can be just as much a stage as Broadway. If I were an acclaimed playwright I should like to strut about and crow my successes from the rooftops. I want to do that as an actress, for God's sake. Nobody in this blasted version of Manhattan seems to know who I am. Well, to be truthful, as I always am to you, my dear Playwright, not nearly enough good folks in my Manhattan had the chance to know me either, to know me as the great actress I wanted to be. You are aware of this already. There is something damned soothing about confessional writing, I must admit. The echo of the crash heals the crash itself, or some such thing.

Where was I? Oh: Manhattan, how do I love thee? Let me count the ways. I confess I had a weakness for the poetry of Elizabeth Barrett Browning as a girl. It was probably part of my downfall. When I met Robert, I felt fate must have brought me my very own Robert

Browning. Yes, too many hours sitting in an apple tree reading love poetry is what did me in. It skews a young girl's mind. It turns her into an idiot. It makes her believe that there is a man out there who smokes a pipe that smells just like her father's. That this nice, pipe-smoking man will love her and never lose his temper. Good thing I murdered my girlishness. Good thing I am a fighter; I know how to dig a trench and charge out firing.

Today I walked to Forty-Second Street so I could stand outside the New Amsterdam. It's become a regular pilgrimage. They are playing some show I've never heard of called *Mary Poppins.* Some woman floating along while holding an umbrella aloft. Looks rather fanciful. She makes me sad, this phantom lady I do not recognize. I almost went inside. I wanted to climb on the stage, stare out at that magic spot above the invisible heads of the crowd. I have every move of *Follies* memorized. I could have played every part, even though I wasn't a Follies girl for very long. I'm a quick study, as they say.

Don't worry, I refrained from storming the stage. But oh, what price. How I wanted to go inside. I forget, you know, I forget most of the time that my city makes strange with me. Who would want to remember such a thing?

I stood in front of the theatre a dreadful long time, looking mournful. A man came up to me and asked if I was lost. New Yorkers are good that way; they like to give directions. But I was insulted that he thought me a tourist. Do you think once you finish writing my play I will be allowed to come back here? I know I'll be living here on the stage, which rather thrills me, but it isn't the same as walking the streets. I know you've said muses never come to opening night, that they usually disappear as soon as you've written the final lines. Yet I wonder, do you think an exception might be made? I hope, oh, how I hope. Your apartment isn't half so nice as the nest Robert feathered for me, but it will do in a pinch and I just want to wander these streets always.

My eyes are hurting, and I am tired of typing. Please read my diary entries right away. I expect steady progress from you. My story is getting too heavy for me to carry all by myself. Well, I know you've got bits of it, but I am still doing the heavy lifting. My rather boyish body is a bit on the frail side, though pleasingly in step with fashion. Robert says I am cut from the pages of *Vogue*. I confess to a weakness for silver tongues.

Anyway, here are the pages.

Love, Maxine

July 26, 1925, Part II

Robert has gone. I expected him to stay all evening. I'm teary about it, really I am. He said he must take his wife to her favourite restaurant as she's been blue. I started to cry. Two can play at being blue, you know.

"I feel sorry for her, Maxine. She's still grieving our son."

Son? What son? Which is exactly what I said.

"Our son Charlie. He died ten years ago. My wife has never gotten over it. She's not as strong as me, not by a mile. I am sure you understand." He smoked his pipe, calm as calm could be.

Understand? I should like to wax poetic about the full flowering of sympathy that burst from the bud of my heart at that moment. Oh look, I just did. It's a lie, though. All I felt right then was resentment. I'm only confessing this to you, this page, of course. I don't need the entire world knowing I'm a louse of a person.

I had too much giggle juice before Robert arrived. I was starting to feel dizzy. "I'm sorry...about your son. How did he die?"

"Consumption. He always was a sickly boy. Wife went mad with grief."

I don't know his wife's name, and I don't intend to ask.

"And you think taking her to dinner will make a difference?" My voice came out whiny and petulant. Not what I intended. I'm not prepared for the slap across the face, my drink falling out of my hand. I scampered away holding my cheek.

"Yes," said Robert, sipping his drink. "I do. Do you have a problem with that?"

Perhaps he has mistaken me for a weakling.

"You don't love her anymore. She's in love with her Bible. That's what you said."

Robert shrugged. He seemed a bit amused. I wanted to punch him, give him some real chin music.

"She's still my wife. I have my duties, Maxine, as we all do. Now are you going to come and sit down like the sweet girl I adore? I've missed you."

So I did. I guess I am indeed a weakling. I have a crazy weakness for him, as he has a crazy weakness for me. No, correction: I like to think his weakness for me is the most natural, sensible thing in the world.

He kissed my face where he'd slapped me, and the sting was gone. I lay back and he reminded me how wonderful his hands are. The chandelier sprayed light that dazzled my giggle-juiced eyes. It looks just like the one at The Plaza. Till I came to New York City, I'd never seen a chandelier in all my life. A good chandelier, like a good lover, makes a girl feel anything is possible.

Robert held me very tight afterwards, like he was afraid to let me go. He always seems younger after, maybe because I can feel how much he needs me. I think there must be something a woman gives to a man, something nameless, that money can't buy. I am giving him something worth more than a whole block of fancy apartments on West Fifty-Seventh Street.

When he finally lifted his head, he said, "You make me so happy. You help me forget the bad times."

"I really am sorry," I said. "About your son. I didn't mean to—"

Robert kissed me then. "Hush. It's all forgotten now."

"I'm nervous about tomorrow, about being a Follies girl. Do you think the director'll like me?"

"Of course Julian will like you. You got the face of an angel, sweetheart, and a body to match. Besides, all you have to do is pose in the tableaux. It's about beauty, not talent."

"But I do have talent, and I want him to see that."

"Baby, your talents will be on full display."

I sat up. "What's that supposed to mean?"

Robert moved to touch my face. I pushed his hand away. "Don't touch me. I thought you believed in me as an actress. That's what you said, I'm captivating in the limelight."

Robert sat up and grabbed me by the shoulders. "Hey, easy. Cool it. Of course I believe in you, princess. That's why I think being a Follies girl is a waste of time. I want to see you do more than parade around in next to nothing. But do you see me stopping you?"

"I've gotta start somewhere."

"Start somewhere? Look at this nest. Carnegie Hall is right out there. And you're the belle of the Cotton Club. You're damn lucky to be starting at the top, baby, and don't you forget it."

"I know, I know. I mean, I love this apartment and I'm grateful for everything you've done for me. I meant start somewhere on the stage. I came to New York to be an actress. I wanna work my way up, make it on my own merits."

Robert kissed my forehead and pinched my cheek. Sometimes he makes me feel like a little girl, a little rube girl from the middle of nowhere who doesn't know anything about anything. In those moments, I have a mind to punch him. My right's pretty good.

"Sweetheart, it isn't about merits in this town, it's about who you know. Stick with me and I'll make sure you climb the ladder."

He pinched my cheek again. I balled my fist, itching to lead with the first two knuckles. The first two knuckles hurt the other guy, the last two hurt you. Papa taught me that.

"Look at you, all rosy and glowing. I've got magic hands. Listen, darling, it's been swell, but I gotta blouse, as the youngsters say. The wife needs me, I know you understand."

My face was red because I was mad. Perhaps it's for the best he thought it was from fucking. I kept silent.

Robert dressed quickly. Once he makes up his mind to do something, he doesn't waste time. I covered myself with the embroidered shawl he had presented to me when he walked through the door.

It's cashmere and silk, you know. Soft on the skin, warm and safe. Nothing very bad could happen to you inside a cashmere shawl.

"Don't get up, princess," Robert said, bending to kiss my mouth. "I'll see myself out."

He didn't wait for me to speak. He turned on his heel and was gone.

For a long time I sat on the sofa, trying not to cry. I gave in, wiping tears with my shawl.

I'm better now. Writing always helps me stop crying—tears quickly become impractical when one is trying to see the page. I bought this new velvet-covered diary as soon as I heard that I'm a Follies girl. Well, I guess Robert bought it, to be exact. He is very generous with my allowance. Anyway, I want a posh place to record my new stage experiences. I'm nervous so I just poured another drink. My dizziness is wearing off; I may as well replenish it. I can't take a twirl at the Roseland Ballroom tonight—I want to arrive at my costume fitting tomorrow looking fresh as a daisy. Hmmm...I suppose more than this one last splash of giggle water might wilt my petals. I must be disciplined in my approach to my stage career. And I will be, I vow to be. It's just that a drink gives me such a romantically warm feeling inside. Especially champagne and gin, both of which Robert has got me positively in love with. Robert says Prohibition is proof that stupidity often wins the day.

I am in my boudoir now. I am still reeling that I have a bedroom I could aptly call a boudoir. Everything has happened with such haste. Romance is better when it happens quickly. Of course, I lack the experience to make a firm judgment on that, but fast in general is much more exciting than slow.

This velvet-covered diary would not be as sacred without a description of the room in which I rest my head. Robert's decorator did a most magnificent job. How did said decorator know I adore butterflies? I wept when I first entered this room. On the wall behind the bed, rising almost to the ceiling, is the most exquisite rendering of a butterfly, a true artist's interpretation. The bed, enormous and black with an enamelled panel of lilies set into the headboard, is covered with the most luxurious Oriental-themed spread, gold on black. Birds painted on silk watch me from the walls on either side. Their eyes seem to move. It doesn't alarm me; I find it quite comforting. I always thought if I had a sprawling closet, as I do now, it would be my favourite room. It turns out this bedroom, with its butterfly and majestic pillar candles and inlaid ebony vanity and huge bed pillows I can hug when Robert is scarce, is the happiest place on Earth.

I have arrived.

July 29, 1925

I am officially a Follies girl. I don't think I've ever been officially anything in my life, and I must say it is a glorious feeling. On Monday morning I arrived promptly for my costume fitting. In truth, I stood outside the New Amsterdam for an hour before I was scheduled to arrive. Not just because I was afraid of being late—imagine being fired before one makes a start!—but because I wanted to inhale every molecule of that morning, soak up every bit of blessed Broadway glamour with my name on it. There is only one first time for everything, and first times are what you think on when you are about to die. Or so I imagine. First times echo till the final silence.

People must have thought I was lost or loony, I stood in front of the theatre so long. I couldn't tear my eyes from the marquee. Couldn't stop myself tracing the letters of *Ziegfeld Follies* with a finger through the air. When I at last went in, I was taken to the dressing rooms to meet a costume assistant, Mrs. Whiting. She is a square woman with a military frown. Been a costume helper since ancient times. She looked me up and down, frowning.

"You're well dressed for a chorus girl," said Mrs. Whiting. I was wearing a blush-pink silk crepe de chine dress Robert had chosen.

"You're pretty, I'll give you that," she continued. "Costumes'll fit. You dance?"

"I'm an actress, not a dancer. But I can do some steps. I'm a natural."

"Right. Well, doesn't matter, you're just parading. Careful with the costumes. Gentle with the beads and feathers."

"Yes, ma'am. I am always very careful with my attire. I adore fashion too much to ever be rough with it."

"Fair enough. Go with Millie, she'll help you change."

A black woman stepped forward. I hadn't even noticed her. Stout and sullen; she didn't smile at me. She turned and walked away with a curt, "Come, miss." I looked back at Mrs. Whiting, but she was already bustling off, me long forgotten.

My, but you've never seen so many feathers and beads and jewels in your life. I nearly went screwy. I gasped and had to choke back tears. Such beauty!

Millie stared at me. "You're exactly her size, miss," she said.

"Who's size?"

"Anna, the girl you replacin'."

"Oh yes, right. The girl who got in trouble."

"She ain't in trouble, she dead."

"She's what?" I was astonished.

"She went to get her problem fixed and they did a bad job. Be careful, s'all I'm sayin'."

Turns out the wardrobe women are the unofficial secret keepers. It figures. They see all us girls right down to the skin in more ways than one.

"Sweet girl, she was," Millie said. She looked awful sad.

"I'm sorry," I whispered. Suddenly I felt damn guilty about being the new Follies girl.

"Well, keep your legs crossed and you won't got to have nothin' to be worryin' 'bout. Now let's get you changed and see if we need to be fixin' anythin'."

My first costume is the biggest feather headdress I've ever seen and not much else. To be accurate, it is the only feather headdress I've ever seen. Truly, it staggers the eye. Strange, but I felt shy wearing such a bit of nothing, more shy than when I am really wearing nothing.

"Don't hunch, girl," said Millie. "You got to stand tall and show your stuff. And it's the only way you gonna keep those feathers on your head."

I looked in the mirror and saw my dream coming true. I was shivering, not just from the cold of the dressing room, but from something else.

Your dream is coming true, Maxine. All your dreams. So why the hell do you feel so damn scared?

ACT II
SCENE 4

Lights up on the DOCTOR'S *apartment.*

PLAYWRIGHT

I'm only doing what Anais wants.

DOCTOR

I have never known anyone by that name. Look, I'm not sure exactly what you're going through, but I'll be able to assess you better when we get you back to the hospital. Obviously, your meds need to be adjusted. But whatever you're feeling right now is valid and I support you in every—

PLAYWRIGHT

Oh, stop with the psychobabble already. We're past that, you and me.

DOCTOR

I understand why you're upset. You have every right to feel—

PLAYWRIGHT

Shut the fuck up!

(Beat)

Now: I suggest you drink some water to ease the pounding headache of drunkenness.

DOCTOR

I'm not drunk. I got sober as soon as you showed up. The headache I've got sure as hell isn't from alcohol.

PLAYWRIGHT

I don't plan on leaving. I've never had someone who knew one of my muses standing right in front of me. I want the story. She wants you to tell me the story. And if you so much as reach in the direction of that telephone, I will scream this place down and make sure the world knows a few more things about you than it does right now.

DOCTOR

Who the hell would believe you? You're a psych patient. I'm a doctor. And whatever you think you know, it's some fucked-up fantasy. It's not your fault. I can help—

PLAYWRIGHT

You met her in a café. She was writing about you. You had a copy of Henry Miller's Greek travelogue in your bag.

(He glances toward the phone.)

PLAYWRIGHT

Don't even think about it. And I'm not a psych patient. I'm a playwright. Check the *New York Times*. I'm a damn good writer who enjoys exercising her health insurance by dropping into her local nuthouse for a periodic constitutional.

(Beat)

Anais wants to know where you got your medical license.

DOCTOR

She knows where I got— I mean— Fuck! I can't do this. I can't help you. I don't know what you think you know, but you don't know anything. Not about me. You need to leave or I'll call the cops.

PLAYWRIGHT

Go ahead. I'll tell them all about Anais. But she doesn't want me to. She still loves you.

(Beat)

DOCTOR

What did you say?

PLAYWRIGHT

She still loves you. Never stopped.

DOCTOR

She said that?

PLAYWRIGHT

Yes. She's been emailing me for a while, since before I came to the hospital. The new muse always shows up before the old muse has finished with me.

(Beat)

I never thought I'd meet the living story. Not in my wildest dreams. Surprise never dies.

DOCTOR

What else...did she say?

PLAYWRIGHT

She said to tell you something.

DOCTOR

What?

PLAYWRIGHT

Storytelling is healing.

Blackout

DOCTOR

WHAT THE FUCK am I gonna do with her?

She said her name. How does she know her name? How does she know—?

How does she know anything?

She doesn't, she guessed.

No, she didn't guess, how could she guess?

She's crazy. She's fucking crazy.

I need to get her out of here. I need—

She said her name. She knows her name.

She said her name. She knows her name.

She said her name. She knows her name.

I'm crazy. I must be crazy. This isn't really happ—

"Are you just going to stand there and stare all night? You look like a crazy person. Drink some water. I won't hurt you. Anais wants you to talk to me. You know she does."

Okay, this psychiatrist jig is up. I've gotta get the hell outta here.

Run. I've done it before, I can do it again. Run. Man, I'm fucking exhausted.

She is staring at me, calm as a buddha or some other irritating symbol of tranquility. She has a repulsive look on her face, repulsive because it resembles sympathy, or worse, pity. No patient of mine gets to pity me. No fucking way.

I can't think straight. I can't—

Anais. Anais. Anais. I haven't said her name out loud since last century. When I was a different person, in a different place. I've missed the sound of it. So. Fucking. Much.

"Are you hungry? Do you want to eat something? I'm a lousy cook, but there must be something edible in such a beautiful apartment."

My hands twitch. Her neck is very small. No. No. No. The stars hate me—No. She has a message. A message from Anais. Maybe Anais doesn't hate—What the fuck am I talking about?

I don't know what to do. I can't breathe. I can't move.

"Anais was a great cook, wasn't she? She likes to write about food. I'd never read such a moving description of moussaka. It actually brought tears to my eyes. Me, a person who forgets to eat more often than she remembers."

–

WE ARE IN HER KITCHEN, Anais and I, eating leftover moussaka and drinking wine. Anais licks her fingers. She is giggling. Her rough, scraping laugh sandpapers my skin in the best fucking way ever.

Her laugh is a drug. I haven't used a lot, but I've used enough to know which poisons I like best. She makes me feel something new. I want to take her laugh and stick it in my arm.

I phoned Marie last night while Anais was in her garden picking out stuff for dinner. Anais has a good long-distance plan so she can talk to her brothers and her best friend back in Toronto. I don't know why I said that. An attempt at sounding nice? I would've phoned whether she had a long-distance plan or not. I don't want to hurt her. That's what I'm trying to say. I've never had that thought about a woman before. Well, I didn't want to hurt Marie either. I wanted to save her. I tried to save her. But still, my feelings for her were different, somehow. I want to protect Anais in a way I didn't know you could want to protect someone. It's fucking terrifying. I can't hurt her. I promise I won't hurt her. I mean, I don't go around wanting to hurt any women, I really don't. I didn't mean to. I've never meant to.

I asked Marie if things were cooling down.

"Cooling down? I'm in fucking Mexico. It's a hundred degrees."

"You know what I mean."

"I don't watch American news. What's the point? They're not gonna keep broadcasting what happened. What more is there to say? They don't know who did it, and they're not gonna find out. Maybe you'll come home one day."

"I don't want to go back. There's nothing there for me. I like Greece. And Greece likes me."

"You met a girl."

"I didn't say that. But if I can stay away, why wouldn't I? Fuck. How did everything get so fucked up?"

"Ours is not to reason what the fuck."

"Then what is ours to reason, Marie?"

"Don't ask the why of life. That'll get you nowhere fast."

"Shit happened. I'm in Greece. Doesn't that call for a little introspection?"

"It was an accident. You didn't mean to fire."

"Yeah, but I did fire."

Marie paused. I could hear her breathing. I knew she didn't know what to say.

"Sex with Lark is amazing," is what she came out with. I'd always found Marie's amoral compass to have a comforting sedative effect, like a human Quaalude. But we are bad for each other. That's what I told her the first time we had sex. She agreed and we were both hooked. "I'm glad I convinced her to move down here. We're having a blast."

"So you're gonna stick with women for a while?"

"No. I'm not sticking with anyone. But I like Lark. Oh, and I'll stick with you. As a friend. Like glue. I don't want anything bad to happen to you. You're one of the few people I have actual feelings for." She chuckled her bitter chuckle. "You remind me of me."

"Thanks. Bad things have already happened."

"Yeah, but it could be a lot worse. You could've been caught."

"You too."

"I'd get off a lot lighter."

She had a point. Fuck. I fucking hate trusting someone who has less to lose. Marie's Quaalude effect was gone and I could feel a hit of adrenaline, a buzz in my ears.

"I've gotta go."

A moment of silence.

"Don't worry, babe, your secrets are buried deep. I'm a walking grave."

"I'll be in touch if I can. Marie? Take care of yourself. Or let Lark take care of you. Don't do anything stupid."

"Baby, I never do anything stupid. I just have a really low tolerance for boredom."

Click.

I stared down the barrel of the receiver until the dial tone smacked me in the face. I was sweating, but not from nerves. Shapeshifters don't sweat. Marie gave me that line. It's the truth. The sun was sinking and it was hot in the house; "the sear before the surrender" is how Anais describes sunset.

–

I MET MARIE IN A BAR before I dropped out of med school. "You? A shrink?" she scoffed when she asked what I was doing with my life. "One lost soul to rule them all."

"What makes you think I'm a lost soul?"

"I'm a magnet for them."

A purple gem studded her nose. Not everyone can pull off face jewellery. She pulls it off. Way off. Turned out she's a performance artist and aspiring thief.

"You don't really want to be a doctor," she said, knocking back rye straight up. "So why play that game?"

"I don't know. I'm smart enough. I like the idea of being called 'Doctor.' I like abnormal psychology."

"'Course you do."

"Do you always assume you know things about random people you meet in bars?"

"Yeah. And I'm usually right. You're bored. The buttoned-up life ain't for you. Get out while you still can."

She had short hair, shorter than mine, which somehow made her look more feminine, the delicacy of her face cresting into high cheekbones that emptied into wide, shiny, long-lashed basins. A fierce china-doll face, the kind that preys on fools dumb enough to take her for fragile. A lace dress and combat boots. Biceps and tiny wrists.

"Are you always this bossy?" I asked, finishing my drink. I'd been drinking beer and felt pedestrian next to this rye-swilling pixie.

"Oh, you have no idea," she replied, and we ended up fucking in the bar's unisex bathroom, the broken light flickering on and off, our image in the mirror tattooed with lipstick graffiti.

That night, I dropped out of med school. The decision was literally orgasmic.

I was bored, and then there I was, fucking adventure personified.

I don't think you'd call Marie a kleptomaniac, because the things she liked to steal—say, money—were always useful. Kleptomaniacs steal stuff like salad dressing. Still, the act of thievery never failed to get her charged up. Then she'd do something like paint herself red and pierce her navel while chanting Buddhist mantras at the freakshow art bar where she gigged part-time as a beer slinger, when she wasn't exhibiting weirdness and calling it art.

I didn't know any of this, of course, that night in the bar bathroom. I just knew she was bad news and I was hungry for bad news.

A week later we were living together. I had the money my father had given me before we quit talking. Shacking up with abnormal psychology was more interesting than reading about it.

Our apartment was grungy. Slumming it was romantic. It made it easy to imagine I was Henry Miller when he first arrived in Paris with nothing, or even before that when he was slumming it in New York. Except we sure as hell weren't in New York or Paris. But when you're young and she's young—come to think of it, she's older than me—and you're surrounded by takeout boxes and half-finished art projects, and you think you've cut loose, and you come face to face with intimate piercings for the first time—she did them herself!—everything has a gritty glamour which it doesn't deserve. Being stoned helps too. Though even then I preferred alcohol. My father only drank good scotch. I was raised with standards.

Those were heady days, man. That's how I talked, back then. I adopted Marie's hippie-artist-stoner speak, tried it on for size like a costume. A far cry from the articulate, stiff doctor I would later become. I don't think anyone ever really knows who they are. Not all of who they are. We just drift, seeping and bleeding into each other. So we may as well fuck strangers, because in some ways, that's all the other person will ever be to you. Psychiatrists exist because people don't accept this.

Forgery was one of Marie's many talents. "I have mercurial handwriting," she liked to say. "My ABC's can be whatever I want them to be." She was dabbling in cheque forging when I met her, and had a sideline in fake IDs. You'd be surprised how many people want a fake ID. Not just kids who want to buy flavoured vodka. Lots of people want to be somebody else. Lots of people want to disappear. Marie was only too happy to help them do it. "It's a calling," she once told me. Spoken like humanity owed her a fat debt.

Marie has always been far ahead of her time. I mean, she was tops at identity theft in the early '90s, before it all got so high-tech and easy. A real visionary in some ways. Too bad she had psychopathic leanings. Leanings, mind you, not full-blown psychopathy, which is far less sexy. She had redemptive glimmers. It was a heroin-esque combination. And yes, I know what my attraction to her says about me. I didn't care at the time. I'd come back to our falling-apart digs and she'd be standing in the middle of the living room naked and painted purple, smoking a cigarette and filming herself for some performance-art project, a bunch of forged cheques arranged in a sunburst pattern on a table just off camera. She could be cold, like my folks, but she could also be hot and I needed heat. If you're gonna go down in flames, do it with someone who's got style.

"Come here," she'd say. "It's urgent." Fucking a purple woman was something new. It turned me into a purple man and I realized how easy it was to become someone else. Quit school. Cut ties. Shack up with a weirdo. Pretend to care about art. My voice sounded different. My eyes looked different. Maybe that was the bond between Marie and me—we could shapeshift, be whoever, and people believed us. And we liked that.

–

"DID YOU CALL SOMEONE last night? I thought I heard you on the phone." Anais is still licking her fingers, but the giggling has stopped. Her dark-blue eyes peer at me over the rim of her wineglass.

"I, uh, yeah. My friend Mary. She was having a hard time before I took off for Greece. Just wanted to make sure she's okay."

"What's wrong with her?"

"Uh, bad breakup. I've known her a long time. She lives in Atlanta. I met her at Emory."

"Is that a university?"

"Yeah, where I went to med school."

"So, I'm learning something about you. Was Mary your girlfriend?"

"No, just a friend."

"I think you're lying."

"Why do you think that?"

"Told you, I've got my grandmother's intuition."

"Why would I lie?"

Anais shrugs. "Look, I don't care if she was. I just want to know more about you. Since you happen to be living in my house. For now."

"For now?"

"Well, yeah, for now. Don't you have to go back to the States? I mean, we both know this is just a bubble."

"I like bubbles."

"So do I. But bubbles burst."

"What's the point of knowing more about me if this is all going to disappear?"

"Only a very lonely person would ask such a question."

Anais stares at me for a long moment. She's had too much wine and her eyes look teary.

"Are you sure, Doctor, that you're really a shrink? You don't seem healthy enough to be telling other people how to live."

"I don't tell anyone how to live. I write prescriptions."

"That sounds bleak."

"It is."

Anais touches my face. "No wonder you needed to run away."

I slip her finger in my mouth. It tastes of cinnamon and nutmeg and eggplant and cheese.

"Don't you have any faith in the redemption of humanity?"

"Psychiatrists aren't faith people."

"I bet I can restore your faith."

"In what?"

"Healing."

"Shouldn't I be healing you? You're the one who's grieving."

"You're grieving something too. I don't know what. But I know you're too broken to heal anybody."

There is a strange pressure behind my eyes. And then I realize: tears on the ledge, threatening to jump. I haven't cried since I was six. I forgot what it feels like.

Anais squeezes my hand. "It's okay," she says. "I cry all the time."

"I don't," I reply, choking on my voice.

"I'm going to read your cards tonight. A reading would help."

I don't answer. Fuck this. I hate tears. I pull her to the floor and drown my sorrows inside her.

–

"DOCTOR? Hello?"

My patient is staring at me, her expression somewhere between amused and worried. The air is thick. I see her mouth moving, but I can't make sense of her words.

"You've been spaced out for ages. Thinking about Anais, I'm guessing."

I flinch at the sound of the name.

"You should sit down. You look like you might faint. I don't want you to hit your head."

I sit because I can't think what else to do. Curse? Fuck. Fuck. Fuck.

My patient sits across from me, her face now composed of doctorly empathy. I'm going to vomit. I need to get her out of here. I can't move.

"She's dead, isn't she?" My patient is speaking very softly. "I mean, she must be, it's only dead people who contact me, wanting to be muses. But she's fine. She wants me to tell you she's fine. Would you like me to tell you what else she said?"

I must be crazy. Insanity must be catching. Wake up. Wake the fuck up. This isn't happening. You are alone in your apartment. There's no one here. She's not here. I'm drunk. I'm hallucinating. She's not really here. This isn't real. It's a dream, a dream about Anais.

If it isn't real, then what's the harm?

"Yes," I say.

ACT II
SCENE 5

Lights up on the DOCTOR'S *living room. He huddles on his couch. The* PLAYWRIGHT *is perched on a chair.*

PLAYWRIGHT

I'm glad. Anais wants you to hear what I have to say. What she has to say.

DOCTOR

She...she doesn't hate me?

PLAYWRIGHT

You tell me. Should she?

DOCTOR

I would hate me. I...

PLAYWRIGHT

You what?

DOCTOR

Tell me more. Prove it.

PLAYWRIGHT

Prove it? That she really emailed me?

DOCTOR

She didn't have email when I knew her. No one did.

PLAYWRIGHT

Right. Well, she has it now. It's anaisingreece@playmail.com. If you want to write to her. I'm sure she'd love a letter from you. She chose that address because she was happiest in Greece.

DOCTOR

I know she was.

PLAYWRIGHT

Of course you do. You were happiest there too, for a while.

DOCTOR

No one had ever cooked for me before. I mean, no one who wasn't paid to cook for me.

PLAYWRIGHT

It's a primal need. Someone to offer you food, and to wonder where you are when you don't come home at night.

DOCTOR

That's what she— How do you know?

PLAYWRIGHT

How do you think? I've composed a scene of your time with her, based on what she sent. Do you want to hear it?

DOCTOR

A scene?

PLAYWRIGHT

Yes. A scene in a play. It goes like this:

ACT I
SCENE 1

Lights up. The DOCTOR *and* ANAIS *sit in her kitchen. Tarot cards are spread on the table.*

ANAIS

Hmmm... A lot of pain. Something tragic. Did someone die? There's a death you haven't told me about.

DOCTOR

Sure I did. My mother. Died when I was a kid. And how can you see death in a bunch of playing cards?

ANAIS

They're not playing cards, they're tarot. You should be more open-minded. And I'm not seeing your mother. There's another woman who died. Who was she?

DOCTOR

I have no idea—

ANAIS

You feel guilty. Why?

(He stands. His chair falls over. He puts it back in place.)

DOCTOR

Look, I don't wanna do this. I don't believe in this shit. I need some air.

(He exits to yard. Anais stares after him, then looks back down at the cards.)

ANAIS

Should this man be in my house?

(She pulls a card from the tarot deck.)

Blackout

PLAYWRIGHT

I TAKE A SIP OF DOM and think of Henry. Maxine's been chattering on about him, says she misses my beloved something fierce. That's the trouble with multiple muse disorder—grief comes in bulk.

On that note, I take another sip and nearly choke. Henry's twin has just walked into The Ritz-Carlton. Not his literal twin. Someone who looks just like him. Or is it—? His hair is longer, wilder, like he's been hiding out, but—it's Henry, it's gotta be. I'm clutching the stem of my glass so hard I might snap it. I've never seen anyone who looks like Henry. It must be— No. Yes. No, because—because he's looking right at me, but he doesn't see. Like he doesn't know me. Or doesn't want to.

The Ritz-Carlton is a staid, boring hotel. Until it isn't. Until it is the most interesting and devastating place in the cosmos.

A waiter is touching my arm. He's saying something but I don't understand what.

"Are you all right, ma'am? I asked if there's anything else I can get for you."

Am I all right? No, I'm not. I can't remember how to speak. I need Maxine to do the talking. Maxine, though, doesn't show up when I want her to. She's got a sense of timing all her own.

The waiter walks away and I'm not sure if I interacted with him in a socially acceptable manner, or if I interacted at all. Oh well.

A waiter in New York is well versed in the eccentric.

Henry's double has ordered champagne. I taught my love the necessity of bubbly for sanity.

So it's him. And I am unwanted.

Henry wouldn't do that. Wouldn't just disappear, pretend I don't exist. So it's not him. It can't be.

He looks up, turns, looks right at me. Tilts his head, the way Henry does. I should smile, but I can't feel my face. He smiles and nods, as to a stranger, goes back to drinking. I want to talk to him. I must talk to him. To say what? You look just like my vanished love? Does your name happen to be Henry? Will you come home with me and make everything beautiful?

–

HENRY SOON GAVE UP his apartment. It had bedbugs, and why wait for fumigation when you can move uptown for love? I told him about the muses—I had to, obviously. Abandonment is the cutting currency of love, and I decided I would rather pay and bleed. Even when you know someone will leave you, the hope that they won't infects you like a parasite. Henry hadn't met my muses yet, so he had no clue what I was talking about.

"Every artist has muses," he says when I try to explain that he's moving in with more than one person. "You're mine."

"Yes, but I won't take over your body."

He laughs. "You already have."

He stops laughing when he sees the tears in my eyes. "Babe?"

"If you want to leave and never come back, I'll understand."

"What are you talking about? I gave up my apartment. And not just because of the bugs. I want to be here, with you."

"I know. And I want you to be here too. I just don't want you to be afraid of me."

"Well, I suspect you may be concealing a decent right hook, but I'll take my chances."

"Sometimes, when I'm writing, or even when I'm not writing, the people I write about come through me, step into me like a costume. And then I'm not me anymore, I go somewhere else. Not sure where. I mean, my body is here, it's just...I might speak with a different voice, come from a different time and place, tell you my name is something else. But I'll always come back to you."

Henry's eyes are a bad combination of goggly and frozen.

"I don't know what to say. You don't look like you're kidding."

My face is blotchy with tears and my nose is starting to run. I'm not an elegant crier.

"You're an artist, so I'm banking on your love of the cutely kooky. Sometimes more kooky than cute. It will never be boring here, I can promise you that. And you don't have to be scared of me."

"Babe, I'm not scared of you. What do you mean, like, you have personalities...like multiple...?"

"No, I mean like dead people. I have dead people."

Henry looks more curious than unnerved. "You mean like ghosts? You mean like you're possessed or something?"

"Or something. I mean, we're not talking *The Exorcist* here. I love my muses. I couldn't live without my dead people."

"Have you seen someone about this?"

"Like who? A ghostologist? I do take meds sometimes, but I don't like them. I can't write when I'm on drugs. The *New York Times* says I'm brilliant. But I'm not brilliant without the muses. Good writing has a price. Sometimes unpayable. Usually just when I'm writing the climax of a play, a muse may do something...dramatic. Then I need a doctor and some meds. Or a tourniquet."

Silence descends like a sandstorm: it gets into everything. No traffic noise, no sirens, no New York. I wait for Henry to get up and get gone. I stare past him to an empty bottle on the kitchen counter. The green glass shot through with waning day. I have an urge to break it over my head. That would feel better than waiting for Henry to leave and never come back.

But Henry doesn't leave. Instead he takes my hand, squeezes it.

"I don't know what to say to all that. So while I'm thinking of what to say, I have a very important question."

The room starts to spin. Love is the worst idea I've ever had.

"Do you have another bottle?"

Is he serious?

"I think we need it, don't you?"

Henry is getting up and going to the kitchen. He isn't leaving. Traffic noise comes back. A siren blares by. Maybe that's what abandonment will do to me one day: deafness. Maybe that day isn't today. Maybe Henry will stay.

The word "maybe" is an incurable and fatal disease. An artist makes beautiful the pox of petrifying possibility.

The cork pops and Henry returns to the living room and refills our glasses. "How many people know about your...the way you are."

"Sam. Nobody else. I don't let most people get close enough to find out. I'm sure I've said or done odd things to people and they just assume I'm eccentric. My neighbours must think I'm nuts. I don't know. That's the good thing about New York: you never really get to know your neighbours."

"But you want me to live with you. Why me?"

"Because I've just told you something crazy and you haven't left yet. Instead, you seem very calm and you're tilting your head in that way I love and all that makes me want you to stay here forever."

He takes my hand. Maybe he's just being kind before he bolts. Maybe he's one of the few men on Earth who knows how to deal with a crying woman. Just because a man is kind doesn't mean he wants to move in with me and my characters.

"Well..." he says.

I'm going to be sick. All over this mammoth sofa. What the fuck was I thinking? I'm doomed to be alone. I should never have—

"I've never known someone who... I've never seen... And I think it would freak me out." He pauses, and the room starts to spin again. "But being freaked out is not always a bad thing. Right?"

The room stops spinning.

"Right." My voice is an unfamiliar croak.

"I've been freaked out pretty much ever since I got to New York. Sometimes in bad ways, sometimes in good. I guess I want to believe you're one of the good ways. And I don't know if there's any more to say. Right now, I'm happier holding your hand. If that changes, I'll let you know."

It's possible, of course, that he isn't recoiling in horror because he needs a place to live and I have a nice apartment. And because, by some miracle, he hasn't yet met my muses, so he might think I'm exaggerating. None of that matters. A geyser of relief surges and I leap up, charge into the bathroom, and vomit beside the sink. I've never been so happy to see my stomach's abstract art, or to have to erase it from the floor.

–

HENRY'S DOUBLE KEEPS glancing at me across the lounge. He must know I'm staring at him. I should stop doing that. But I can't. A snippet of a Bach sonata drifts through—my mind or the room, I'm not sure. I should pay my bill and leave. I should get the hell out of here. But I can't. I can't. Just one more time. I've so wanted to see him, just one more time. Not even talk him. Not even touch him. Just see him.

–

IT WAS HENRY WHO CLEANED the vomit off the bathroom floor. Ever after, I've associated romance with Pine-Sol.

"Just lie down," he says. "But I'm taking the booze away."

It's only when he's busy getting up close and personal with the contents of my stomach that it occurs to me to wonder if he's too good to be true. If there's something seriously wrong with him. If he's a sick lunatic. Or maybe Canadians are even nicer than I thought.

That strange and wondrous thing called happiness, though, that elusive thing my muses have described so many times and in so many ways, trumps any trepidation about potential lunacy. Good feelings can be just as dangerous as bad.

–

HENRY MET MAXINE the night he moved in. Fred, my gay British muse, was gone—I'd finished his play and he was satisfied with my work. Maxine, unlike the others, showed up a long time before I commenced writing her story. Her early letters explained she was auditioning me, wasn't sure yet if I was the playwright she wanted. Yes, she was a demanding bitch from the get-go.

Darling Playwright,

My name is Maxine Doyle, and I am a lauded actress. I would have been more lauded, were it not for my untimely— Forgive me, that introduction was not what I intended. My nerves have been dreadful ornery, and the doctor's remedy has had little effect. One would think that in these modern '20s, medicine could fix a thing like overwrought nerves in a jiffy. Not so.

I have seen by way of the *New York Times* that you are a playwright of some note. I want you to turn my story into a play. A play that Broadway will adore. A play that will make my torment worthwhile. A play that will make people understand me—understand me, and remember my name.

Thus, I am auditioning you for the job. I have never been a director before. I must say, I rather like being on this side of the table. Commencing soonish, I shall send you notes on my story. Please don't be too harrowed by the drama I shall unfold for you. You will need to get over any shock in short order if you are to bring the events of my life to the stage. There is no rush to start writing, mind you. I want you to know and understand me first. If I come to feel you are suitable, then all shall be well. For you, I mean. Nothing can ever be entirely well for me. Unless, of course, you write my story as a play of which I approve wholeheartedly—then I shall be restored to happiness. If you are not up to the task, I will have to recommence my search for the appropriate playwright. After I recover from the devastation of you disappointing me. But really, as long as you do everything I say, I am optimistic we will get on fine. I expect a response by the end of the week. Send a telegram to The Plaza. I prefer it there. Your taste in decorating grates on my nerves.

My story is worth writing. It is worth putting on the stage. My last hope of being a Broadway star.

Yours sincerely,

Maxine Doyle

It took a hell of a lot of grief to convince Maxine to stop spending my money by staying at The Plaza. My muses might bankrupt me before they kill me.

–

HENRY'S DOUBLE IS STARING at me now. The room starts to spin. Not vomiting at The Ritz is the best I can hope for today.

–

HENRY DIDN'T HAVE MUCH in the way of movables. He hadn't brought furniture from Canada, just a suitcase and his violin. I know men had drifted in and out of my life, and maybe I even liked having sex with some of them, but my memories of encounters with testosterone were sketchy at best, too vague to consider myself a woman with a past. If I'd ever done couple stuff before Henry, like make French toast and watch documentaries about the ruination of the environment, I had no memory of it.

And now here is a man, a man with flaming hair like mine, standing in my bedroom unpacking his underwear. I don't think I will ever forget this sight.

"I don't have much stuff. I won't get in your way," he says, poking his finger through a hole in a pair of polka-dot boxers.

"I want you to be in my way. I wish you had more stuff so I could trip over it."

Henry tilts his head and grins. "I've never had anyone say that to me before."

"Have you ever lived with a woman?"

He nods. "For about a year. Bad idea."

My heart hits my stomach and stays there. "Are you worried this is a bad idea?"

Henry holds out his arms. "Maybe I should be. But I'm not. Come here."

My small nose fits in his bony chest like there's a notch carved in his bones just for me. A man with a notch in his chest—the best treasures are ones you never would have thought of.

"Let's not worry," he says into my hair. "Let's just live."

"Okay," I say into his chest. "Let's live." His arms are snug around me. So this is the feeling everyone makes a big deal of. I'm an insider now.

The smell of Henry's shirt—a chypre with a dose of peppery Henryness—is the last thing I remember about the day he moved in.

I vanished, and Maxine made an entrance. I'm glad I wasn't there to see the look on Henry's face. Don't know if he recoiled or gaped or what. He didn't leave, that much I do know. It's the part that matters. Mattered. Past tense. No, present. For me, Henry is present tense. But if you're still reading, you know that already.

So my face was buried in Henry's chest, happily ensconced in his nose-notch, when Maxine took to the stage and then Henry wasn't holding me at all, he was holding some other woman with a different voice, a woman he'd never met before. There was a scene. Henry told me it went like this:

ACT I
SCENE 1

Lights up. The PLAYWRIGHT'S *apartment.* MAXINE *pushes* HENRY *away.*

MAXINE

Who the hell are you?

*(*HENRY *says nothing.)*

MAXINE

I said: who are you? And what are you doing in my playwright's apartment? Answer me this instant.

(He continues frozen and silent.)

MAXINE

You have exactly five seconds to identify yourself before I start screaming. One—

HENRY

My name is Henry.

MAXINE

Henry. Henry.

(flips through her mental card file)

Wait a minute. Are you her lover? She sent me a note about you. She asked me to treat you with kid gloves. Damn, I've made a mess of things and we've only just met. I do apologize. It's just that there was one time when I came to in the presence of a man— Never you mind. How do you do?

(MAXINE steps forward and offers her hand for Henry to kiss. Instead, he awkwardly shakes it.)

MAXINE

Whatsa matter, you shy? You look like you've never seen a lady before. Well, perhaps I'm not a real lady, but you catch my drift.

HENRY

A real lady?

MAXINE

You know, lily-white and all that jazz. Never mind. I do hope we can be friends. My playwright has a soft spot for you. More than a spot, actually—every inch of her.

HENRY

Really? She said that?

MAXINE

Don't you know it? So don't break her heart or I'll break your face. Oops—that wasn't part of my kid-gloves routine. But I need to level with you: she's my playwright and I need her to tell my story. Truth is, I wanted her to steer clear of the male persuasion, but I wilted like a damn pansy. Anyhow, she'll be no use to me with a broken heart.

HENRY

I...understand. I think.

MAXINE

Good. Now we've gone and got that all straightened out, is there any giggle water in the joint? A little toast to us meeting seems in order and you can tell me all about yourself. I'm an actress. Gosh,

I don't think I told you my name: Maxine Doyle. She must have mentioned me. I'm a gal who likes to be mentioned. *(winks)* I was a Follies girl until— Anyway, let's skip to the toast. I simply can't draw another breath without tipping a Sarah. My idol, Sarah Bernhardt, was crazy about champagne, you see, so whenever I drink it, I'm "tipping a Sarah." And tipping an imaginary hat in tribute, obviously. It's a little ritual I adore.

HENRY

What's a Follies girl?

MAXINE

Oh my God in heaven, where have you been? Take a long look, sweetheart.

(MAXINE struts across the room, does a slow turn, and poses.)

MAXINE

This, my darling, is a Follies girl. One of the best. I don't believe in false modesty, I believe in tellin' it like it is. You've never been to the *Ziegfeld Follies*? And you live in New York?

HENRY

Um...actually, maybe I *have* heard of the Follies. Didn't those shows close, like, decades ago?

MAXINE

Close? Darling, they've been going strong for near twenty years, since 1907.

HENRY

Twenty years? But it's—

MAXINE

You from out of town?

HENRY

I'm Canadian. From Toronto.

MAXINE

Golly, I always wanted to go up there and see some Eskimos. I'm from upstate, apple-knocker country, but I never made it across the line.

HENRY

We don't call them Eskimos. They're Inuit, and most of them don't live in Toronto.

MAXINE

Whatever the hell you call them, let's have a little drink to those charming folks and to us finally makin' our acquaintance.

(MAXINE sashays into the kitchen, pops a cork, and pours. HENRY follows her.)

MAXINE

I've heard so much about you. Well, read about you, to be precise. She and I must communicate through letters, obviously. She's never been in love before. Poor thing doesn't know what hit her.

(hands him a glass)
Cheers. You ever been in love?

HENRY

Yes. She left me for another guy.

MAXINE

Ouch. Love's the bunk. Pardon my *français*. But I hope you two will be very happy together. Just keep her smilin' and you and I will get along fine. Don't be put off if she gets shy sometimes, acts like a bit of a cancelled stamp. She isn't a gal who's used to bein' in love.

(HENRY *hasn't taken a drink yet.)*

HENRY

Uh, do you plan on dropping by often?

MAXINE

'Course. I've got to look in on things, tell her my life story, look over her notes about me, how else is she going to write a play about my life? She needs my direction. I have final script approval, it goes without saying. I always dreamed of having script approval. Thought I would go into the movies, you know. Life had other ideas, damn it all to hell. And I had to keep Robert happy.

HENRY

Robert?

MAXINE

My sugar daddy. A theatrical producer. He cast me in my first role, the same part Tallulah Bankhead played her first time out in 1918. So I understand about the money.

HENRY

What money?

MAXINE

Well, she told me you don't have any money, but she doesn't mind. She's got money. As long as you love her, or pretend to. I understand what it's like, bein' in need of dough. I was crazy for Robert when I let him set me up in a beautiful love nest. Golly, was I ever.

HENRY

Look, I don't know what you think, but I'm not moving in with her for money. I'm not that kind of—

MAXINE

Simmer down, sweetheart, I didn't mean to rile you. I know you're not a good-for-nothin' dewdropper. And your eyes are too soft to be a cake-eater. I bet you're a hopeless romantic, poor sap. I'm a realist, that's all. I've seen too much not to be.

HENRY

I'm not some gigolo, for Chrissake. I'm a violinist—

MAXINE

And a damn good one, according to her emails. You know it took me ages to learn how to use that email contraption, but I'm so glad I did. I love the little smiley faces and flowers you can put in your letters. They're awfully sweet. What will they think of next? I'm not a very good typist because I never imagined I'd do anything but be on the stage—

HENRY

Look, it's been nice meeting you, but can you bring back my girlfriend? I just wanna settle in and put my arms around her and celebrate our first night of—

MAXINE

(suddenly cold and harsh)
She comes back when I say she comes back. You got it? I came here to tell you what's what. She belongs to me first. She works for me

first. She does what I say first. You might think you're in love now, baby boy, but life has a way of makin' you sorry you were ever born. You don't have to love her forever, you just gotta make her believe you do. I just need her to do this one job for me. But it's a big job. An important job. It's not too late for me to be a star.

HENRY

Who the fuck do you think you are? You don't tell me what to do. And you don't tell her what to do. She's a playwright. She doesn't work for you, she works for herself.

MAXINE

(laughs)

Wrong. Oh, how wrong you are! You're all wet! She works for her muse. Which is me. Ever thus, ever will be.

(HENRY downs his drink.)

HENRY

What the fuck? Who the—? I just— Where—?

(to himself)

Who the fuck am I talking to?

MAXINE

Maxine Doyle. I'm an actress, remember?

HENRY

Are you dead?

MAXINE

Well, that's a rude question.

(HENRY grabs MAXINE and shakes her.)

HENRY

Stop this! Stop it! Where are you? Come back!

MAXINE

Unhand me this instant.

(HENRY continues to clutch her.)

HENRY

(to himself) I don't get it.
(to her) I don't understand.

MAXINE

You don't need to understand. Just love her till you don't. But don't stop loving her till she's finished my play. Really, it's a small favour I'm asking. And you do seem like a nice man. I haven't known many, but I still know one to see one. Now please take your hands off me. I want us to be friends.

(HENRY remains frozen. Then raises a hand and touches her cheek.)

HENRY

Friends?

MAXINE

Yes. Very, very, very dear friends.
(smiles) Can we? Can we be friends?

HENRY

I thought I was moving in with a lover.

MAXINE

You are. She's just offstage right now. We share the limelight.

HENRY

I don't know how—

MAXINE

Neither do we. But we muddle through.

HENRY

But I can't—

MAXINE

She wants to muddle through with you. Don't let her down. You have a kind face. There's nothing worse than a disappointing man with a kind face.

HENRY

Are you going to be here every day?

MAXINE

Possibly. Depends how lucky you are.

(downs her drink)

Anyway, darling, it's been delightful meeting you. Mind what I said, now: don't go breaking my playwright's heart.

(She takes his face in her hands.)

MAXINE

You really do seem like a good man.

(kisses his cheek)

You might be the last one on Earth. Now: I must away to the scene of the crime.

HENRY

Scene of what crime?

MAXINE

Come to the premiere of my play. Then you'll know what crime. It was in all the New York papers, 1925's sordid news story. It's masochistic, I know, but I like to stand outside the hotel where it took place, stare up at the suite. You must relive the awful things to make art of them.

(kisses his other cheek)

Lovely meeting you, baby.

(MAXINE heads for the door.)

HENRY

Hey, wait. You can't leave. We were supposed to celebrate—

MAXINE

Celebrate what?

HENRY

Moving in together.

MAXINE

Baby, you and I ain't movin' in together. Ha! They'll be sculpting snowmen in hell before I get tangled up with another man. So long.

(MAXINE waves and exits the apartment. Henry stares after her. Then he picks up the champagne bottle and smashes it against the fridge.)

Blackout

I CAME BACK TO MYSELF outside The Plaza. I checked my phone: 3 AM. I was pretty sure the date was the same as what I last remembered: Henry-moving-in day. Fuck. I figured it was now Henry-moving-out day.

I took off running. Don't remember getting in a cab but I got out of one in front of my apartment and went tearing inside. I literally knocked Henry, who was pacing in the front hall, to the ground, sprawling in a jumble of limbs. We both sat where we fell. There was only one light on. Despite the mercy of shadows, he looked older, his skin growing shadows of its own. I tried to touch his face, but he pulled away.

"Are you you? Or are you Maxine? 'Cause if you're Maxine—"

"I'm me! I'm here, I'm back! I'm sorry. I'm just, I hope... I'm sorry."

Henry ran his hands over his face, tugged at his hair. Then he burst into a peal of high, hysterical laughter.

"Interesting character, that Maxine." His voice was hollow.

"Uh, yeah. I mean, she's more than a character, she's a real—a woman who needs... Should be a good play. Look, if you want—"

Henry put a hand up. "Don't talk. Please. I just need to sit here for a minute."

I was suddenly ravenously hungry. I wondered if Cosette had dropped by with food; I couldn't remember.

The wood floor was cold. I looked past Henry's shoulder and out the living room windows: the moon was round as an eyeball and too close, like it wanted a front-row view of the ridiculousness of my life.

Henry reached out and touched my face. I flinched, but his touch was soft. He smiled with the corners of his mouth curved down, the way people smile when they're sad.

"You're back," he said, like I had done something unexpectedly amazing. He pulled my head to his chest, to the notch where my nose fit. "Thank God."

"You're happy to see me?" I asked. Not what I was expecting.

"God, yeah. I thought you...she...Maxine might have... I don't know. I didn't know what to do."

"You don't have to do anything, remember? I always come back. And now I have the best reason in the world: you."

So Henry moved in with two women on the same day. There would be other characters who came and went—I think the men freaked him out the most—but Maxine hogged the limelight. He actually started writing notes to her, and they became friends. They were, it should be noted, banned from having sex.

–

HENRY'S DOUBLE HAS ASKED for his bill. Panic rises. Should I walk over? Ask him if Henry will ever come back? How the fuck would he know? But what if he does? What if—?

"You're a playwright, correct? I was just reading an article about you. Sorry if I'm disturbing you, I just had to say hi." Henry's double is looking down at me with a fond, gentle, slightly awed expression. He tilts his head just like Henry. He sounds just like— I can't find my words. "I saw your last play. It was amazing. It's an honour to meet you."

"Thank you. I'm glad you liked it." My own voice sounds hollow and echoey, like I'm in a tunnel hoping my words carry to someone unseen at the other end. "Are you an actor?"

"No, I'm not. Oh sorry, did you think I was looking for a job?" Henry's double grins. "Don't worry, I'm a violinist. Just wanted to tell you I'm a fan."

"Thanks. People don't usually recognize me. It's easy for a playwright to fly under the radar."

"Well. Your picture stuck in my mind. And we've got the same hair. You know, us redheads gotta stick together."

"True enough."

"God, it's great to meet you. I'm sorry, I don't want to freak you out."

He's my Henry. But how—?

"It's just, your play really inspired me. Wow. I saw it right after I got out of the hospital. Was exactly what I needed."

"Hospital? Are you okay?"

"Never better. It's a bit of a story."

"I like stories." Can it be? "You look like someone I know. Used to know. Exactly like someone I used to know."

–

WE'VE BEEN LIVING TOGETHER for three months, Henry and me. I'm so happy I wake myself deep in the night, climbing out of the labyrinth of a lucid dream so I can cup a hand under Henry's nose and catch his breath. I do this often.

"What are you doing?"

Henry sits up, looking alarmed. I guess you would too if you woke up with a hand hovering over your face.

"Nothing. Sorry. I was watching you sleep."

"Watching me sleep? Or suffocating me? Because—"

"Suffocating—no, what? Seriously? I just... I just like feeling your breath."

My face is hot, it's turning the same colour as my hair. Darkness, at this moment, is my friend.

Henry stares at me, his bony silhouette backlit by the snatches of urban glare conquering the pashminas that serve as curtains. I wonder why I've never thought to get blinds, and then I wonder why I've never wondered this before.

"Can I try it?" He's smiling.

The warm water of relief rushes through me. I nod and lie down. Henry cups his hand under my nose.

He starts to laugh. "Yes, I can definitely see the appeal."

I push his hand away. "Shut up. I'm happier when you're breathing. So sue me."

"I'm happier when I'm breathing too. And when you're breathing. Now: can we breathe together while sleeping?"

Henry reaches for me. He's asleep before I've even finished getting comfortable. I'm wide awake. Something foreboding settles on my chest and I don't think it's just a natural allergy to contentment. Maxine left a note in my purse that I've worked all day to forget:

My dear Playwright,

I went to a fortune-teller. A Greek. She had strange eyes. Sort of half asleep, or half zozzled. Strange eyes are a good sign in a fortune-teller. I wanted to know if our play will be a grand success. It will be, according to the Greek. Hallelujah! (Or, to be Grecian about it: Eureka! I have found my playwright!) But, alas, she cast a dire augury for you. About Henry, you and Henry. Perhaps I shouldn't tell you, but I feel it is my duty to protect you, at least until you finish writing my play. The Greek said there is a shadow hovering over your bed. A shadow that grows. Please tread with care.

Love, Maxine

A shadow? A growing shadow? *Love, Maxine*? What the fuck am I supposed to do with that?

Damn right she has a duty to protect me, and not just till I finish writing her damn play. Selfish bitch. Sometimes I hate my muses. Sometimes I want to kill them all. Frequently, in fact. I wonder: why must destruction lie in bed with creation?

Henry is snoring, soft wisps of innocent slumber. Or maybe guilty sleep, who is to know? Love is innocent; no person is. So many shadows have hovered over my bed, taken over my body. I no longer have the energy to be afraid. I hold Henry's hand, trying hard to imprint the feeling of my fingers curled 'round his palm in the deepest well of my memory.

–

"DO YOU MISS HIM?"

Henry's double is talking. I can hardly hear him above the buzz in my ears.

"The guy you used to know. The guy who looked like me."

I understand what he's asking now. I want to reach out and cup a hand under his nose, feel his breath on my palm.

"Yes, I miss him."

But he *is* him. Fuck, I must be hallucinating. Don't wake up. Keep right on dreaming. A frisson of wonder surges through me, prickling my flesh into miniature hills and valleys.

To my embarrassment, I feel the hot pressure of tears. "Could you— Do you ever play Ravel?"

"I love Ravel."

"I know."

"How could you know that? You just met me."

"Lucky guess." Fuck, don't cry, don't cry.

"Hey, are you okay?" His dark-honey eyes widen in sympathy.

"Yeah. No. I mean... It's a long, long story."

"I like long stories. Especially as told by great playwrights."

I smile. He has Henry's genuine earnestness, a belief that gallantry is comatose but not dead. "Don't worry about the feelings of a strange woman."

"Can I ask you a question?"

"Ask."

"What happened to the guy who looks like me?"

I stare at him a long moment. I don't know what to say.

"You don't have to answer. I'm sorry, I don't want to upset you, I just—"

"He was murdered."

"Christ. I'm so sorry. No words for that."

"Can I ask you a question?"

"Of course. Anything."

"Why were you in hospital?"

"Busking in the subway."

"Busking?"

"Can be more dangerous than you think. Guy mugged me. I got whacked in the head. Brain bleed."

"How awful."

"Hey, there's a bright side to everything. Now I know what it's like to be dead."

"Dead?"

"Yeah. But—ta-da!—here I am. The docs brought me back to life."

I can't speak.

"Oh, I'm sorry," he says. "I forgot to introduce myself. My name's Henry."

ACT II
SCENE 6

Lights up on the DOCTOR'S *apartment. The* DOCTOR *sits on the couch. The* PLAYWRIGHT *pulls a throw blanket off the back of the sofa and drapes it around his shoulders. He flinches. Long silence.*

DOCTOR

She loved those stupid cards. What are they called?

PLAYWRIGHT

Tarot.

DOCTOR

Right. Fucking tarot. Do you believe in that shit?

PLAYWRIGHT

I totally believe in that shit. Look, your dead girlfriend is emailing me. It stands to reason I believe in more stuff than you.

DOCTOR

She can't be. That isn't—

PLAYWRIGHT

Possible? Who are you to say what's possible? Enough denial. It's time for show and tell. I'll show and Anais can do the telling. I need to borrow your laptop.

(His laptop is sitting on an end table. She opens it.)

PLAYWRIGHT

Her latest email arrived this morning. Checking email is part of my hospital therapy. It's working miracles.

DOCTOR

(to himself)

Real fucking miracles.

PLAYWRIGHT

Okay, hold on a second. Are you ready for this?

DOCTOR

I don't... Fuck, I don't know what's happening.

(The PLAYWRIGHT *hands him his laptop.)*

PLAYWRIGHT

See. Read her email.

(He stares at the screen. He looks up.)

DOCTOR

She didn't write this.

PLAYWRIGHT

Then who did? How could anyone else have written that?

DOCTOR

I don't know.

(snaps the laptop shut)

But I'm sure as hell going to find out.

PLAYWRIGHT

You do that. You find out. We've exchanged quite a few emails, Anais and me. She has lots to say. Maxine's even written to her. Although I get the impression they might be in the same place. Still, Maxine likes to read my email and respond to anyone she finds interesting.

(The DOCTOR yanks the blanket from around his shoulders and throws it on the floor.)

DOCTOR

Oh, for Chrissake.

PLAYWRIGHT

Anais says the house on Corfu is still there. And so are the bones. You saw what she wrote: "I need you to bring me back to him." She wants to talk to you. Through me. You should be happy. You should be grateful. Your lost love still loves you. Even though...

(There is a long moment. Then the DOCTOR springs from the couch and lunges at the PLAYWRIGHT.)

Blackout

MAXINE

September 1, 1925

BENNY SHOWED UP alone with the giggle juice. I thought it strange; I've only ever seen him and Ronny together. But why should that be strange? Ronny could get the influenza or something. People miss a day of work now and then. Still, when I opened the door and saw just Benny standing there, something felt worse in my bones. Worse than what I already felt, which was saying a lot. I'll get to that part.

I've got a bit of the second sight, you know, a—what do they call it?—oh yeah, a sixth sense. Sometimes, I know a thing before it happens. It seems to work best with bad things. When I get excited about something good happening, well, I guess I should stop doing that. Things had already gone to hell in a handcart before Benny and his bloodshot eyes showed up. When I saw him, I knew I hadn't seen nothing yet.

It seems impossible now to remember the good feeling I had only days ago, the real good feeling about my big break coming. I mean, being a chorus girl in Follies is a break, but I didn't come to New York to be in a chorus. Now I wonder what the hell I was thinking, coming to New York at all. I think about dancing in the chorus—I can't help feeling jealous of that girl Louise Brooks, she being a featured dancer and all. She's attracting all kinds of attention. Too pretty for her own good, mark my words. There's something tragic in her face and I don't know if life is going to be real kind to her. It's a feeling in my bones. Or maybe the feeling is jealousy, nothing more. All those thoughts seem very far away now. It's funny what you think about when you think everything is going to turn out grand. I'd been feeling so damn hopeful. It helps to wake up in a bedroom with a giant butterfly painted on the wall. I've had enough of being a caterpillar; I'm ready for gossamer wings and bright lights. Or I was, anyhow. What had really made me hopeful those days was my upcoming meeting with Vance Campbell, producer extraordinaire—a film producer, you hear?—and learning he wants to give me a bit part in a Lillian Gish picture. My charisma, according to Mr. Campbell ("Call me Vance, darlin', I like the sound of my name on your lips."), leaps from the stage, and I'm a cut above—way above—the other girls. He had a very sweet way and didn't give his attention to every sheila he came across, that was plain. I didn't see him talking to any of the other dames. He said he adored my chocolate-box face. Apparently, he likes all the other parts of me too. More on that later.

I was smoking a Lucky Strike and pacing up a storm when the bell rang. Life had dealt me a raw blow and I didn't know what to do with myself. I was trying to carry on as normal. Makeup was helping in that regard, bless Saint Max Factor. I opened the door to find Mister Muscles standing there alone. Benny has always been the quiet one; Ronny is the talker. *Always*—it's not like I've lived here all my life, for pity's sake. It just felt like it, like I'd lived here forever, the feeling of being a feather-boa Broadway baby for the rest of time, even though the show closes this month. Life is better with feathers. And then life plucks you all to hell.

I knew he was drunk when I opened the door. His eyes, protruding out of his swarthy square face, were glazed. He pushed past me and set the case of bootleg on the floor.

"Spare a cup uh water?" he said, removing his newsboy cap and wiping his heavy, hairy brow. "It's hotter 'n Hades out there." I knew he had a Brooklyn accent, but this was the most I'd heard of it. Ronny usually did the talking.

"Uh, well, I'm just on my way out." I wanted to get rid of him fast as lightning.

"Aw, come on, I'm dyin'. Just uh cup."

Goddammit. "All right, sure thing. But just one and then I've gotta skedaddle."

But I had a bad feeling in my stomach, kind of squeezing hard like when my monthly is about ready to bleed all over the damn joint.

"Where's Ronny today?"

"He's under the weather." *Unda the wedder.*

I fetched him the water and he stood there drinking it, watching me with his shiny zozzled eyes. Hurry up, goddammit. I wanted him to scram real bad.

"What's in the case?" I don't usually have trouble making conversation, but there was something about his eyes that was giving me gooseflesh, so I didn't feel like talking beyond platitudes. Plus, I was already treading the depths of almighty hell. I'll get to that.

"The usual: champagne, gin, whisky. I sampled a bottle on the way over. You won't tell Robert, will you?"

Why had I never noticed his strange eyes before? Benny had always seemed like a lump hanging from a newsboy cap, nobody worth paying attention to.

"Robert'd be real sore if he knew. Why'd you do that?" If his eyes hadn't been making me so nervous, I would have flown into a fit and given him what for. I'm good at rage. Strange, the feeling of being afraid of someone you'd thought was just a piece of furniture. Sometimes furniture grows scary eyes and then you'd better watch out.

He shrugged and looked around the apartment, taking his time like he wanted to drink it all in.

"More water. Please. Ma'am." He spat the words, holding out his cup.

"Well, Benny, I really must be running along, I was on my way to a fitting for a new Follies costume. I'm going to be late—"

"That's right. You're going to be late."

I took a step back. Jesus, Mary and Joseph and all the fucking saints too. What was he on about?

"Look, I'll get you a little more water and then I really must be on my way."

I got to thinking he must have sampled more than one bottle. Robert would fire him, no question. He always says it's hard to get good help these days.

I filled up his cup only halfway so he would down it and go. He took it from me, turned on his heel, and went into the smoking room, plunking himself on my beautiful gold damask sofa like he owned the joint. That's when I got mad.

"What's the big idea? I told you I have to go. And look! You've got mud on the floor! I'm not asking nice now, I'm telling you—get out!"

He didn't move. He kept on sipping his water and looking at me without blinking. Strange, this was the first time I'd really noticed his face before. I notice more when I'm mad—anger makes my brain sharp. His eyes were dark green, kind of jewel-like in his brown face. His jaw was very heavy and strong and his mouth full: a touch of the Italian. Men seem more handsome when I'm raging at them; I can't for the life of me figure out why this is so.

Benny spoke in a calm voice. "We need to talk."

"About what? What in the world could we have to talk about? You brought the bootleg and now you've gotta scram. There'll be hell to pay if I'm late for my fitting. And there might be a director there scouting girls for a picture. I'm telling you, I've got to go. So scram!"

The bastard didn't twitch a muscle. "We need to talk."

A four-word string that ought to be removed from the English language: nothing good ever comes of it.

I blistered the air with an oath.

"I may look like a lady, but I wasn't raised to be one. You have five seconds to cross from here to that fucking door or I will scream this place down."

Four seconds of silence went by and then: "I know what you did last night."

"What the fuck are you talking about?" My blue mouth was in full swing then. Sometimes a sheila has to swear like a sailor to gain the upper hand.

"I followed you. I know what you did at the hotel."

It was very quiet and then there was a rushing in my ears. A police siren sounded in the distance and I wondered, for a fleeting moment, where the stickup was, or the murder.

"You're lying. I don't believe you. You didn't see nothing. Anything. You didn't see anything 'cause there wasn't anything to see."

"No use in fussin'. You know what I'm talkin' about. And I'll make this real plain: I want payment. You can start with that pretty gewgaw around your neck."

My hand went to my throat, protective-like. "There's no fucking way I'm giving you a cent. You know nothing and you are nothing and you can get the fuck out of my apartment."

My ears were steaming and the hot rushing racket drowned out the noise of my knees knocking together, trembling like leaves in autumn. I wanted to slug him bad, but the brute would've flattened me in a second. Benny lays no claim to height, but he makes up for the shortfall by the width of his shoulders.

I took a step back and tried my damnedest to stop shaking. I was even more shaking mad than shaking scared. How dare he threaten me! Imbecile! Robert's pathetic minion threaten me? Bunk!

"You heard me! Scram!" I stood my ground like a real David, piercing Goliath with my eyes. It turns out Papa taught me lots of useful things, though I can't praise his methods.

"I ain't goin' nowheres. You're prepared to deal, I can see it in your eyes."

"You can see nothing of the sort. I'm warning you, I'll scream this house down."

"And then what are you gonna tell your sugar daddy, huh? Think he'll take a shine to the truth?"

"You really think Robert will take your word over mine?"

"Yeah, I do. A man knows the truth when he hears it."

"Ha! Men hear what they want to hear. Robert's crazy for me."

"Maybe he is. You wouldn't wanna break his heart. It's a damn cold world out there, baby. This town's no place for a girl all by her lonesome."

"You don't scare me. I'm tougher than I look."

"Oh yeah?" He stood up and took a step forward. "Wanna test that theory, sweetheart?"

Fuck. There was no other word for this, schoolmistresses be damned.

"Look, you've got nothing on me because I haven't done anything wrong."

"I followed you last night. Right into that fancy-pants hotel. With a man. And he wasn't Mr. Sullivan. You were too goddamn giggly to notice I was right behind ya."

"So? So fucking what? So I went to a hotel for tea with a film producer to chat about him putting me in his next picture. Mr. Vance Campbell is his name, and he says I have star quality."

"Yeah, and what about afta tea, huh? I saw you go upstairs with 'im."

My stomach fell through the floor. Did he really know what had happened?

"We wanted to have a business discussion in private."

"Bullshit. Business discussion, my ass. Mr. Sullivan is gonna hit the roof. His little china doll is a floozy."

"You shut your mouth! You don't know anything!"

And then it dawned on me: he really didn't know what I'd done, not the whole story—thank the Lord. And then something else dawned on me.

"Did Robert ask you to follow me?"

"Sure did. He doesn't want his investment whoring around."

Bastard.

It was then I realized what I already knew: New York isn't about love, nor romance neither. And maybe men aren't about love. They don't need it to get ahead in this world. Well, neither do

I, goddammit. I've always done without, and I've made it this far. Robert can kiss my—

"Give me your necklace."

"What?"

"You heard me. Give me the gewgaw and I won't squeal to the boss."

"And what do I say when Robert asks what happened to it?"

"Tell him ya lost it."

"Go to hell."

"Gladly. But first I want your necklace."

"Or what? Robert will never take your word over mine."

Even as I said the words, I knew they were a lie. I was sweating, and not in a dewy attractive way.

"Oh yeah? He'll believe these."

Benny pulled an envelope out of his inside jacket pocket. Out of the envelope he pulled photographs of yours truly and Vance Campbell getting into the hotel elevator, enroute to his room. A hot feeling started to sizzle my insides, the same feeling as on the many occasions I wanted to brain Papa with a right cross.

"You fucking bastard. How dare you? Just who do you think you are?"

Benny winked at me. "Just doin' my job, ma'am. Now pay up and I'll keep quiet."

My Manhattan story has turned into something bad, not a one-time bad, a long-time bad.

I don't think I did a damn thing out of place by going to Vance Campbell's room. I was just stupid, that's all. A girl's got to survive in this world, and the bastard Robert didn't even tell me he's married. I don't want to be on the nut, for the love of God. I've had my fill of being poor. Papa liked the giggle juice more than he liked food; I like both. Which brings me to Vance Campbell, who was charming enough that I didn't notice he was evil. Not in the way Robert is—was—charming, that heavy-browed swagger. No, Vance's act was softer, like an old teddy bear. When a film producer invites me for tea, what am I going to do, say no? He worked with Lillian Gish, and he said I have as much charm.

"Darlin'," he said in his Louisiana drawl, "you got more charisma in your little finger than all the other Follies dames combined. You belong in pictures."

"Why, Mr. Campbell, thank you, I don't know what to say."

He put his hand on mine. His eyes were blue as a cloudless day and webbed at the corners with wrinkles, presumably from boyhood squinting in the Louisiana sun.

"Say yes. Say yes to my offer. A bona fide film contract. You'll start as an extra, of course, I can't guarantee a speaking role right off. But with that face, darlin', and those gams too, I'll be damned if you don't knock that Lillian Gish right off her pedestal. Heed my words, Uncle Vance is a bit of a seer, and my crystal ball is seein' stars for you."

Vance had poured gin in my teacup from a little bottle he kept hidden in his jacket pocket and I was seeing stars too. I drink too fast when I'm nervous, and how on this mortal coil could I not be nervous when I might be on the verge of becoming a Hollywood star? Exactly, it's not possible. My mind was swimming, and my eyes were swimming too—the room tilted and did a bit of splashing around. Naturally, under these circumstances, it seemed a damn fine idea when he said:

"Baby, let's mosey on up to my quarters so as we can discuss important matters of your life and future stardom in a more private setting. Cheque, please."

I stumbled a bit as I was getting out of my chair, much to my everlasting mortification. Golly, I don't recall having a truly obscene quantity of gin-spiked tea—don't know why I felt so zozzled. I guess I was dizzy with the magic of it all. Vance grabbed my arm and kept me from falling and making a disgraceful scene. I was terrified he might change his mind about me knocking Lillian Gish off her pedestal, but he was ever the gentleman. Or so I thought.

"There, there, baby, easy does it. I'll fix you a nightcap upstairs to get you settled. Hang on to my arm, that's a girl."

The lobby, all gilt and glittering with possibility, did the breaststroke before my eyes as Vance guided me to the elevator. Still, it was a grand moment, like arriving at the end of a rainbow and finding more gold than you could ever have imagined in a lifetime of imagining. With all that glitter and my head aswim in giggle juice, how would I have noticed that Benny the Rat was snapping pictures? Not that there was much I could have done about it even if I had noticed. You can't stop dominoes from tumbling, so one may as well sit back and watch the show. Maxine, darling, one must live dangerously if one is to live at all. Nobody ever climbed the Hollywood ladder by playing it safe. Golly, I'm stupid.

Vance held fast to my elbow as we rode up in the elevator, as though he were suddenly afraid I might get away. Why would I want to get away? I confess to a certain mental image of Lillian Gish toppling over a cliff as I stood triumphant, gazing out at the expansive view more full of stars than ever before. I wondered if Vance had an actual contract in his room. If so, I was ready to sign it.

We entered to see all the lights of New York beyond the window doing their starry best. It really was just like being on the edge of the cliff I'd been imagining, except there was no Lillian Gish to shove off it.

"I've got something better than gin, darlin'," Vance announced as he steered me toward a sofa. "Wait here," and he disappeared into the bedroom. There may have been butterflies behind my bellybutton. But I was still dizzy, too dizzy to notice their fluttering. City lights exploded in melting haloes like they were putting on a show, trying to keep time to the chorus of horns below.

"Better than gin!" Vance came out of the bedroom with a bottle and a cloth in his hand. "Gin fizz got nothin' on this, baby girl."

I didn't recognize the bottle, so at first, I assumed it was a new brand of whisky. He wasn't carrying glasses, though, and the cloth puzzled me.

"Have you ever tried this, darlin'? It's heaven in a bottle."

Chloroform. I've seen it around the party circuit, of course, but I've always stuck to giggle water. I don't like the idea of putting something over my face. Reminds me of that time I nearly suffocated in a haystack, gasping and reckoning that Papa would probably be none too sorry to see me go.

"I've never tried it. I like champagne." There was a knot in my stomach. Never would have taken old Vance for a sniffer.

"Baby, you don't know what you've been missing. This here'll put you on a pink cloud the likes of which you have never floated on before."

He unscrewed the cap and poured some on the cloth.

"Ah, Mr. Campbell—"

"Call me Vance, darlin', I insist."

"Ah, Vance, I really do prefer champagne. And about my contract—"

"Contract?"

"My film contract. You said—"

"Darlin', you can't rush these things. I can see your star quality, but I want to get to know you better. I mean, we've barely had a chance to get real well acquainted, and if I'm going to make you the next Lillian Gish, I need to know you real intimate-like."

He put his hand on my knee. It was big and I could feel its dampness through my silk crepe de chine.

"You only take a tiny sniff, otherwise it's lights out." He grabbed the back of my head and pressed the cloth to my face for a moment. There was a faint sweetness, a chemical edge to the sugar. I pushed his arm away and jumped up.

"You do what you want, but I think..." The room started to spin.

"Darlin', this'll make us nice and relaxed. It's always better, I find, to talk moving-picture business when everyone involved is mellow and happy as a clam. This magic stuff takes the edge off everythin' and makes doin' business a real pleasure. Surely you'll agree."

It was then that I had enough sense to be afraid. I was dizzy and his eyes were floating before me. They had changed. No longer the crinkled blues of a Southern charmer. They were hard, hard and amused. Fuck, Maxine, what now? That's what I was thinking. You need to gather your gams and get the hell out of here.

"Forgive me, Mr. Campbell, but I'm suddenly indisposed. I'll bid you goodnight."

I turned and walked toward the door, quickly, wanting escape more than dignity. I was nearly at the door when I felt his hands on me, stronger than I would have thought for a man with white hair. He spun me around. My head was already spinning something fierce.

"Now just where d'ya think you're goin', little darlin'? We were havin' such a lovely time."

His blue eyes seemed greyer now, as if they'd turned to a steel plate of sea in the hour before a storm.

Did Lillian Gish look into those grey eyes before she signed to do a picture?

My right's pretty damn good—pretty damn good if the room ain't spinning like a tornado. The only thing that jumped out clear as day were Vance's eyes. They weren't blinking.

It was then or never, so I yanked my right arm away and wound up for a punch. He knocked me off balance and I fell against the door. Damn if I wasn't going to go down fighting. I pushed against the door to right myself and gave him a swift kick in the shin.

"Owww! You fucking little bitch!"

He clipped me in the jaw. I screamed.

"Help! Help! He's tryin' to k—"

He grabbed me by the neck and clamped the cloth over my nose and mouth. I held my breath for as long as I could, which wasn't long as I was struggling so hard.

"You want to be an actress?" he kept saying. "You want to be in pictures?"

I kicked and kicked. I kept seeing his steely eyes floating in front of me, just the eyes all by themselves, without a face. A sweet smell filled my nose and throat. Blackness came quickly.

–

I WAS LYING FACEDOWN on the bed when I came to. His bed. Vance Campbell's fancy hotel bed. I tried to move fast. I couldn't. My limbs felt like lead.

I was alone in the bed. That much I figured fast. The clock said it was still deep night.

My head throbbed, a pipe upside my temple. The right side of my face felt bigger than my left. I touched it, gingerly. There was a marshmallow where a cheekbone used to be. My lip was sore, all bitten up.

I tried to assemble pieces in my mind. My head was fuzzy as a broken radio. There was a sweetness in the back of my throat.

Next thing I knew I was sitting on the edge of the bed, staring into a mirror edged in roses, lit by the glow of the bedside lamp.

I was ugly as hell. My right eye was shadowed, a black rose on my cheek. Dried blood rouged my mouth. I wasn't giving Lillian a run for her money.

I stared at the girl in the mirror and wondered why she kept twitching. She looked due for the asylum, and I wondered who was going to cart her off, and when.

Nice girls don't twitch. Nice girls don't wear blood for lipstick.

I'm not a nice girl. Let's face it. I came from an ash heap, and to an ash heap I shall return.

Where is that bastard? That's what I was thinking. Where the fuck is he?

I was sore something awful. My underclothes felt crusty, hard.

I pushed myself off the bed, swaying like a baby giraffe. I've never seen a baby giraffe, but I imagine they sway something wild when they're new at standing up. I was wild at swaying, my head in one hand, the other hand trying to breaststroke something fierce against a black tide that came rushing all at once. Stubborn gal and a strong swimmer: I kept my head above water and managed to get on my feet. That fucking bastard.

The light was on in the fancy powder room. I stumbled toward it. Everything in me and on me hurt. The mirror in the lav was no kinder. But I didn't cry. I feel proud about that now. No siree, I didn't shed a tear. Instead, I looked at my eyes and saw they were lit with a queer burning light. Those eyes were eyes I'd never seen blinking out of my face. Blue fire. If the Devil were a woman, she'd have eyes like those. My eyes were speaking. They were telling me something. They said two words in a cold, hard voice: "Kill. Him."

Where the hell is he? Those were the next words my eyes said. He must have hightailed it out of here.

Next thing I know, I was standing in the sitting room. And there the bastard was, his back to me, eyes to the bright lights of Manhattan, sipping gin as calm as you like. The sight of him took away all feeling in my body, save for the burning in my eyes, so hot they were melting my face.

I wanted to jump on him right then and there, poke his peepers out the back of his head. And I might've, too, if the cold, hard voice coming out my eyes hadn't ordered me to retreat to the bedroom, which I did, silently. The bastard never turned around.

"Fireplace," the voice said. "Fireplace." We were in the fanciest hotel suite I've ever seen, with a marble hearth in the sitting room and one in the bedroom too. I stared at the beautiful mantel. When I think of it now, I miss the ugly woodstove of my girlhood.

My eyes came to rest on the fireplace poker, fancy like every other thing in that goddamn place. I don't remember crossing the room. The poker was just in my hand as if it grew there, cold and heavy, though strangely as easy to lift as a feather.

"Wait," said the voice. "Wait."

I froze, breathing hard.

"I'll tell you when," said the voice.

I haven't the faintest notion how long I stood there, seething and breathing blue flames, while the cold, hard, calm voice ordered me to stay put.

It must have been a while.

And then I heard the voice say: "Go."

I didn't need further instructions. The strange being who had looked at me in the bathroom mirror knew what to do.

I crept to the door of the bedroom and peeked out. There he was, sprawled out on the sofa, his empty glass on the floor beside him. He was snoring, the same grating long blubbery exhale Papa used to do.

Perhaps my heart was pounding. I didn't feel it. I didn't feel fear. Only rage. Not a hot rage, no nail-spitting. An icy rage, a curled fist frozen.

He looked like an ugly baby in his ignorant sleep. A dead baby.

I could hear the cold, hard voice in my head doing something, and at first, I couldn't figure what it was. Then I realized what: laughing. The voice was laughing, a low, vicious rumble. I stood there relishing the sound.

Beyond the dead baby and the cold cackle, the lights of the city dazzled. They were different. Sharper. Scores of swords to fall upon.

I felt nothing as I raised the poker above my head. Except wonder at how light it was.

Then I don't know what happened. Or, at least, I don't remember it. When I came to, so to speak, I was standing over a terrible mess, huffing hard. For a moment I waited for a curtain to drop, for the character sprawled on the sofa to get up and walk off the stage, bound for an intermission nip of bathtub gin. I waited for the voice to tell me what to do next. The voice was gone.

I dropped the poker like it was on fire. Next thing I knew, I was hanging over the edge of the bathtub, sure I was vomiting up my heart. After I stopped heaving, I checked the contents of the tub—my heart was beating so loud I was sure it was beating outside my body, half expected it to be sitting there on a nest of vomit, ticking up at me. Nah, it was still where it ought to be. Goddammit.

I marched myself to the mirror, even though I was damn scared about what it might show me. No queer hard eyes, just my usual ones, the big blue things Robert says belong in the face of the cherub on a box of chocolate. Those eyes could never do anything very bad. I was sweating and my hair looked a sight but otherwise there wasn't much mess on me, because it was that other girl who done it and not me, I never did a thing. Even then I wasn't sure who would believe that.

Maxine, you better blow this filthy joint, before all the filth blows on you. That's what I was thinking. Blow it fast. Fucking fast. I swear, my mouth gets fouler by the day. With good reason.

So I washed my face and salvaged my hair. When you've got chocolate-box features, you clean up well, even when you've taken a beating. I was squeaky-church-clean in no time. Mister Max Factor's marvellous makeup did a fair job covering Vance's mess: I was angelic in a jiffy. You could have glazed me and stuck me in a stained-glass window.

I washed the vomit out of the tub. Then I had to face Vance, or what was left of him. I shielded my eyes and crept into the sitting room.

Through my fingers I saw the poker first. I ran and snatched it up, as if I still needed to defend myself. No need, Maxine. Vance was a lump, slumbering in mashed-up fashion forevermore.

I felt nothing as I looked at him, except perhaps curiosity because I'd never seen a dead body before. If it's true that some people look peaceful in death, he wasn't one of them. Nor had there been much handsomeness to ruin with a poker and final repose. If I should have felt sorrow or pity, I didn't. I felt only fear.

Jesus fucking Christ, Maxine. If ever there was a time to take the Lord's name in vain. What now? I needed to get the fuck out of there.

His pocketbook had fallen on the floor and his clams were there for the plucking. I figured I had better use for the dough now than he did. Also, you know, maybe it's better it looked like a holdup gone bad. Old Vance, he carried a lot of dough. I guess, though, everyone's a pauper in the end. Vance, you poor bastard, Lillian Gish sends her regards.

After I'd collected Vance's fat wad of clams, I washed and shined the poker till it gleamed and replaced it by the fire. Next, I scrubbed down the bathroom and everything else I could think I might've touched. Never thought I'd see the day I'd depend on what I learned from detective stories in penny dreadfuls. But depend I did. In the moment, I didn't feel sorry for the lifeless gobbet on the sofa, and cooler heads prevail in the absence of pity.

Cleanup done, I stood awhile at the front door, perhaps just a minute or two—it felt like an eternity in purgatory—listening for footsteps outside. 'Course, I didn't want anyone to see me leaving Vance's once-classy joint. I kept reminding myself what Robert had told me, back when I was believing everything he said: You got the face of an angel. An angel, Maxine. You're a goddamn angel. I hoped to hell that would be enough to get me through, should anyone happen across my path.

The hallway outside the suite seemed quiet. Sweat from my palm had soaked through my glove, and I felt to keel over in a dead faint as I turned the doorknob. I opened the door a crack. Nobody afoot. The suite was around the corner from the elevator. Not on your life was I going fraternizing with the operator. So I turned left instead of right and fled into a stairwell.

Dammit, Vance, you had to be in the damn penthouse. It was a long way down. Staircase after staircase. I took them fast, stopping whenever I could stand it to see if anyone was coming. The lighting was dim, of course, so thank my stars I've always been pretty fancy on my feet and managed to break neither neck nor ankle.

When I got to the bottom, I found a door that emptied me out into the alley behind the hotel. The heat had broken and I was glad for the chill wind, which gave me a normal reason to tremble. A drunk was half-asleep at one end of the alley, mumbling to himself, and he paid me no mind. I hotfooted it in the other direction, trying to remember how the hell to get home. Everything looked clearer, sharper, and yet I couldn't think what damn street I lived on. Slow down and breathe, girl, act normal. Though at that wee hour the streets weren't full of what I'd call normal people, anyway. Once I figured out which way was home, I decided against a taxicab—didn't want the driver to ask what a sweet sheila like me was doing out on the street at this hour. I kept my head down as I walked, collar up, cloche pulled low. It was a long, long walk. It was the longest walk of my life.

When I rode my elevator up to my apartment, Stan, the kind operator, tried to make conversation. I think he's sweet on me. He's used to my late hours, and thinks I lead a terribly exciting life. Which I do.

"Swell party?" he asked, in his lilting Irish voice.

I assured him it was the best party I'd ever attended.

I kept my head down, but I could feel him taking a closer look at me. My face was banged up, no question.

"Miss Doyle, are you sure you're all right?"

I nodded. Then I blew him a kiss as I left the elevator. Damn, I'm an even better actress than I thought. Fuck you, Lillian Gish, there's a new game in town.

Oh my. There's a hot hammock in hell for me.

When I was safe inside, I fell to the floor. Two minutes, I told myself, you can lie in a sobbing heap for all of two minutes on this here floor before you take this fucking dress off and burn it.

Up and at 'em, Maxine. By God, I did pull myself off the foyer floor and, in two shakes of a lamb's tail, had a roaring fire stoked in the fireplace I used to love but can never think of in the same way again. There was blood on my dress that I'd failed to notice back at the hotel. I peeled down to my favourite cami-knickers, the pink silk ones Robert bought for me, and then decided I'd better burn those too.

So there I was, naked as the day I was born, watching my fine clothes burn. I kept one pearl button from my dress. I don't know why. I just wanted to.

As the sun came up, the fire burned low. My eyes burned as I stared at the dying flames, the painful red of the embers. Now what, Maxine? One way or another, I think my goose is well and truly cooked.

I tossed for an hour and then I was up, pacing, the sounds of the city splitting my head from all sides. Life in New York goes on, and I don't know how this can be. But it cannot go on for me. I knew this the moment Benny darkened my door, my death knell ringing in his eyes.

'Course, I didn't think he knew anything, I just had a lowdown bad feeling soon as I saw his face. I already felt like hell, naturally, when I answered the door, and he sure as sugar was no saint come to wash my sins away. I'd bathed and dressed and troweled makeup on my bruises. I figured I should act as normal as normal can be. True, I've got experience pretending bad things never happened, but nothing like this, not even close. This is a whole other world of pretending, the likes of which no stage nor screen has ever seen.

So then he sprang his blackmail on me, and the fight was on. It was obvious he didn't yet know that Vance was dead. Perhaps no one did, it was still early. Soon, the coppers would be hunting for his killer. And Benny would figure it was me.

I had to think fast and talk faster. By gosh, I was up against it. Well, as I write this, I still am. Some jams you just can't wriggle free of. Not entirely. They put marks on you that aren't ever going away.

My first thought was to run for the bedroom and pull out my baby automatic, plug Benny on the spot. Robert had insisted I keep a gun in my night table for protection; he sure as hell never figured on me needing it for this reason. But Benny might've been carrying, and... well, I lost my nerve. Besides, people in the building would have heard the shot, and then how would I get his body, which probably weighs a barrel of bricks, out of my apartment?

I figured I had to play his game until I could think of something else, get him somewhere else. Jesus, I was trembling, every muscle screaming from trying not to let him see the shakes.

Finally, I said: "Maybe we can work something out."

"Now you're talking," said the louse.

"What do you want?"

"For starters, that gewgaw around your throat and five hundred clams."

"You want five hundred fucking dollars for a few lousy pictures? How dare you!"

"No, I want five hundred—to start—for not telling Robert his doll is a tramp. He'll toss you out like yesterday's trash, and you know it. Then what'll you do, huh? You ain't no movie star. There's a pretty good brothel in Chinatown. A class joint. Baby-doll puss, eyes of blue. Maybe they'd take you."

Bennie started to laugh. My hand twitched, longing for my baby automatic. Right between the eyes.

No, Maxine. You got to play this smart. That's what I was thinking as I reached up and unfastened the gewgaw from around my neck, all the while glaring daggers at Benny. One of my favourites, that necklace. The one Robert gave to me on closing night of *The Squab Farm*. Rubies, because red was my favourite colour till I saw Vance Campbell lying in a pool of it.

"Here. Take it. Now get out."

"What about my money?"

"I don't have five hundred here. You'll have to wait."

"I ain't waitin' around. So you bettah act fast, little lady. These lips won't stay closed for long."

"And what am I going to tell Robert if he asks where five hundred clams went?"

Benny chuckled. "That ain't my problem, now is it? I want the money by tomorrow. And that's just the first payment."

"You're lowlife scum."

He shrugged. Scum is a costume he's comfortable wearing.

"My mother raised me to be smart, not nice."

"Fuck your mother."

He took a step toward me, menacing-like, and I took a quick step back. Right between the eyes, pal. Just you wait.

"I'll meet you tomorrow," I said, my voice all hollow and echoing in my head. I needed time to think.

"What time?"

"I don't know. I'll telephone you. Tell you when and where."

"What's wrong with here?"

"I don't want scum in my house."

"This ain't your house, baby, it's your sugar daddy's."

"Get the fuck out of my house."

The smirking son of a bitch paused, looking me over like I was a dumb side of beef. Then he strolled past me to the front door, all relaxed like some lollygagger on a summer's day.

He turned at the door and smiled. "I'll be waitin' by the phone, dollface. And remember: I don't like dames who don't play by my rules."

And with that, he made his exit. Now how the hell was I going to fix his final curtain call?

My thoughts on how to answer that question were interrupted by the telephone. I didn't feel like chatting, to put it mildly. That said, I needed a distraction, and I'd received so many godawful shocks I answered it half insensible to what I was doing. I forgot to say hello. There was a pause, and then Robert's voice.

"Hello? Maxine? Hello?"

I should have hung up and curled up on the floor.

"Hello, Robert," I croaked. My tough voice failed. My nerve was gone. My eyes started to leak.

"What's wrong, sweetheart? What is it?"

What's wrong? Him being married used to be the limit. Yesterday was a long time ago.

"Uh...nothing, I just...need..."

"What is it, my love? You're not still angry, are you? Maxine, I may have commitments elsewhere, but I've given you—"

"No, it's not that," I managed to shove out of my throat. "I just... I think I've got a touch of the influenza. You should stay away for a few days."

"Influenza? My God, I'll ring the doctor. Are you in bed? You should be lying down."

"No, no, don't call the doctor. I'm sure it's, uh, nothing. I just need a rest. I'll have to miss a Follies night or two. Hope they don't sack me."

"Don't worry about that, dear, it's time you moved on to greener pastures. Are you certain I shouldn't ring the doctor?"

"I simply have a headache and need to go to bed. Please don't call the doctor. I'll ring him myself if I need to. And please don't come 'round till I say. I wouldn't want you to get, uh, sick. So long, Robert."

"So long, kid. I'll speak to you soon. Rest well."

On my way down to complete collapse on the floor, I managed to hang up the phone. If I'd had something in my stomach, I would have thrown it up on the beautiful soft rug. I've never been much of a praying gal, but right then I asked God to strike me with influenza and let me die quick. Or a bolt of lightning. Nothing happened. Yeah, I always knew God was a bunch of bunk.

There was no time to wallow and whine. On your feet, Maxine. You've felled one good-for-nothing bastard. Why not two?

September 2, 1925

I spent much of yesterday pacing, dithering, fretting, and taking baths trying to get the filth of Vance Campbell off my skin. Every rosewater spritz and lavender bath oil I own were of no use—his damn filth doesn't budge. Perhaps that is for the best, at least right now. It keeps my rage hot. I feel guilty of nothing.

I have the dough Benny wants under my mattress. Could've handed it to him yesterday, but that doesn't fix the problem. Why give meat to a rabid dog?

Today my first order of business is to get a newspaper. Vance would have been discovered yesterday, and I need to know what the coppers—and everyone else—are saying. I hope to hell there aren't any pictures. I'm done with looking at that man's blood.

Except for a handful of minutes, I still haven't slept. Tough as tough can be to take care of this kind of calamity without hardly a wink to give me strength. Who, I ask you, could sleep or eat at a time like this? I forced myself to choke down toast and black-as-the-Devil coffee. The coffee-crazed, empty-bellied state made me feel so mentally defective I had to fight back with ham and eggs. At this moment, a piece of pork is the only thing standing between me and lunacy.

Dawn has barely knocked out night and I am ready to go. Enough red lipstick and Jicky perfume to play the part of an elegant young lady out for an early morning stroll and newspaper. Though Stan and Mr. Reece are used to me coming in at this hour, not going out.

7:11 AM

I'm back with the newspaper, not sure whether to feel better or worse. Stan did look at me sideways when I went down, and so did Mr. Reece when I passed by the concierge's desk with an overly cheery "Good morning!" They're the least of my worries.

The headline reads: "Movie Producer Croaked in Apparent Robbery." Underneath that are the words: "Coppers on the Hunt for Vicious Assailant." And underneath that is a photo of the crime scene.

Jesus, Mary and Joseph. He was the vicious one, not me.

More photos of the crime scene on page two. Vance sprawled all bloody and lumpish. Coppers with grim looks. Then an editorial about the lawlessness of New York City, how all the mentally defective criminals are ruling the streets and making life hell for ordinary decent folks.

The coppers noted that Vance's pocketbook had been rifled through by the horrible intruder, the robber-turned-killer. Mr. Campbell was a Hollywood luminary, they said. Produced films starring Gish. A spokesperson for Vance's studio said the world of cinema had suffered a tragic loss of inestimable proportions, that a bright light had been dimmed forevermore. He was a visionary to all who knew him.

Christ Almighty, my ham and eggs are about to make an encore all over the carpet. I need a swallow of gin to keep me steady. That said, this is good news. They think it was a robbery. And I'm sure nobody saw me leave. True, folks in the lobby may have seen me go into the elevator with the dirty scoundrel. I'm not sure. But who in tarnation would suspect this skinny little thing of bashing a man's head in? You've got to keep on thinking that, Maxine. Don't know what else to do. So my problem remains Benny. Surely he, like everybody else under the sun, would never think me capable of doing what I did. This scrawny kitten with the big blue eyes picked up a fireplace poker and—never! Well, that'd better be the case. Thing is, though, he knows I was there and he wants money, and I don't see an end in sight.

At this moment, I am more alone than I have ever been upon this mortal coil.

The newspaper quoted the chief of police as saying they are going to hunt down the rabid dog who did this fiendish thing to wonderful Mr. Campbell, and make sure the evil, dirty culprit goes straight to the electric chair. I don't think they would send a woman to the chair, do you? Come to think of it, there have been a few of the fairer sex to fry.

If I left town, where would I go?

How would I live?

I don't need to leave town, nobody knows I did Vance.

But Benny. Benny's a big fat problem.

A problem yours truly knows how to set right.

But I'm not some mental defective who just up and croaks men and goes along her merry way. (Well, Vance wasn't just any man, he was a louse and he had it coming, and Benny is a louse too!)

So what's the story, Maxine? Go south to Florida? Hide out in a swamp town? Survive by stealing oranges? And then what?

A fine fucking kettle of fish.

I don't fancy suicide. Why should I be forced to croak myself? I'm the victim!

That's final—I'm neither opening my veins nor the gas. This cookie's too tough for such awful jazz.

Perhaps it's best to pay Benny today, buy more time to think things through.

Now you're on the trolly! Get a wiggle, Maxine. Pay him half, that's the ticket. To show him I'm not a simp who's going to wilt entirely. And take along my bean-shooter just in case I need some muscle.

The last time I fired a gun I was standing beside Papa taking instruction and blasting a row of bottles on the fence, thinking maybe, just maybe, one day I might practise on him.

So it's been a while, but I can take care of Benny if I have to. Just because you can, Maxine, doesn't mean you want to shoot a man. It's cleaner than what happened to Vance.

What you can't remember, you didn't do. When a person is justified, they are not a murderer. The Bible says an eye for an eye, and this is a Christian country. Robert says I have the face of an angel. An avenging angel, apparently.

Damn. All my gaspers are gone. I've smoked the whole pack without noticing. Little wonder my throat is a sore mess of burning tar.

8:18 AM

Pulled some dough out from under the mattress. Counting clams is soothing at a time like this. Counted to five hundred and then started over. Did it six times. I should pay the full price, no sense in getting him sore.

There was more money in my bed than I thought. Robert's generous, I'll give him that. He'd be horrified if he knew I'm keeping some of his cabbage in my bed. But when you've never had money, you want to keep it where you can see it anytime you want. You don't want to hand it to some stranger in a bank and trust they're going to keep it for you. I make sure the seventy-five a week I earn from Follies is kept at the opposite end of the bed, separate from Robert's allowance. It tickles me to see my stage earnings growing, even if I'm really only making peanuts. It's my own peanuts, and that little pile of green used to give me a thrill and pour fuel on my limelight daydreams. Was all a lifetime ago. The life of a very stupid little nobody.

Now I've got to figure where to meet Benny, and how I'm going to play the scene. I don't want to hand him the five hundred and invite him back for more. So out comes my bean-shooter. I've got to say, I feel a damn sight taller with that thing snug in my hand. I think all ladies should carry a gun, and no men should. The world would be a much nicer place.

It was while I was posing with my gun and pretending to shoot

Vance Campbell first and Benny second that the phone rang. It was Robert.

"Have you seen the paper? What am I saying, you never read the morning paper. Vance Campbell, the film producer, was brutally slain in his hotel suite. Can you imagine? A shocking business. I met Vance dozens of times. He produced the last Lillian Gish picture."

I didn't say anything. My palm started to sweat against the handle of my gun.

"Maxine, are you there? By the way, kid, how are you feeling?"

"I'm, uh, a bit under the weather. And that's real bad, about Mr. Campbell."

"A beastly business. Criminals are running amok in the streets of Manhattan. None of us is safe. I mean, if a man isn't safe in his hotel room, what is the world coming to? I suppose one of the staff is the culprit. You know, looks like robbery. Some rotten bellboy drunk on the idea of easy money."

I was silent. My heart was pounding and I was scared if I opened my mouth, my damn heart might shoot up my throat and swan dive right off my tongue, crazy as that sounds.

"Sweetheart, are you there? Are you sure I shouldn't fetch the doctor? I'd like to call on you later today."

"No!" I burst out. "I mean, I don't want you to get whatever I've got. And don't bother the doctor. I'll bother him if there's need. But there isn't, at least not right now. I'm going back to bed. I'll say goodbye."

"So long, kid. I'll ring you later. Have a little brandy and some tea."

A little brandy. All the brandy in the world wouldn't salve this gaping wound of a disaster.

9:03 AM

I made more coffee to pacify the six swigs of gin I couldn't help but imbibe. I'm in front of the empty fireplace, gun beside me like my new and only best friend. I haven't been in the city long enough to have any real best friends. Everything's happened so fast. There are a few Follies girls I like, as well as a lot of gossips in the bunch. None that I would call on to help me out of a fix. Especially not the worst fix in the world. I've just got to believe Benny won't connect me with what happened to Vance, and then I have to figure a way to put an end to his blackmail. Which is easier said than done. My mind is swimming, my body shaking. I have nobody in this whole wide world. It's a pretty sad business when your heart belongs to your diary and your gun.

I want to go back to the innocence of feathers at Follies, of sparkling costumes and thinking I was the next Lillian Gish. The innocence of being jealous of that beautiful Louise Brooks, prettiest girl in the whole Follies show, as if being second-best was the worst problem in the world. You can't go back to innocence when something hideous happens. Even at my lettuce age, I know that like I know my own heartbeat, and I learned it long ago.

Benny lives in Brooklyn and I'd rather meet him there. He and the dead louse have tainted Manhattan all to hell for me. It's easier to pretend I'm just acting in a play if I go to a whole other place.

So that's what I'll do. I'll get in a taxi and go to Brooklyn and then—and then what? I want to stomp on his face like I would stomp on a cockroach. Make hash of it. Maybe I can. There is something in me that can do anything, do things I'd never thought of before.

In the ashes of the empty fireplace, the ashes that were once a dress I adored, I can see Benny's face becoming a godawful corned-beef hash under the heel of my satin shoe. What terrible things now soothe my heart.

Burn the newspaper, right, that's what I should do. If nothing else, to stop me vomiting over the glowing descriptions of "one of motion-picture production's leading luminaries," and to temporarily distract myself from the notion of smashing Benny from here to the nonexistent hereafter. There is a part of me that terrifies me. I don't know what it's going to do next. Perhaps I've always suspected it was there, saw glimmers of it once or twice, especially that time my fingers itched to pick up Papa's hunting rifle and blow his drunken head clean off. Now those terrifying glimmers feel like some blasted inferno searing me from the liver on up. It's the inferno, I reckon, that's keeping me kicking.

If the Devil does exist, maybe he's just misunderstood.

3:59 PM

Benny called five minutes ago. I knew it was him and almost didn't answer. What would be the point, though? He'd just keep calling, or arrive on my doorstep.

"Ya got the money?" he growled, by way of hello.

"I'll meet you in Brooklyn. You're not welcome here."

"You're always welcome at my place, baby."

"Shut your yap. What's your address?"

"Fifty-Three Madison Street. In Bedford."

"I'll see your sorry mug at midnight."

"Remember, it's five hundred clams. And another gewgaw."

"Hey, you never said nothing about more jewellery!"

"I drive a hard bargain. I'm Italian."

"Fuckin' wop."

He started to laugh. "You're mighty cute when you're hot undah the collar."

"Fuck you." And I slammed the phone down.

He's going to keep asking for more. I've got to get myself together. To get ready for a dogfight. To dope things out and figure what's what. To coat my face in a fresh ton of pan-stick and so much face powder I'll be called a flour lover, all so nobody sees the marks Vance put on me. I'm so goddamn tired I can hardly see straight. My mind is a dumb Dora mush. I'd be feeling mighty sorry for myself if I had the time, time to hide out in my big bed and cry to the big butterfly that stares with no feeling. That's what I'd be doing if I didn't have fear wringing me limp from head to toe. Think, Maxine, you got to think real clear now.

So here I am huddled in front of a roaring fire, a cleansing fire that burned up the newspaper with Vance Campbell's blood splashed in black and white, staring into the flames and willing them to tell me what to do.

All I know is I'm going to Brooklyn. And my baby automatic's coming with me.

ACT II
SCENE 7

Lights up on the DOCTOR'S apartment. He has her by the shoulders. Then he shoves her away.

DOCTOR

Get out. Get out of here. I don't care where you go. You're not my patient.

(The PLAYWRIGHT doesn't move.)

PLAYWRIGHT

What if I'm the only person who can help you?

DOCTOR

You? Help me?
(to himself)
I'm losing my mind.

PLAYWRIGHT

No, you're finding it.

(Beat)

Tell me.

DOCTOR

Tell you what?

PLAYWRIGHT

Tell me what happened. You saw her email, she doesn't hate you. She wants you to know she's fine. The night before she died, she read her tarot cards. She pulled the Strength card, one of her favourites. A good omen, she said. She wants you to know she's too strong to hate you.

(There is a long silence.)

DOCTOR

I hate me.

(Beat)

Look at me. I died long ago. And I went to hell.

Blackout

DOCTOR

IT WAS MARIE'S IDEA to use real bullets. It was her idea. It was her idea. I said let's just use empty guns. Why do we need bullets? We're not going to fire. But she wouldn't hear of it. I'm a just-in-case kind of person, was her rationale. Just in case? We're not killing anyone. There is no "just in case."

Marie got the guns—well, actually, one gun—from a guy she knew through the art bar, a gun collector who had the hots for a purple-painted woman. She'd slept with him twice, before she'd met me, and found out he was boring. "But he's got great guns, I'll give him that," she said.

She already owned one gun, a leftover from another ex-boyfriend. She kept it under her pillow for protection. My WASPy parents weren't gun people. I'd never seen a gun up close till I met Marie. Sleeping with one right next to my head was a bit disconcerting at first. And then it was kind of hot.

By this time I'd blown through much of the money my father had given me, on alcohol, cocaine for Marie, and general hedonistic joblessness. Man, I was happy. Or maybe not happy. But alive. Awake. High on a woman who was high on everything.

Marie had been talking about hightailing it to Mexico since I'd moved in with her. Starting over. Eternal summer. Getting out of the United States of Banal, as she put it. I figured out what the obsession with Mexico was about when I realized she was being stalked by yet another ex, a nightmare of a pusher with a tattoo down one side of his face. He showed up one day at our apartment about two months after we'd shacked up. Before then he'd come around when I wasn't home or show up at her bar. I told him to fuck off. He broke my jaw. And my arm.

"Forget going to the cops," Marie said, crying like I'd never seen anybody cry. "He'll kill us both."

If, by hooking me into living with her, she had thought she was getting a bodyguard in the bargain, she misjudged. I mean, I can throw a decent right hook, and my jab isn't too shabby either, but I'm no match for a born streetfighter who spent time in prison working on his boxing.

"I shoulda shot him," Marie sobbed, as I lay on the floor. "I'm sorry, I'm sorry. I just don't wanna go to jail."

Now I should have packed my shit and gotten the fuck out of there. But I wanted to protect her. See, I'm not a bad man. I'm not.

Even then, as a twentysomething college dropout, I don't think I was enough of a romantic to have said Marie was the love of my life. The idea of a love of one's life was bullshit. But she was a high, a speedball high, and then a dreamy apple-pie-in-my-belly haze, like the morphine I was shot up with when my jaw was being wired.

She nursed me back to health. I was impressed, because she's not the nursing type. Her cooking leaves something to be desired, but on the upside, every night she insisted on rubbing my chest with Chinese liniment, like that could somehow make my jaw and my arm stop hurting. "I'm fixing your qi," she said. "I picked up Chinese wisdom somewhere along the way." Nobody had ever nursed me before. It was a weird feeling. Weird and awesome.

We were hiding out at her friend Lark's place so Marie's crazy ex wouldn't show up and finish me off. And her. "He's been wanting my ass dead a long time. He's warming up to it. The bastard still loves me. Love can be a real killer."

In a fog of painkillers and aching bones, Mexico started to look pretty damn appealing. I admit, though, that our gritty cheese-straws-

and-whisky lifestyle was already starting to wear on me. I was born to moneyed cold fish. I'd never known grit, at least not in a material way. Medical bills had been a fresh drain on resources. We needed to get serious about cash.

Hell, maybe I *am* a romantic—I wanted to run off to Mexico with a coke-snorting woman I'd been sleeping with for two months to save her from her villainous ex. It was the stuff fairy tales are made of.

"Imagine, we could get a boat and live on it, wouldn't that be cool? I've always wanted to paint and float at the same time. Float on a perpetual wellspring of inspiration."

"Stop, stop."

"What? It's a fucking brilliant idea."

"No, I mean stop with the Chinese stuff already, it's burning my skin."

She got up and opened the living room window. We were on Lark's pullout couch.

"It does reek of camphor in here. But it's making you better."

"What would we live on? In Mexico."

"Well, you've got some money."

"We've burned through a fuckload of it."

"Well...I guess I could bartend part-time. I speak some Spanish. *Te amo.*"

I rolled my eyes. "That's not a plan."

"I hate plans. You make plans to break plans."

"That's your life philosophy?"

"My philosophies are very malleable. I consider chameleonism my greatest strength."

"And what would I do in Mexico?"

"Drive the boat."

Marie started laughing hysterically.

"You're fucking crazy, you know that, right?"

"You love crazy. That's why you're here."

She had a point.

"Oh, come on, laugh! We've been through hell, we need to dream a little. And we need to get the fuck outta Dodge."

She was undressing as she spoke. Slowly, without breaking her gaze. There was black stuff smudged around her eyes. It made them stand out in a glowy alien kind of way.

"I'm gonna make you feel better," she said, her voice unusually soft. "And then I'm gonna tell you how we're gonna get some money."

She got the car. She got the guns. She got the bullets. But I got in the car. After I picked up the gun. After I loaded it with bullets.

–

7 AM ON A FRIDAY and I'm shaking and thinking what the fuck are you doing, man. And I keep right on doing it. It's exciting, in a sickening kind of way. In the moment, it all makes perfect sense. Mexico is calling. You can be anyone you want to be in Mexico. Right? A new life. A new start. A sailboat. A purple-painted sex-crazed woman you need to rescue from the fuckhead ex who wants you both dead. Right?

I'm innocent. An innocent boy. An innocent med-school dropout.

Marie is talking. I can't hear what she's saying. My thoughts are too loud, drowning her out.

Focus. It's too late to back out now. The plan has claws, it's got me in its grip, I don't have a choice. It's pulling me along. I don't like being dragged so I'm going to take control, get some balls. Do what needs to be done.

–

9 AM. THIS IS IT.

Marie talked the whole way there. Almost. Until I yelled at her to shut the fuck up. She didn't seem nervous at all. Lack of fear—a psychopathic trait. She was almost chipper, actually. "It was really nice of Ed to get us this car without charging. He boosted it from that lot across from the library. He totally owes me this favour and more."

I was driving. I prefer to drive. I hate being driven by a woman because they usually suck at it. This is still true even though you can't say it out loud anymore.

"Ed has no clue what we're using it for, obviously. In case you're worried. You look worried. Relax, for Chrissake. We'll be in and out in the blink of an eye. Would you quit looking like a fucking zombie, it's really giving me the creep—"

That was when I lost it. After that I had two minutes of blessed silence and then we were there.

We get out of the car. Leave it running. Stride to the door. Pause for a moment, pull our balaclavas down. And then it's on.

"Everybody on the ground!" Marie yells.

Guns drawn. I'm in a movie. It's a fucking movie. Christ, what a high.

There are only four customers. They hit the floor, covering their heads.

There are six tellers. They throw their hands up and get on the ground. A man is still standing, hands up, shaking.

"You the manager?" I growl. I have a different voice in this movie, a voice I don't recognize.

He nods.

"Vault!"

I follow him to the vault while Marie covers the others. He's a short man with wire-framed glasses. Blink, blink, blink, blink—he's sweating so bad it's messing up his vision. His spastic hands are fumbling with the lock.

"Hurry up!" I have the gun pointed at his ear. I've never waited this long for anything. It feels like a year just dragged by.

Then it opens. Thank fuck. Nobody has to get hurt. We're almost there.

I hand him a burlap sack. It once held potatoes. Marie made scalloped potatoes for me when my face and arm were busted up. An image of her standing at Lark's stove, smoking a joint and smiling, flashes through my mind.

"Faster! Move!" The manager is putting money in the sack. He's shaking so bad he's vibrating. Shit, don't pass out. Keep it together. He drops a stack. "You wanna bullet in the brain!" I scream in his ear. I don't know why I did that. It just came out. It just came out.

The sack is full. I snatch it and back out of the vault, training my gun at the poor guy's forehead. Wet saucer eyes. He's crying now.

I turn and run to the main part of the bank. Tellers and customers still on the floor. "You all start counting to five hundred!" Marie hollers. "Let me hear you!"

We start toward the door. Then a woman walks in, head down, fumbling with her purse. She almost walks into me. "Get down on the ground!" I scream. Her head jerks up and she screams bloody fucking murder. And then I hear a sound like a firecracker. The screaming woman falls. Did Marie shoot her? No, it's me—it's my gun. I didn't pull the trigger. I didn't pull the trigger. The bullet, it just came out. It just came out.

I back away. I don't know. I don't know what happened. I don't know.

"Holy fuck!" Marie shrieks. "Let's go!"

We run. We fly into the car. I peel away. Start screaming.

We dump the car at an abandoned warehouse outside of town. Put the money in two backpacks. "Oh my God, holy fuck, holy fuck, holy fuck..." I keep saying this till Marie slaps me hard.

She grabs my face. "Listen to me. It was an accident, right? Shit happens. Pull it together. We've gotta move."

I nod. "Accident, accident, accident..." My new mantra. Everything is an accident.

–

WE DUMP THE GUNS in the river and head back to Lark's place. Good thing Lark is outta town. I'm losing my mind.

When we get close to town Marie suggests we get a cab.

"Are you fucking crazy? A cab? The driver's gonna know it was us!"

I'm sweating like a pig. I keep walking.

A couple minutes later she grabs my arm. "Stop. Stop! Listen to me. Nobody's gonna know it was us. We were wearing masks, remember? We were wearing gloves. What happened wasn't your fault. You gotta put it outta your mind because we gotta be smart. Okay? Are you with me?"

I stare at her. My fingers twitch. I want to rip her face off. "You're right, it's not my fault—it's your fault! You were the one who wanted bullets! We didn't need loaded guns, I told you that! And you were supposed to lock the fucking door! Fuck you!" I start walking.

"This is not my fucking fault! It's nobody's fault! It was an accident!"

"An accident? Yeah, tell that to the woman lying in a pool of blood!"

"We don't know she's dead. She might be alive! We can't think about it right now. Okay? Let's just get home."

"Home? Where's that? Just shut the fuck up and keep walking."

Not another word passes between us till we get to Lark's place. All the way here, walking on backstreets and side streets, I've been glancing sideways at anyone we passed, trying to see if they were looking at us funny. Nobody was. It's the weirdest feeling. Bad shit goes down, and life goes on. Why doesn't the world stop turning?

We get inside and I turn the deadbolt. Like that will protect us from what we've done. From what I've done.

"What now?" I say softly. "What the fuck now?" I'm tired as hell. I want to sleep and never wake. I want to cry but I can't.

"Mexico," Marie says, taking my hand. "Sailboat."

"I don't want to go to Mexico. Fuck the boat."

"Where do you wanna go, then?"

"I don't know. But I've gotta get the fuck out of here."

I let go her hand. Turn away. And throw up.

We switch on the radio, tune into the news station. I refuse to count the money till we know. Till we know about the woman. Every time I hear a sound outside, I jump. Marie seems strangely calm, and it's making me fucking furious.

"Maybe we should turn this off," she says. "I mean, what good will it do you to know?"

A woman's voice comes over the radio: "There's been an armed robbery at Bank of—"

"I really think—" Marie reaches for the dial.

I smack her hand away. "Shut the fuck up! Ssshhh! Listen!"

"Police say two armed robbers, a male and a female, made off with a substantial amount of cash. Shortly before leaving the bank, the male suspect shot a customer. The victim, a woman in her forties, was pronounced dead at the scene."

I get up. Put my fist through the wall. And scream.

I'm on the floor. Marie just decked me. Not a slap, a punch.

"Do you want the cops to show up? Do you? Get a hold of yourself! What's done is done. It was an accident. I know that. You know that. Now let's pull it together. You can't fall apart on me now. No fucking way. Get up."

I don't move. I was already on the ground when she punched me. It seems like a good place to stay for the rest of my life, this old wood floor. A life I hope ends soon.

"What if she had a husband? What if she had kids? Holy fuck..."

"We don't need to know. What good would it do to know? It was an accident. Now we move forward. Like we planned. Okay?"

In this moment, I can't remember why any of this happened. Any of it. It's all a blank.

I vomit several more times. And then we count the money. We can't think what else to do. There is nothing else to do.

Holy fuck. We count it again—two hundred and twenty-two thousand dollars. I may have grown up with everything money can buy, but I've never seen this much hard cash before. It's like Monopoly money.

Marie keeps fingering it like she doesn't quite know what it is. "Jesus fuck, holy Jesus fucking Christ," she keeps whispering, over and over.

Vodka. There's vodka in Lark's freezer. I pour a tumblerful. "Don't drink too much," Marie barks. "I know you're upset, I'm upset too, but we need to keep a clear head. Let's pack our stuff."

We'd bought nice luggage, Samsonite, happy and giggling while we picked it out, as if we'd soon be on a honeymoon at some all-inclusive resort with nonstop lobster and mariachi.

"I'm fucking serious. Put the booze down. We're in this now, and we're gonna see it through. We have to."

It doesn't matter whether my eyes are open, or whether I close them—I see blood.

"Focus!" Marie orders. "Let's do this."

We don't have a lot of stuff. It's mostly the money. Oh, and new swimsuits—we bought those while on our luggage-buying excursion. We also have new baggy pants into which Marie sewed secret compartments for some of the money.

"I wanted to be a fashion designer," she had commented while sewing. "You know, punk chic. Who knew my skills would come in so handy one day."

I had laughed at the time, happy to see her happy and not worrying about her lunatic ex or looking sorrowful while she basted me with liniment. A woman's happiness can get you so gloriously stoned.

"I'm not going to Mexico," I say. "Fuck Mexico."

"But...but that's what we planned," Marie sputters. She seems more dumbstruck than when I shot someone.

"I don't care. I'm not going. Anywhere but there." I dump half a glass of vodka in the sink. My head is humming. I'm ready for a fight. Try me. I've got nothing to lose. What a weird fucking feeling.

"What the fuck are you talking about? All of this, we did it so we could get the hell outta Dodge and go to Mexico. Start over. Be safe. Be happy. Be whatever else it says in the brochure. You ain't backin' out now."

"You've got the money. What more do you want from me? You can go to Mexico, you can go anywhere you want. You'll be safe. But you saw what happened. You saw what fucking happened. And the fucking bullets were your fucking idea. I can't just go off into the sunset now like everything is fucking fine. I can't—"

"You're blaming me? It was an accident, you didn't mean—"

"You said that already. I'm not going to Mexico."

Silence so heavy suffocates the room, a hot sickening smother. Marie's face is twitching. So is mine. Our flesh doesn't know what it wants.

"We'd better pack," I say. "We've gotta get out of here."

"Where are we going? I still wanna go to Mexico. I wanna stick with the plan."

"Then stick with it."

"What are you gonna do?"

"No fucking idea. But I'm taking my share of the money and getting the hell out of this apartment. Out of this city. Out of this country. Off this fucking planet."

We divide up the money. It feels strangely, sickeningly domestic, like we're used to sitting side by side and organizing our spoils.

Then I drag out the suitcases and rip off my clothes. I never want to touch these filthy rags ever again. There's no blood on them. But still. I put as much cash as I can into my new pants with the secret compartments. Pack some other clothes. A toothbrush. Books by Henry Miller. Put the rest of my money in a carry-on bag. I feel alone in the world. Marie may be in the room, but I can't feel her. To me, she is gone. Everyone is gone.

If I live through the next few days, I may have to take matters in hand. But I can't think about that right now. All I can think about is getting to the airport.

"So that's it? You're abandoning me?" Marie's voice filters into my head, as if from far distance.

I zip up my carry-on. "You've got everything you need. You've got money. You've got a ticket to Mexico. Everything you need is sitting on that table right there."

Marie stares at me. "I don't wanna go to Mexico by myself. I wanna go with you. That's been the plan all along."

"Plans change. You saw what happened today. Right fucking in front of you, you saw what happened. She's dead. That poor woman is dead. Everything's changed."

I put on my coat. "Are you gonna pack or not? Your flight leaves tonight. You do whatever you gotta do, but I'm outta here."

Marie's eyes harden. She bites her lip. "Fine, fuck it, I can't stop you. So where are you going if you're not going to Mexico?"

"I'll decide when I get to the airport."

"Fine, great, whatever." She starts stomping around, throwing stuff in her suitcase.

In the cab on the way to the airport, we don't speak. What's there to say? I wonder where the fuck I should go. Besides off a cliff.

Henry Miller. I've been reading *Tropic of Cancer. The Colossus of Maroussi* is in my suitcase. Henry went to Paris. I'll go to Paris. Decision made.

"So this is it," Marie says, now that we're inside the airport. "This is goodbye."

I shrug. "It's goodbye for now."

"Where are you gonna go?"

"Wherever Henry Miller went."

"Huh?"

"We'll be in touch."

"How? How are we gonna be in touch?"

"Lark."

Marie nods, doesn't speak. Her fierce pixie face looks sad and fragile. I hug her. It feels like the last time. "Stay low. And I hope you get your sailboat."

The words seem hollow and ridiculous. All I can see is a woman's body on the floor. Her blood.

I turn and walk, don't look back. There's no looking back.

—

IN A HOTEL IN PARIS, I stay in bed for four days. It is September 1991. I wonder if I'll be alive for Christmas. Not that I like Christmas. If I want to off myself, it's either a belt or a razor. Neither option is appealing, so I guess I don't really want to kill myself. I can still hear my gun going off, see the woman hit the floor, but there is a blur around the edges of the picture. It's already starting to fade. I didn't do it. It wasn't me. I wasn't there.

The Colossus of Maroussi is beside me. I've underlined passage after passage. I flip through: *"At that moment I rejoiced that I was free of possessions, free of all ties, free of fear and envy and malice. I could have passed quietly from one dream to another, owning nothing, regretting nothing, wishing nothing. I was never more certain that life and death are one and that neither can be enjoyed or embraced if the other be absent."* I am free of ties and most possessions. But as long as I live, my life will be no concatenation of dreams. Of this I am certain.

"There are so many ways of walking about and the best, in my opinion, is the Greek way, because it is aimless, anarchic, thoroughly and discordantly human," Miller advises. Forget Paris. I'm going to Greece.

–

ANAIS HAS NO CLUE how much cash is inside a suitcase under her bed. I keep waiting for her to find it, keep thinking about what I'm going to say when she does. Or maybe she won't. Maybe we will live happily ever after. Whoever invented that phrase should be dragged into the street and killed.

I've been living in Anais's house for eight terrifyingly happy months. I'm in a Greek Henry Miller dream and I am petrified of waking. In my mind there is a tattoo on my arm, the outline of her long fingers, at the place she clings to when she sleeps.

We are at the farmer's market in Corfu Town, a town Henry Miller disliked but which has become frequent witness to my astounding happiness. Anais is buying flowers—she insists on a fresh bunch every week. I used to hate flowers. My mother kept bunches everywhere, and floral wreaths, like in a funeral parlour. It's one of the things I remember most clearly about her—obsessive flower arranging. I guess she would have approved of the nauseatingly fragrant floral bomb that exploded all over her coffin.

"I could pick some from a field, but these ones seem to want me," she says, handing over money in exchange for wild irises. For eight months I have watched her place flowers in the kitchen window, cook eggplant, and talk to goats. What would Henry Miller say right about now? *"Though it has been practised on me time and again I never cease to marvel how it happens that with certain individuals whom I know, within a few minutes after greeting them we are embarked on an endless voyage comparable in feeling and trajectory only to the deep middle dream which the practised dreamer slips into like a bone slips into its sockets."*

Happiness, apparently, can come to the undeserving. Anais has pulled me into a deep middle dream and I wait for its end as the brimstone prophesier waits for the end of the world.

The middle dream is not without its shadowy reapers. I get nightmares. More now than right after the robbery. Anais is a sound sleeper. I don't think she notices.

"So are you going to tell me what's waking you up at night?" Anais is looking at me over the tops of the irises, her eyes that deep dark-blue blueness, an extension of the petals.

"Sorry. I didn't think I was waking you."

"Oh please, how could anyone sleep through you thrashing around? You could wake the dead."

"You should have said something sooner. I can sleep on the couch."

She raises an eyebrow like "yeah, right."

"I don't want you to sleep on the couch." She touches my forehead. "Tell me what's swimming in your cranial fluid."

"Nightmares don't live in the cranial fluid. They don't backstroke."

"This way." Anais pulls my arm. "We're out of cinnamon." The spice market is her favourite place. I swear she gobbles cinnamon straight from the jar, just so she can come here more often. Anais doesn't just buy spices and split. She touches every damn thing in the store, and has long conversations with oregano, thyme, mint, dill, cloves, nutmeg, and the sage leaves she makes tea out of. She grows her own herbs too, but that doesn't replace her need to visit her spice lady, a warm, broad-faced Greek named Akantha.

"Hello, my loves!" This is Anais, talking to several jars of oregano. Akantha waves and smiles from the back of the shop.

"Tell me, sweet boy," Anais continues, cradling thyme against her heart, "what have you been dreaming about? It scares me. Last night you almost shoved me out of bed."

"I'm sorry, baby. Just kick me."

"It must have been awful, your dream."

"Uh, I don't really remember."

"Liar."

"Hello, lovebirds." Akantha's heavily accented tongue interrupts, her big, long arms suddenly squeezing us both at once. She learned to speak English in London, she said, where, as a young girl, she worked in a Greek restaurant. "Are you having a spicy morning?" Her laughter erupts in a volcano of head shaking.

"Very spicy," says Anais, pinching me. She winks at Akantha who winks back, and suddenly I realize I have, in absentia, been the subject of many spice-store conversations.

"Ah, I love to see love. Food for my widow heart." Akantha turns to me, eyes sharp. "You take care of her, you hear me? Don't be dog boy."

I put my hands up. "No dog boy, I'm not dog boy." Anais lets loose a peal of laughter.

"You know what they say," says Akantha, "you never know what skeletons are hiding under the bed."

Anais laughs. "In the closet, but yes, you're right, you never know what skeletons."

Nausea fountains up toward my throat.

"Now: I'm making papoutsakia this evening and I've run out of a bunch of stuff. I need oregano, cinnamon, nutmeg, and cloves." Anais and Akantha leave me standing with the Aleppo pepper.

The money has been under the bed for months, slowly being changed to drachmas. There's a shitload left, of course. I could bury some, I guess. When I wake from the dream, though, and have to bolt, I don't want to be digging up cash. When Anais is in the yard with the goats, I touch the crisp bills and see blood. Never thought touching money could feel so fucking awful.

On the street in front of the spice shop, Corfu is rolling out of bed and stretching to life, a collective cat languid in the glassy Greek morning light. Old men gather for coffee; women sweep their storefronts. Life is addicted to getting on with it.

Anais takes my arm. "I went a bit crazy with the spice-buying. Let's go get lemons so I can make avgolemono."

We turn and wave to Akantha, who is near the back of the store, sweeping. "Remember," she calls, "don't be dog boy!"

Anais laughs as we step into the sunlight. She squeezes my arm. "Yeah, don't be dog boy."

"Never," I say, my hand moving to the back of her neck. She says she hates her hairy Greek neck. In this moment, the downy hair under my fingers is the best thing ever.

–

"TWO TABLESPOONS SALT, no more, no less," Anais announces, sprinkling it over the chicken that bathes in her big soup pot. "You'll adore this. My mum made avgolemono every Friday night when I was little. My dad was crazy about it."

Anais sautés onions. Weird, the sight of her wielding a spatula makes me hard. Who knew?

"After they died, Fridays were Hungarian-mushroom-soup days. My grandmother was a maestro with paprika and dill."

"My mom didn't cook, or if she did, I don't remember. My dad definitely didn't. He hired a woman to feed us. A Jamaican lady who kept a flask of rum in her apron. She was nice. Her cheek-pinching used to piss me off."

"You've never mentioned her. You've lived here for eight months and I know almost nothing about you. And yet I don't want to throw you out. Strange. No matter what the cards say."

The fucking tarot cards again. Haven't heard about them in a while.

"The cards love me. And so do you."

"The cards don't love you. But here I am, making you Greek lemon soup anyway."

"Soup is love, baby."

"Seriously, what do we talk about? I keep waiting for you to stop being a mystery."

"You don't really want that. You talk, and I put my hands on you. That's the way we are."

"The way we are?" She slices lemons in half. "There must be another way." Long pause, a lemon-squeezing silence. Then: "Nice to have someone to cook for. Humans need two things: someone to feed them and someone to wonder where they are when they don't come home at night. That's what my grandmother used to say."

For a moment, there is such naked grief in her face it burns my eyes. She turns away, presides over her broth. "I'm thinking of writing a cookbook. Pottery is kind of dead to me right now. Don't feel like putting my hands on clay. I'd like to feed people, like my grandmother did. Like my mother did." Anais turns back to me, spreads her hands. "What do you think?"

"Sold. Brilliant idea."

"Really?"

"You're the best cook I've ever met."

"I'm the *only* cook you've ever met. Well, except for the cheek-pinching Jamaican lady."

"Everything you make is amazing. You've saved my life. The world needs your food."

"I've saved your life? Seriously?"

"Seriously."

An incandescence spreads across her face. "I like saving you. What am I saving you from?"

"A life of broken wandering."

"Greek lemon soup can fix most things. Except death."

"I know."

"I wanted to write a cookbook with my grandmother, her recipes. Magda's recipes. What do you think about Hungarian and Greek, together?"

"Perfection. Like you."

"I asked the tarot cards about it. I got the Empress card, the creative mother. It's time to give birth to this. Will you help me?"

"I'm your official recipe-tester. My qualifications as a professional eater are legion."

Anais laughs. Her laugh is as much a turn-on as her spatula-wielding. Can't stay out of bed much longer.

"No, I mean with writing the descriptions. And anecdotes. You know, family food stories. Maybe short histories of ingredients. I suck at writing."

"What makes you think I don't?"

"Well, you were in med school. You must be able to write better than I can."

"Doctors aren't writers. I wrote stuff about schizophrenia and manic depression, not lemon and dill."

"Doesn't matter. I asked the cards. Which told me, some months ago, to throw you out. Obviously I didn't listen. So I asked them again yesterday and they told me if you're going to stay here, you've gotta help me with this. So that's the new deal."

"There was an old deal?"

"Of course. Every relationship is a deal. I cook and you fuck me and I talk and you don't answer many questions and possibly feed me bullshit and I want you anyway. That's our deal. The cookbook is an amendment to our contract."

Those eyes, heavy-lidded, always wet, always shining. If I believed in love and bullshit like forever, then I would lo—Jesus fucking Christ.

"I would love to help. Sign me up. Where do we start?"

"Right where we are. With Greek lemon soup. And soon, stuffed eggplant. You can help me scoop out the flesh."

"Nobody's ever said *that* to me before."

"It's your lucky day. And tomorrow, we'll test out some Hungarian. Starting with paprikás csirke, Magda's favourite."

After our morning visit to the market, we'd spent the day

swimming and lying naked on a deserted beach. Her skin had turned a deeper, richer bronze, her eyes an even darker blue. Now, the afternoon sunlight through the kitchen window cuts across her face, bones in high relief, the face of antiquity. I would rather die than leave this place. Than leave her. Than leave her.

–

"THE FIRST THING is the fat. Lard is essential to life. Are you writing this down?"

"Lard? Who cooks with lard?"

"Hungarians. Magda wouldn't dream of making paprikás csirke with olive oil. We're doing things her way. Another essential: you must use Hungarian paprika. Thank God I brought some from home. I brought all Magda's spices with me. My suitcase hardly had room for clothes."

"You're too hot for clothes."

"I know. Now put the pen down and cut up the chicken."

One of our neighbour's chickens lies dead and naked on the counter.

"I've never cut up a chicken."

"Today you're going to learn how."

"You want me to be the cookbook writer and the butcher?"

"I want you to be the everything. Get over here."

I come up behind her and put my arms around her, my face in her neck. What is it with a woman's neck, the smell of it? It's the best goddamn thing ever. Anais doesn't wear perfume, none of that flowery shit I remember my mother dousing herself in. No, Anais is all herself, just skin that smells of nothing else I've ever known.

"Would you come to Toronto with me?"

My head jerks up. Fuck. Pit of my stomach might never cope with food again. "What? Why?"

"Well, I was thinking maybe I should go for a visit, see some friends, my brothers. I mean, I don't want to stay there for more than a week. But I thought it would be nice if you came with me. There are people dying to meet you."

"You've told people about us?"

"Well...yeah. Haven't you?"

"Uh..."

"I know you don't talk to your dad. But I've heard you on the phone, aren't you talking to your friends? Don't they know where you're living?"

"Uh...yeah, of course they do." She's staring at me, and for once I don't want to look in her eyes.

"So why do you think it's weird that I've told people about us? I didn't tell them you moved in five minutes after we met. But I told them I have someone."

"I guess I just thought, I don't know, I mean, I guess, well, what did you tell them about me?"

"That you went to med school to be a shrink but you're taking a break. That you're handsome. That I'm happy. That I love to cook for you. My brothers are happy, they feel better knowing someone is looking out for me over here."

"Oh. Well, yeah, I'm happy to be the one who looks out for you."

"Are you?"

"Yes. Happiest I've ever been."

"Really?"

"Happier than I ever thought possible." This seems even more true now I've said it.

"So you'll come to Toronto with me?"

"I... Well, I just... I left the U.S. because I wanted to get the hell away. And stay away for a long time."

Anais cocks her head and smirks. "Toronto's not in the U.S., it's in Canada. I mean, I know all Americans think Canada is nothing but an extension of themselves, if they think of it at all, which they generally don't."

"Hey, no Yankee-bashing."

"Seriously, it's another world up there north of the forty-ninth."

"I know, I just..."

"Why are you so weird about this?"

"I'm not weird. I just love it here. Don't wanna step out of paradise, even for a week. I want you all to myself." I kiss her. I'm not purely a manipulative asshole, what I'm saying is true.

Anais kisses me back. "That's selfish of you."

"I know. And I'm not even a tiny bit sorry."

"You're a bad boy."

"You have no idea."

"Should I be afraid?" She is smiling. I feel like crying. Wish I still could.

I kiss her again. "No. Nothing to be afraid of. Now: are you still forcing me to carve up this dead bird?"

"Damn straight. Let's cook."

She moves out of my embrace and picks up a knife. "Here, like this. Cut the breasts in half, cut the legs in half. Save the bony ends of the drumsticks for stock. And the breast bones, those find a home in the stock pot too."

"What's stock?"

"Are you serious?"

"Deadly."

"Oh my God, you *were* a deprived child. That's so sad. How can you not know what stock is?"

"Stock is something you buy and hope it goes up."

Anais rolls her eyes. "Soup broth. Haven't you ever had real chicken soup?"

"Does Campbell's count?"

"Yuck. You poor sweet kid. Here, do the cutting."

I don't think I've ever touched raw chicken before. Kind of gross, kind of cool.

"You look like you're enjoying that." Anais is dicing an onion at top speed. I keep waiting for her fingers to end up in a recipe.

"It's getting me in touch with my hunterly primal nature."

She rolls her eyes. "You didn't actually do the killing."

My stomach drops again, my knife hand goes weak. I need a case of amnesia something fierce.

"What's wrong? Careful, don't cut yourself."

"Nothing's wrong."

"Then why do you have a weird disturbing look on your face?"

"I don't. I'm concentrating. This is my chef look."

"Well, you'd scare the kitchen help with a face like that."

"A chef is supposed to be intense. I'm intense."

"Okay, Chef Intensity, you can intensely put the chicken pieces in the pot in a minute. I'm just gonna let these onions sauté a bit more."

It's burning hot in the kitchen. I'm cold all over. Cold like that woman. The woman in the bank is very cold right now.

"Earth to butcher man, put the chicken in. We don't want burnt onions. You look, like, a zillion miles away. What are you thinking about?"

"I'm, uh, summoning every culinary bone in my body."

"Yeah, right. You don't have any culinary bones. Okay, we're going to sear the chicken for a couple minutes to seal in the juices. Meat juices are essential to life."

I wash my hands and put one up her dress.

"Not yet, you can tend to my juices later. Right now, it's all paprika, all the time."

"Yes, Chef."

"Now we add the paprika, salt, pepper, caraway seeds. And then the tomatoes and peppers. We should be using Hungarian peppers, but we'll have to make do with these."

"Smells awesome."

"Magda's kitchen always smelled awesome. Paprika is the scent of my childhood."

"My childhood smelled like my mom's sickeningly sweet perfume.

Until she died and the cook quit and my dad hired Nellie, the Jamaican. Then it smelled like jerk chicken."

"Why did the first cook quit?"

"She probably thought after Mom croaked Dad would marry her. He liked to diddle the staff."

"That's disgusting."

"That's one word for it. There are others."

"You're not like him, are you?"

"A staff-diddler? I don't have any staff."

Anais punches my arm. "Seriously."

"Can't you see I'm not an asshole? I'm a nice cooker of paprikash and writer of cookbooks. And addicted to you." I kiss her mouth but she pulls away.

"I can see you're a mystery. That's what I can see." She heaves a sigh. "Oh, fuck it. We need to add water to the paprikash."

She pours and stirs, I kiss her neck. Oh, that scent.

"We need to bring this to a boil."

"Yes, ma'am." I reach under her dress.

She pushes my hand away. "Later. Right now, we boil and simmer. And turn on the oven."

"That's what I was trying to do."

Anais laughs. "You're incorrigible. What can I do to concentrate your mind?"

"I can think of a few things."

"Concentrate on cooking. I'm trying to teach you. Who ever heard of a cookbook author who can't cook?"

"What does 'simmer' mean?"

"Are you joking?"

"No. I have no idea what it means. I can't cook, remember?"

"Jesus. Okay. It means we let it gently bubble. Put the lid on."

"It's too hot to use the oven."

"You should be used to it by now, baby. And anyway, when you taste this, you won't be sorry."

I am here in this kitchen in this cottage in Greece with this woman in my arms, she of the hooded iris eyes, she who offers me food and sleeps soft against me. Lightning is going to strike. And I will have to say goodbye. I know it's coming.

"Now: pick up your pen. I'm going to make nokedli to go with the paprikash. Egg dumplings, Magda's answer to all that ails you. I want you to write down her recipe."

–

ANAIS LIGHTS CANDLES every night before dinner.

"I used to be afraid of fire," she said, the first time I saw her strike a match. "But look at me now—fearless!"

"Why were you afraid of fire?"

"Fiery crash. My parents."

"Oh."

"But it's not the only reason I was afraid. I was born that way. Maybe a past life."

"A past life? What are you talking about?"

"Maybe I had a horrible past-life experience with fire. Like I was burned at the stake or something."

"You believe in past lives?"

Anais flashed me a teasing smile. "Don't you, Doctor?"

"There are meds for delusion."

"Hindus believe in reincarnation."

"Do I look like a Hindu?"

"You don't think you could have known me in some other time, some other place? Don't I seem familiar?"

"Well, yeah, you seem familiar, but that's just attraction, sexual chemistry. It doesn't mean we were walking hand in hand across a meadow in the year 1250."

"So you moved into the home of a woman you just met because of pheromones."

Her shining eyes shone a bit more, in that edge-of-tears kind of way, and I felt like an asshole. I mean, I think I'm pretty much an asshole most of the time, but I didn't want her to agree with my assessment.

"No, baby, it's more than that. I just, I don't know how to explain it. There's something about you." I wasn't lying when I said those words.

Now she's lighting candles and I'm watching her like I'm watching a ritual, some temple thing. An image of me kissing the hem of her dress flashes through my head. It kind of weirds me out. Who knew such a creature could come out of such a tapioca-seeming place as Canada?

"Dinner should be a sacred ritual, that's what Magda taught me. Worship at the temple of food. The way to the spirit is through the flesh."

"I wish somebody had taught me that. Our cook didn't talk much, and my only living grandparent was in a nursing home and half out of her mind."

"I'm teaching you now."

"I'm remembering everything you say."

"Okay, let's eat."

The sun is down, the room dark save the candlelight. Every once in a while, a goat bleats, then silence. This paradise goes on and on. It's terrifying.

"We would eat this meal with sour cream if we were being strictly Hungarian. But since we're in Greece, I'm feeding you Greek yogurt I soured with vinegar and lemon juice."

"I'm going to get fat if I stick with you. I've never eaten so much in my life."

"What do you mean, *if*? Going somewhere?"

"Only where you go."

"I needed to fatten you, you were too skinny. Nobody likes a gaunt-faced man. Besides, a cookbook author should be a bit chubby. Otherwise, it looks like they're not enjoying their product."

"Good point."

The first bite of paprikash is the best thing ever.

"See, it's just like being cuddled by my grandmother. Magda used to say, 'If you meet a good man, feed him paprikash and he'll be your slave forever.' I want to put that in the book."

A wave of sadness hits me so hard I almost choke. I reach across the table and take her hand.

"Whatever happens...thank you. For this. For...all of this."

There's a weird feeling in my eyes.

"Baby? Are you okay? You look like you're gonna—"

I blink back the feeling. "I'm fine. Way better than fine. This is the best dinner of my life."

Anais searches my face, squeezes my hand hard. "Then it's the best dinner of my life too."

She keeps searching, that blinkless searching look I've never seen on anyone else. I'm a shit. Wish I could be better. It's too late. It was too late when I laid eyes. If the whole past-life thing is true, which it isn't, I hope I was once a better man for her.

I have to look away. A plateful of egg dumplings bails me out. "Mmm... these are awesome." I fork so many in my mouth I almost choke.

"Food can be healing in every way." Her voice is low and soft. "Magda's food was, my mother's was, mine is."

Silence, save for the sound of my chewing. And the sound of her mind. And the sound of my heart.

"You think I need healing?"

"I'm not stupid. I know when I'm nursing a wounded soldier."

"If that's what you're doing, you're good at it. The best."

"Thing is, I need someone who's gonna nurse me back. Otherwise, I'm just the idiot who makes paprikash for the unworthy."

"I can be that person."

"I want you to be that person. So I need you to tell me who you are."

"I've told you things."

"Yeah, but there's something you're not telling me and I want to know what it is." Her face softens into a smile. "I mean, we can't write a cookbook together and have secrets. Magda wouldn't approve. It would be culinarily sacrilegious."

An egg dumpling catches in my throat and I choke. Anais jumps up and comes around behind me, whacks me on the back. The coughing fit subsides. She kisses my temple. "You okay, baby?"

If we could just freeze here, this moment, stop time, just like this, could we please stay like this forever?

"Yeah, fine, it's just, you're too good a cook, I can't eat this stuff fast enough, it's amazing." My words sound lame and hollow, the smoking gun of ineptitude.

I kiss her hand, take her fingers in my mouth. They taste of spices. If love had a taste. Just like this, forever like this.

"Baby, eat the food now, me later."

I look up at her, keep her fingers in my mouth. She giggles. Damn, that sound. Forever that sound.

Anais kisses my forehead, pulls her fingers away. "Don't let it get cold. Would break my heart if you don't finish every single scrap." She resumes her place across the table. "And don't forget about the halva and bougatsa. We should really be having dobostorte for dessert. Hungarian seven-layer cake. Magda's was sublime. Mine is a pretty close second. Guess we're being fusion this evening."

"Greek wine and paprikash. That's our cookbook in a nutshell, right?"

"Precisely. Magda on Corfu. Hey, there's our title. What do you think?"

"Perfect. Just like you."

Anais smiles, iris eyes aglow, fine webs of happy crinkles.

"Wish that were true."

"It is. I don't know a damn thing, except that. Except that. It's the only thing I know."

A breeze, cooler than usual, finds us through the open kitchen window, tugging on the candle flames, dragging them in its wake. I shiver, even though I'm not cold.

"So come to Toronto with me. Will you? I want you to meet people I love. And they want to meet you."

"Okay." I know as I say it I'm not going to go.

"Really? It'll be fun, I promise."

"When do you wanna go?"

"Soon. Before the worst of the summer. I'd take Greek heat over Toronto humidity any day."

"Sounds good." The paprikash is churning. It may come back up.

"More wine, baby?"

"Yeah. Yes. Please."

Anais pours, stopping just short of overflowing. "I'm so happy right now."

"Me too."

"Do you ever get homesick? Long for Yankee soil?"

"No. I feel at home here."

"You have no plans to leave?"

"No. Why would you ask me that?"

"Well...you're not actually supposed to be here. Tourists can't stay forever."

"I took care of it."

"What do you mean, you took care of it?"

I knock back some wine. "I want to stay here with you. For as long as you'll have me. So I had no choice. I bribed a guy at the Aliens office for a two-year visa."

"You what?"

"Well, what was I supposed to do? I don't want to leave you."

"How much did you pay?"

"Doesn't matter. I told you: I come from money, I have money, I solve problems with money. So: problem solved."

"If you get caught—"

"I won't. And you're worth it."

"What about your career? Being a shrink and all."

"I don't want to be a shrink. I want to be a cookbook author."

"You have enough money to just stay here?"

"Yup. And if I hadn't bribed the guy, how could I go to Canada with you? The Greeks wouldn't let me back in."

"True." She pauses, her eyes huge and shiny in the candlelight. "Thank you. I'm happy."

"Good. That's all I want."

Two tears race down her face. She doesn't wipe them, just watches me. After a moment: "This calls for bougatsa."

"No. It calls for this." I get up, pull her to her feet, find her tongue with mine. Want to swallow it. Whole. Want to swallow her. Whole.

"Not on the floor, the tile is cold." Her voice in my ear, teeth in my neck.

A moment of blur carries us from the kitchen, carries us to profane the Greek crosses on her bed.

We are both slick, salted by the hot night. Taste of paprika. Paprika and wine. Paprika and wine and sweat and the very skin skinness of woman. This woman. The only woman. And. There it is. That deep taste. Deep woman taste. Anais taste. A scent. To crawl inside. To possess. To die in. To drink. Sharp sweet salty raindrop earth honey. Legs wrap. A cry. Hot. Dark. Grab. Take. Mine. She. Up. Up. Up. Star. Leap. Fall. Save. Ours. Light. Burst. Burst. Burst. Light. Float. Gone.

She is mine.

We don't speak for a long time. I keep her folded to me, head against my chest, her hair the only scent in the whole wide world.

Smokiness drifts in from the kitchen—the candles have gone out. Dull blue buds snuffed. All is quiet.

I can feel her heart fluttering, a caught bird. My bird. Mine.

Paprika. Wine. Eggplant. Cinnamon. Lemon. Olive. Moussaka. Love. I love her. Anais. Love, this woman. My heart, a caught bird.

Have I ever really held a woman? If I have, I don't remember. Gone. All gone. But this.

The bird, the bird I'm holding, she stirs. "Mmm...baby? You're not allowed to move. Just stay like this. Don't move."

"I'm not going anywhere."

"Ever?"

"Ever." Love and lies fit neatly together, sweetly together. Lies are soothing, reassuring, a post-coital digestif. Lies can be true. I mean what I say. I'm just lousy at keeping promises. And she means what she says. Because she doesn't know what I've done.

So we lie wrapped in our heat and the hotness of the Greek night. Damn, all this terrifying happiness.

Remember this, I always think when I lie with her. This scent. That one. Her hair. Her neck.

"Wait here." Anais rolls away from me.

"I thought you didn't want me to move."

"You're not moving, I am." She passes by the open window, stops, looks at the sky, smiles, moves to the kitchen, a full, brown, wet, luminous Grecian silhouette. I want her. Again. And again. For a moment, less than a moment, I'm afraid she isn't coming back. I don't know why.

When she returns, she has something in her hand. "I've started keeping them in the kitchen, for luck."

"What?"

"My tarot cards."

Anais stops at the window. "Look at this moon. It loves us, you can tell. It's got big eyes."

I'm nervous now, don't know why. Got a bad feeling. I get out of bed, put my arms around her, stare at a moon I don't love that doesn't love me either. It's big, huge, bigger than I've ever seen it. Still looks like a blind rock somebody plugged in.

"It looks pregnant, doesn't it? It's fat tonight." Her voice is soft, softer than I've ever heard it. A shiver passes over. The room is an oven.

Anais takes my hand and presses it against her belly, low down, that place on a woman which rounds out so sweetly, the place never conquered by crunches, thank whatever gods may or may not be. "I'm getting fat like the moon. Too much moussaka. Or maybe..."

There is a rushing in my ears. I need water. The room is too hot. I'm too cold. "You're not fat, you're perfect. I love a moussaka body."

Long moments pass. Anais doesn't speak. My hands are slick

with sweat. “You okay, baby?” My voice sounds strange and faraway. A Casper-the-Ghost cloud flies across the moon. My voice sounds like it's coming from him.

“Yeah, fine. It’s just... Can you keep your hand here a little longer?”

“Okay.”

“Just ten more seconds.”

I count down in my head. I’m many seconds past ten and she still hasn’t moved. We are frozen in the melting heat.

“Thank you.” I wonder where the gravel in her voice has gone. It’s almost a whisper, a tremulous filament of sound. “I feel safe when you put your hand here.”

She wants to say more, say whatever is pressing down on us like a granite slab. But she doesn’t.

“I’m going to read for you now. You can’t say no.” She takes my hand and pulls me to the bed, turns a lamp on. In the sudden light I see her face is wet. Not with sweat. Her eyes are pinkish.

“Take a deep breath and concentrate.”

“On what?”

“On a ball of white light. A ball of light full of truth.”

I have no clue what she’s talking about. One look at her damp face and I keep my mouth shut.

“Now shuffle the cards till you feel like you should stop.”

The last time I shuffled cards I was playing poker with Lark and Marie and snorting coke between hands. These cards feel hot and wired, like they want to jump from my grasp. Anais has a strange look on her face. She stares at the cards as if she’s in some kind of trance. Don’t want to stop shuffling, scared but don’t know what I’m scared of.

“Okay. The cards are ready.” She takes the deck and lays it out in a pattern on the bed. Her eyes are far away, looking at things I cannot see.

“The Death card is right on top of you. Don’t be scared. Doesn’t mean you’re going to die, or anyone’s going to die. Means transformation.

Something big."

I feel sick. A wave of nausea hits so I tip my face toward the ceiling and suck air as subtly as I can.

"Something bad happened. And I'm not talking a long time ago, I'm talking, like, within the last year. Whatever it is, it's still hanging over. Like a ghost, something's haunting you. It'll make you sick if you let it. But in the future, you've got the Nine of Cups, it means a wish will come true. Something you love will come to you. Could be in a surprising way, it feels like. But first, Death. And you're not sleeping. Why aren't you sleeping?"

"Uh, I've always had insomnia. Ever since...uh...ever since my mother died."

Anais is giving me a look. I can't read her face. "It's not that. Something more recent is keeping you awake. The Three of Swords, the Eight of Swords, the Nine of Swords—that's a lot of pain. A hell of a lot."

"I'll be right back. Bathroom."

I bolt, grabbing my shorts on the way out. I don't want to be naked.

Fuck, I hope she can't hear me throwing up the paprikash. It's all coming up now, all of it.

Breathe. Breathe, breathe, breathe. Slow down. Easy now. Don't hyperventilate, for fuck's sake. But hyperventilating kind of feels good, like it's what I've been wanting to do for a long time. Fuck. Fuck, fuck, fuck. Head between my knees, touching the floor. Anais will show up here if I don't go back now. Just wanna stay in this dark pocket. Even in this darkness, there's blood on the floor. All I can see is her blood on the floor. That woman's, whoever she was.

Get up. Now. Locate your fucking balls and pull yourself together. Wash face. Brush teeth. Soldier on. What's done is done. No use puking over what you can't change.

When I enter the bedroom Anais is dressed. A nightgown covered in big red flowers, a nightie I love. She is staring at me, her iris eyes baffled, poppingly blue, her mouth half open. At her feet is my suitcase, wide open. My suitcase full of money.

I freeze. She looks from me to the money, the money to me. "What is this?"

"Money."

"I can see that. Why are you hiding it under the bed? Christ, how much?"

"A lot."

"My grandmother always said, if you have questions and no answers, try looking under the bed, you never know what might be hiding."

"I'm not hiding it. Why did you go looking in my suitcase?"

She touches her belly, low down. "Because I want to know more about you. And I'm sick of waiting for you to tell me. I never snooped before because I figured there was nothing to find. Or maybe I was afraid. Afraid there really was something. Has this been here the whole time?"

"Yes."

"Whose money is it?"

"I told you, my dad gave me a bunch."

"In cash? To put in a suitcase and travel with?"

"I'm not going back."

"Why the hell not?"

"Because... It's a long story and it doesn't matter. I want to stay with you."

"I've got all night. Start talking."

"Babe, it doesn't matter."

"Start talking or get out of my house."

There is something in her face that scares the shit out of me. Guts wrap around my tonsils. No words.

Time goes by. When next she speaks, I am older.

"I want to know where you got this money and why it's in a suitcase under my bed. How much is here?"

A voice comes out of me, high, thin, some other guy's. "Six figures."

"Holy fuck." Her face is starting to crack. "So what's your story? I want all of it."

"Okay, okay. I didn't mean... I didn't want to upset you. I mean, there's nothing to be upset about. Nothing. I swear. I know this looks weird. But everything's okay, I promise. I promise you."

Her eyes are retreating. She takes a step back. "You can't promise me anything when you haven't told me anything. Did you steal this money?"

"No! No, no, baby, seriously, of course I didn't steal it. It's mine, all of it, mine, it's my money. I wanted to get it out of the country. Because I don't wanna go back, I need a new life. So I took everything and hit the road. And then I found you."

"What about your friends? What are you running from?"

"I'm not running, I just—"

"You can't look me in the eye."

"Yes, I can."

"You're not looking at me. You're not looking me in the eye while you're telling me you can look me in the eye. What the fuck is going on?"

"It's a long story."

"Start telling it. Nobody puts that much cash in a suitcase and flies across the world unless they've done something they shouldn't've done."

"Maybe that's true."

"Of course it's true! Oh my God, what did you do?"

She's crying now and I want to put my arms around her. I take a step and she steps back, jumps back, puts a hand against the wall. Her other hand covers her belly. Shielding it. From me. Paradise is over, and the slow knife of its finale is cutting me wide open. Soon I'll be skinless, and I'll deserve it.

I'm a good liar. No, a great one. I've always been a natural. Not to these eyes, though. Not to this face.

The suitcase has bled money onto the floor. Bled money. Blood money. Can't look at it, can't look at her. The moon is the only eye that is indifferent.

Wish I could collapse on the bed and cry tears of contrition. I can't.

Maybe never will. I am made of stone.

"You have ten seconds to explain yourself. Or leave this house and never come back."

Some guy's voice comes out of me, the hollow, distant voice of a colossal, hateable, unredeemable fuckup. "I was helping a friend. A friend who was in trouble. Serious trouble."

"How the fuck does that explain why you have a suitcase full of cash?"

"My friend needed money. To save her life. It was, it was a life-or-death thing. I had to help her."

"Help her with what? Money for what? Save her from what? If your friend was the one who needed money, why the fuck do you have all this? What did you do, rob a bank?"

I look to the floor for answers. And vomit. Paprikash, wine, nokedli, bougatsa, seemingly everything I've ever eaten in my entire life is puddled between us. It can't get worse. This night can't get worse. This is it. My insides have been ripped out, and they are ugly.

Without raising my gaze, I can see her face. Something has died in her eyes and I killed it. I am the worst person who has ever been.

"Oh my God, oh my God, oh my God." Softly, to herself.

"Baby." Look at her. You have to look at her. Look up, for fuck's sake, you fucking—her eyes. Baffled blue, colour of sorrow. "Baby, I can—"

"Fuck you. Don't call me that. Get out. Get out of here!"

Anais climbs across the bed, avoiding my Technicolor lake of shame and making for the door. I catch her, grab her by the arms. "Wait, let me talk, that's all I ask, I just want—"

"You want what? To explain? What legitimate explanation could there possibly be? Who are you? Medical school? A doctor? Oh my God, oh my God, who are you, who are you, who are you? What have I done? What have you done? What have we done? Let go, let go, let me go!"

She breaks free and bolts to the kitchen. Don't let go. Grab her. Hold her. Touch her. Tell her. Do. Something.

"Wait! Listen! Just listen to me. Please." Her arms in my hands are trembling. I press her against the counter. "I can explain. I want to explain. Everything can be okay. I am who you want me to be. I promise I'm him."

She doesn't speak, just trembles in my hands.

"I had to help a friend. A friend named Marie. So that's what I did. I saved her. And I ended up with a bunch of money. But nobody got hurt. I swear nobody got hurt. And now I can take care of you. That's all I wanna do. For as long as you'll let me. I would never hurt you. Please, please believe me. I need you to believe me."

"You robbed a bank to help a friend? Is that what you're telling me? And I'm supposed to be okay with that? Oh my God, I knew this was gonna happen, that's why I never looked under the bed, I didn't want to know, I didn't want to know, I didn't want—"

"Baby, listen to me. It's not bad like you think. Everything can be okay—"

"So you're wanted in the U.S.? That's why you're here? That's why you have no past? You're hiding. That's why you don't wanna go back. Holy fuck—"

"I'm not hiding! I'm starting over! With you!"

"Did you kill someone?"

The room dies, all sound buried deep in the ground.

The room is black, save for a pair of shining eyes.

My arms go limp. She turns to bolt. I watch myself grab her, make her stay, keep her, tell her, hold her, she's fighting, she's fighting me, she's fighting, can't keep her, watch her fall. See her. On the floor. She's lying on the floor. The kitchen floor. There is an onion skin near her face.

She isn't moving.

Her head. She's hit her head. Is that what happened? I'm not sure. Open your eyes. Open your eyes, goddammit. Open. Your. Eyes.

Anais doesn't move, her eyes lightly closed, as if she's sleeping.

On my knees on the floor, cradling her head. Shake her awake. She sleeps. Fingers on her neck. Nothing. All quiet. All still. All quiet. All still. All quiet—till I hear me. Screaming. It goes on. On. On. On.

Anais doesn't move. She's sleeping.

It was an accident. It was an accident. It was an accident. I didn't. I didn't. I—

Didn't hurt her. Would never hurt her.

Never hurt. Anyone. Never. Meant. Couldn't mean. Not in me. Never in me.

Breathe in her mouth. Fingers on her neck. Breathe. Breathe. Breathe.

Nothing.

Nothing.

Nothing.

Onion skin on the floor. And all is still.

ACT III
SCENE 1

Lights up on the DOCTOR'S *apartment. The* DOCTOR *is crying.*

PLAYWRIGHT

It was an accident. She doesn't blame you.

(Beat)

She says go to Greece. The cottage is alive and well. Her family sold it after... The owners take good care of it. The spice shop is still there. Akantha died ten years ago. Heart attack. Her niece runs it now. It's all in her emails. Her emails that she wants me to give to you. They could fill a book. She has a lot to say.

(Beat)

Anais wants you to read her words. Words of love they are, if I know anything about love. And I think I do. I'm a playwright, after all. What else do I write about but love?

DOCTOR

Where is she?

PLAYWRIGHT

She's in happiness.

DOCTOR

No, I mean, where is she?

PLAYWRIGHT

Where you left her. Her bones. Under the olive tree. Above the beach.

DOCTOR

I wanted her to have a view of the sea.

PLAYWRIGHT

Bones don't have eyes. Doesn't matter where you leave them. Anais can view the sea anytime she wants. One of the many joys of being dead.

DOCTOR

But how can she forgive... How can... Was there...a baby...?

PLAYWRIGHT

Another joy of eternity—forgiveness. Bones don't have eyes, but dead people do. They see who you are, not just what you've done.

(Beat)

Don't worry. I'll never tell. About the other thing either.

DOCTOR

What other thing?

PLAYWRIGHT

You're not really a doctor.

(Beat)

Too bad. I could've used one.

Blackout

PLAYWRIGHT

I'M IN HENRY'S APARTMENT. I had to twist his arm to get here. By "twist his arm," I mean I lied. I told him I might need a violinist for my next play. How about an impromptu audition? He seemed flattered. And kind of skeptical. Probably because I went up in scarlet.

This can't be happening. It is. I'm trying like hell not to tremble.

I shouldn't be here. I should've walked away. I want what can never be. I want life to be what it was.

He must remember me. He must.

Henry plays as if for all the world. When the sonata dies out, he offers a courtly bow.

"That was beautiful. I love it when you play Ravel."

Henry gives me a quizzical look. "Thanks. Hey, is everything cool?"

"No. I mean, yeah."

"You're shaking."

He looks freaked. I need to get the hell out of here.

"I'm just... The violin. It really touches me."

"You know, funny thing is, dying actually made me a better violin player."

"What do you mean?"

"I mean just what I said. Getting bashed in the head and dying somehow took me to the next level. I woke up the best musician I've ever been."

"How long were you gone?"

"I was dead for a few minutes. But I was out for a few weeks. Pharma coma."

"Do you remember anything about being dead?"

"No."

"Nothing?" My heart drops way down low.

"Well, maybe. I don't know. I mean, I feel like I went somewhere beautiful, you know? But I can't say for sure."

"Did you meet anyone?"

"You mean like an angel?"

"Just...anyone."

Henry tilts his head and frowns. "Yeah, I've got the feeling I met people. I don't remember. But they must've been people I loved."

"Why?"

"Because whenever I think about being dead, I feel really happy. It's weird."

I look at Henry and will him to remember me.

"Do you like cassoulet?"

"Cassoulet?"

"Yeah. I know, random question."

"Strange you ask. Before, I'd never heard of it. But ever since I died and came back, I can't get enough. My girlfriend made it for me a couple nights ago."

–

IT WAS A JANUARY EVENING, still early, already dark. It was the night my Henry played Ravel for me before he walked out the door and didn't come back. The air stung. January in New York is not known for mercy. Winter's breath shuttered the windows of every parked car on the block. When the sun was setting I stood at the window looking down at the street, watching the light turn hunks of metal into filigreed things of beauty. Henry was behind me, playing his violin. It was one of those moments when you wish you were dead or wonder if you already are, because you know all moments ever after will pale.

Henry and I and Maxine and maybe a few others had been living together for eight bizarrely happy months. Henry and Maxine got on great. "She's a handful, that broad," he would say. "I like the way she dresses."

"What about the way I dress?"

"Well, I like the way you dress too. But she wears all those great '20s togs."

"Do you know who pays for those togs? With blood from her pen? Maxine is gonna bankrupt me any moment now. And remember, you're not allowed to have sex with her."

"She wouldn't touch me with a fishing rod. I'm not her type." And then, hastily, off my look: "Not that I would want to. I mean, I don't want to touch a soul on this planet but you."

"Nice save."

"Just the truth, my love."

Henry likes to dance. Maxine says his steps need work. She taught him to do the Charleston, which he does in the living room with great animation to music from the antique Victor Victrola phonograph. That thing cost a few bucks. I rue the day Maxine figured out how to do online shopping.

So this must be what a happy family feels like, only better, because it is the most unlikely of families.

I turn from the window and watch Henry until the last notes return to silence. God, this man should be in Carnegie Hall. He will be. I've asked my dearly beloved, long-suffering agent and platonic husband Sam to see if he can pull some strings. He got a strange look on his face when I asked, but he nodded in that sweetly agreeable way he has.

"Let's see what Cosette brought us to eat," I say to my beloved. "I asked for cassoulet, the world's most perfect January feast."

Henry has never eaten so well in his life, he says, since he moved in with me, a declaration I find hard to believe given his obvious and adorable love of food. I've never eaten so well since he moved in with me, this much I know for sure. Love makes one hungry. I've lost a smidgeon of gauntness, which delights me no end. Henry, for his part, has never seemed to mind my insistent bones.

"Sure, baby. Sex and Ravel make me ravenous."

Cosette, bless her *Les Mis* heart, has indeed fitted us out like the luckiest French peasants in the countryside. I set the table, feeling as blissed-out domestic as I've ever felt in my life.

"I've gotta go to Brooklyn tonight and fix some guy's computer."

"Tonight? Can't he wait till tomorrow?"

"No, it's a new client and he's freaking out. He's in the middle of a project."

I like the way he says "project" with a long "o." It's so damn cute.

"Babe, I told you not to worry about taking new clients. I'd rather have you here, eating cassoulet."

"I know, you're sweet. But I'm good at fixing computers. And anyway, this is a referral from a regular."

"Okay, fine. But you'll freeze your fingers off out there. Take your designer mittens."

"Designer" in that they were knitted by me—I've taken up knitting, can life get any weirder? Keeping someone warm and fed is the best thing since the Greek chorus.

I turn on the oven and stick the cassoulet in, feeling all Food Network-empowered, like America's worst cooks who manage, by the end of the series, to go from poaching salmon in a dishwasher to knocking the socks off Beef Wellington. For me, however, pretending to cook is still the best I can do. Maxine has been hanging around like crazy and she hates cooking too.

"Baby," Henry says, coming up behind me and enfolding me in his hot bony embrace, "someone's coming to town, someone who wants to meet you."

"Really?" I turn and press my face into my special nose-notch in his chest. "An adoring fan, I hope."

"Well, she will soon be an adoring fan—my mother."

"Your mother? She knows about me?"

"Of course she knows about you. We've been living together for months."

Panic, not joy, geysers up, taking several internal organs with it.

"Have you told her I'm strange? Have you told her about Maxine? About the others? Have you told her—?"

"Whoa, whoa, easy, don't freak out, no freak-out required. All I've told her is, I'm the crazy one. Crazy about you. And that you're a playwright. And that you've got the best damn red hair in New York City. Maybe the whole world."

My internal organs fall off the ceiling, drop back into place. He's the crazy one? Wow. Bless every single speck of freckle that shadows the light of his skin.

If I've ever met a love's mother, I have no recollection of it. It occurs to me in this moment that I have written scenes of everything that ever happens in life, and lived little of it. Shock of all shocks, this may be about to change. Commence terror and joy.

"So I thought we could all have brunch together, and maybe she could come here for one of Cosette's gourmet reheated dinners." Henry kisses the back of my hand.

"I'll ask Cosette to make another cassoulet. If you promise to tell your mother I made it."

"As far as she knows, I live with a Food Network princess."

"Well, the princess part is true."

"She'll be really happy to meet you. You know, mothers like their babies to find someone."

"Just one condition: don't tell her about Maxine and the other visitations. Okay? Why freak her out."

"I've told her all she needs to know. That you're amazing. Actually, my mum doesn't get weirded out. She was a theatre major."

"Still, nobody knows, except you and Sam. Sam stands on his head to make sure nobody gets a clue about my creative process, as he so gallantly puts it."

Henry draws his fingers across his mouth: zipped.

Then he draws them back the other way: unzipped.

"Cross my heart and hope to die. Now, my playwright, I gotta go before I get zozzled, as Maxine would say, and get fired. Don't wait up, baby, might be late."

He kisses me. And then he's gone.

I drink for the both of us and pass out on my sofa. At 5 AM I wake to an empty apartment.

Henry doesn't answer his phone.

I call the police.

Then, in hysterics, I call Sam.

–

I DON'T REMEMBER the next three days.

The eye-gouging whiteness of a hospital room is what I recall next. And Sam, sitting on my bed in a painfully vivid Hawaiian shirt.

His face is devoid of colour. Whenever I have a meltdown, he channels Casper the Ghost. Damn, what I've put him through over the years.

"Have they found him?"

"Henry?" Sam's eyes are pinkish damp.

"Obviously! Who the fuck else would I be talking about? He's missing!"

"Well, not exactly. I mean—"

"What do you mean 'not exactly'? Do the police know anything? Oh my God, what a nightmare."

"The police..." Sam's face is cracking. "They don't know anything. But I don't want you to worry because—"

"You don't want me to worry? Are you fucking nuts? The man I love is missing and you don't want me to worry? Fuck worry, I'm frantic! Sam, what could have happened—?"

Sam starts to cry. Not slowly and quietly, with controlled rivulets of grief. He is a burst dam, clutching my hand and flooding all over it.

I grab his shirtfront. "Sam, is Henry dead? Oh God, is he dead?"

He shakes his head. The flood continues, wordless. I'm going to vomit.

When he speaks, I am many years older. "You sent me a play four days ago, pet. A love story about a violinist named Henry. He has red hair. Henry is very much alive. In your play, he's beautifully alive. He leaps from the pages. That's the only Henry there is."

I have absolutely no idea what he's talking about.

"I tried to tell you before, but... I didn't know what to do. You seemed so happy, I didn't want to take that away from you. And your play, it's—it's magic. Pure magic."

"You mean— Henry is like— He's just another— Henry is a fucking muse? That's what you're saying? He was never in me? He was always *in me*?"

Sam starts to speak, falters. He's holding my hands. I've seen this look before.

"You know I love you, pet."

I nod. In this moment, it's the only thing I know is true.

"And we're going to make everything okay, we always do."

I jerk my hands away. "Nothing is okay. Nothing will ever be okay."

"Baby—"

"Don't call me that. Henry calls me that."

"I'm sorry, pet."

"Henry dies in my play, right?"

"He's murdered in the final act."

Sam starts to cry again, but quietly, in controlled rivulets.

Before, when characters would barge in and perform a takeover, I'd resign myself to being quirky with a twist of eccentric, a sometimes-medicated woman who relies on a domestic helper with a flair for cassoulet. Not so different, then, from other women in New York.

Now: a hollowed-out pumpkin, that's what I am, a freak of orange against the hospital white. Everything scraped raw, nothing left.

"Your play'll win the Pulitzer, I know it. It's genius."

"I don't give a shit."

Sam wipes his face. I can't cry. No words, no tears.

"I'll come and stay with you for a while, take care of you. I don't want you to be alone."

"I've always been alone. Clearly."

Silence like a shroud.

Art is not enough. Being an artist is not enough. It does not answer questions, only asks more of them, forever and ever.

"I love him. He lives with me. The two of us, in my apartment. For eight months. I could touch him. I *did* touch him. Every single day. And he touched me. For fuck's sake, he wanted me to meet his mother."

Sam takes my hand and I let him. "I know. I never doubt you, pet. And I'm sorry. There are no words for how sorry."

"Did I say anything to them about Henry?"

"To who?"

"The nurses. My doctor."

"No. Maxine had taken charge by the time you got here. She was barking at everyone to keep their filthy paws off her."

"Good old Maxine. She can be counted on in a pinch, when the mood strikes her. Must be trying to protect me, she hates hospitals."

"You did rant to the police about Henry being missing and possibly murdered and God knows what may have happened to him in some dark corner of Brooklyn."

"Shit. Is this gonna be in the papers?"

"I'll keep it out. Don't worry, the public doesn't care about the antics of a playwright, they've got the Kardashians."

"Thanks." The white walls scrape my eyes. "Everyone dies on me. Everyone. Please don't die."

"I'll do my best. And don't you die on me either. The world needs you."

"To do what? Entertain it?"

"Enlighten it. With your words."

Short, high, bitter laugh. "What about what I need? I'm tired. And I'm not going to find love. Not in this world. We both know it."

"You have me."

"It's not the same."

"I know. I know it's not."

"Will you just hold me and not talk for a long time?"

Sam says not another word, wraps me up in his big platonic arms, and I keep my face pressed to his chest till I don't know when, the buttons of his shirt imprinting deep in my cheek.

–

HENRY WAS MY FIRST REAL LOVE. This is the truth, no matter which side of the curtain he lives on.

I think he loved me. I felt like he did, which is what matters. It's a better love story than most people get on this side of the veil.

Sam told Maxine that Henry was gone. She sent me an email of condolence.

from: maxinedoyle@playmail.com
to: rememberyourlines@playmail.com
date: January 22, 2015
subject: deepest condolences

My dear Playwright,

Sam relayed the tragic news. Words cannot begin to convey how dreadful sorry I am. Henry was a lovely man, of a sort oh-so-rare in this strange world, and of the very few things I am sure of, I am sure of this: he loved you.

I was worried at first, as I want you to be so very contented and few happenings can muck up the contentedness of a sweet sheila like a man hot on the scene, but after confabbing with dear Henry a time or ten, I was nothing less than assured of his love for you. I have not found a great love in my life, but I am not so bitter as to be anything but joyful for those who do. I was joyful for you.

Please don't let this put you in pieces, my darling Playwright. I am not asking for me. I am asking for Henry. He would want you to go on being who you are.

With heartfelt sympathy and love,

Maxine

I was numb for months. I stopped writing. I cop to a suicidal thought or two or ten million, but I couldn't settle on the best way and it seemed like too much work. It would have involved getting off the couch.

Sam stayed with me for two months and fed me a lot of grilled cheese. Then I told him to go home. I love him, but he's not the man I want to live with. The man I want to live with is gone.

My play, the story of Henry, will open on Broadway with a cast so brilliant it hurts my eyes. Sam told me to buy a dress for when I accept the Pulitzer. Maxine says she's picking it out. And likely dropping a fortune on it, though she neglected to mention that part.

I want to ask Henry—the flesh-and-blood Henry—to opening night. It's a stupid idea. Why kindle disaster? "Because the show's not over, that's why. Don't ever drop the curtain on your story, kid." That was Maxine, advising me to get my act together and buckle up my dancing shoes. "You're still on the stage, for heaven's sake. Tread the boards. Be the star."

Easy for her to say. "You want to end up like Doc?" Um, no. But maybe it's inevitable.

Besides, I think I already scared here-and-now Henry into the hills.

"My girlfriend's an amazing cook. She nailed cassoulet on her first try." That's Henry, smiling, sticking a knife in my chest.

"Your...girlfriend?"

"Yeah. She's a cellist. Do you like to cook?"

"Uh, not really."

"I guess you spend most of your time writing."

"Something like that."

I'm gonna be sick. Run. Get out of here. Run. Run. Run.

But before I can bolt, two enormous tears make an entrance on my face.

"What's wrong?"

I'm going to vomit, that's what's wrong. That, and everything else.

"Nothing. I mean—sorry. I'm not—feeling well."

Henry looks awkward. Not like before, in our other life. It's all gone.

"I should go." But I can't move.

He tilts his head. His face softens. "I was in the same boat a few days ago."

"Same boat?" Sinking boat.

"Yeah. Just feeling pretty low."

"One of those days."

"My girlfriend." There's that knife again. "She's moving. Job at the London Symphony. I don't know if we're gonna make it work."

"Oh." I can't breathe. "Sorry."

ACT III
SCENE 2

Lights up. The DOCTOR *and the* PLAYWRIGHT *face off.*

DOCTOR

What did you just say?

PLAYWRIGHT

You're not a real shrink. But you know that. Not sure why you look so stunned.

DOCTOR

Why the fuck would you say that?

PLAYWRIGHT

Oh, for fuck's sake. Get over yourself. If what I said isn't true, then why do you look like you're about to die? Anais told me. In an email, obviously. She doesn't hold that against you either. If you ask me, she's too good for you. But love works in mysterious ways.

DOCTOR

Look, I don't know what you think you know—

PLAYWRIGHT

Shut up. This scene is boring already. Anais told me. You killed her. But first there was the holdup. You, a bank robber? That's pretty old-school. And then you ended up here, with me. But you're not a real doctor. It's written all over your guilty mug.

(*Beat*)

DOCTOR

You calling the cops?

PLAYWRIGHT

About? (*shrugs*)
That ain't my scene to write, as Maxine would say.

DOCTOR

What do you want in return?

PLAYWRIGHT

I want you to tell me in your own words. All the world has a story to tell, and they want someone to tell it to. I'm your someone.

(*Beat*)

All my characters once lived here, on our side of the curtain. But I've never been able to talk to them—in the flesh. I'm always with the dead.

(*Beat*)

Except Henry—Henry is the only one who's ever come back. To life, I mean.

(*Beat*)

But he doesn't remember. None of it.

(*Beat*)

DOCTOR

You're still so lucky. I wish I was that lucky.

PLAYWRIGHT

You are.

DOCTOR

I'm damned. That's what I am. I'm a monster. And I'm good at it. I know no one, and no one knows me.

(Beat)

Every night I see her face. I never believed in a soul. Till I lost mine.

Blackout

MAXINE

to: rememberyourlines@playmail.com
from: maxinedoyle@playmail.com
date: December 1, 2015
subject: Benny in Brooklyn

My dearest Playwright,

I took a cab to Brooklyn. Let me start there.

I lost the diary I was keeping—excessive imbibing is likely to blame—so I shall write the rest of it on this contraption.

The wind was up; it cut through me as I went from curb to car. Strange that it was chilly in early September. Perhaps the chill was in my heart, and I am remembering the weather wrongly. I suppose for the purposes of our play it matters not whether it was windy or still.

Darkness was upon me, within and without. Can you believe I remember what shoes I was wearing? How strange. How frivolous. I was wearing hot-pink satin heels, chosen because they gave me courage.

The gun should have given me courage. It didn't—I was depending on the shoes.

It was the most frightening taxicab ride of my life. All I could think about was Benny's heartless eyes. The driver kept running at the mouth: "You all right, little miss? You're mighty quiet tonight." I don't have the faintest notion of anything else he said.

After the driver let me out on the corner I stood there for some minutes, trembling, knocking my knees something fierce. I kept a hand on the gun in my pocket. Hell, who would ever have imagined me as a gunmiss on a Brooklyn street corner. Everything seemed hell and worse than hell. Follies and Lillian Gish were dead to me. Strange, I thought of Celia Cooney, the famous Bobbed-Haired Bandit, handling herself and her baby automatic with steely aplomb—before she got nabbed by the coppers, anyway. Never did I dream I would need inspiration from the likes of Celia Cooney.

I walked to Fifty-Three Madison Street and knocked on Benny's hovel. He answered straight away, as though he'd been standing just inside the door, waiting.

"Fancy seein' you here, little lady. Come on in."

"Don't be crazy, I'm not coming in there. Let's walk."

Benny shrugged. "Suits me."

We made our way down the block. The street was empty and quiet.

"Ya got the money?"

"Yes."

"Ain't that grand."

Out of the corner of my eye I could see him peering at me, like he was trying to figure something. I kept my sight right ahead.

"Say, have ya read the papers?"

"I don't read newspapers. I'd rather spend my time on elocution and other things necessary to the life of a thespian."

"Hmm. Interestin'. So does that mean ya don't know?"

"Know what?"

"Vance Campbell's dead. He got croaked in his hotel room, a real messy scene. Real messy."

I stopped walking and turned to Benny. I had so many damn things to cry about, it was easy to summon the tears. "Oh my God, he's dead? Is it true? God in heaven, how dreadful. What on earth happened?"

"Someone bashed him and took his dough."

He paused and stared at me for what felt like an awful long time. I slipped a hand in my pocket, grasping for the cool touch of my baby automatic.

"Seems you were one of the last to see 'im alive."

"I assure you he was very much alive when I left him."

"I never saw you leave."

"So? Maybe you weren't looking hard enough."

"I waited in the lobby."

"Look, I don't have to answer to you."

"Oh, I think you do. If it weren't for the fact womenfolk ain't killers, I'd wonder about you. But a little china-doll frail ain't the type. So who do ya think croaked Vance?"

"I haven't the faintest. But it sure as hell wasn't me. There's no way I could bash a man with a fireplace poker. Must've been some demented goon, they're everywhere."

Benny looked at me another long minute and then started walking. I let go the steely muscle in my pocket. Everything was going to be—

"Ya sure ya brought all the clams? All five hundred?"

"Yes. I'm not making a habit of it."

"We'll see about that."

We rounded a corner. The street was dark and silent. Not a soul about. We walked for a bit, not a word between us. Strange, like we were a couple out for a late-night stroll. Then Benny stopped dead in his tracks.

"You said ya don't read newspapers."

"That's right, I don't." Stupid me. No idea what he was on about.

"Then how do you know Vance Campbell got croaked with a fireplace poker?"

Goddammit. My heart stopped and for the life of me I couldn't think what to say.

"Whatsa mattuh?" Benny growled, his menacing self in full swing. "Cat got yer tongue?"

I pulled the money out and thrust it at him. "Here. Take it. I guess you're used to taking money from ladies. I've got to be getting back. Robert'll wonder."

Benny snatched the cash without taking his eyes off me. "You haven't answered the question."

"I don't know what you're talking about. Goodnight to you."

I turned on my heel but Benny grabbed my arm, his grip digging deep in bone.

"Answer the question."

"Lucky guess. That's all. Now let go of me or I will scream my lungs out."

"Wait just a minute, sweetheart. This is very interestin' infuhmation. It just might be that a few coppers'll wanna know about your lucky guess. They may wanna see the photos of you goin' up to Vance's room too."

"Fuck you! You filthy lowlife—scram!" I tried to jerk my arm away. Benny was hanging on come hell or high water.

"Relax, dollface. I think it's time we went back to my room and had a proper talk. We got some new things tuh negotiate. Well, well, well, looks like I found my new quiff."

"Fuck you! I ain't nobody's whore!"

"Yer old man would disagree."

I spat square in his face. He wound up and clocked me hard. I fell to the sidewalk. I'd like to say what happened next is blurry. It's not. It's clear as a spring stream. I got to my feet, pulled out my baby automatic, and clocked Benny back with two jabs of lead. Fresh in my mind is the look of pure surprise on his face before he fell. He sure as hell never saw that coming.

My heart was going hog wild. I took a fast gander up and down the street. Silent as the dead. I made sure Benny was croaked, snatched my five hundred clams from his cold clutches, and hightailed it out of there, down the block and around the corner, as fast as my getaway gams would carry me. The satin shoes that gave me gumption in the face of a scoundrel now gave me surprising speed. On second thought, it was croaking a man that gave me surprising speed. My second dead doornail. I did what I had to do.

I ran and ran and ran. I stopped and coughed my cookies, then I ran some more. My heel broke so I hobbled for half a block, till a taxicab came along and obliged my frantic hailing.

"Where to, miss?" The driver's Brooklyn accent was thick as Benny's.

"Mm-man-man-man—"

"Manhattan? Is everythin' Jake, miss? Ya look like you've seen a ghost."

"Everything's f-fine. I'm, uh, j-just late g-getting home. My husband's w-waiting for me."

"Aw, I got it. Hope he's not real sore. I'll step on it."

It took a fierce effort not to cough my cookies again in the cab. Benny's eyes were staring at me, his blank, wide-open eyes. Those eyes been hot on my tail ever since.

The nights are long, dear Playwright, and I don't sleep a wink. I walk that dark street in Brooklyn, I escape the hotel from hell.

When I walked into my apartment, I collapsed in a heap. No chance to have the world's biggest bawl. Robert's voice came sharp from the living room, cutting into the raw bones of me.

"Maxine! Where have you been?"

I jumped up right quick.

Robert appeared in the foyer. "Where on earth were you? You said you had the influenza."

Good goddamn, I didn't need to be afraid of one more man. Don't forget, though—I'm an actress. As if I'd ever let you forget.

"I did. I mean, I do." I bent double and started hacking up a lung.

"Where in God's name did you go? What the hell are you doing out of bed?"

"I-I went for some h-headache p-powder." I didn't have to feign weakness. I felt faint as faint could be. "But I n-never made it."

I collapsed into Robert's arms, somehow having the presence of mind to keep a hand on the bean-shooter in my pocket.

"Oh Maxine, sweetheart, you should have called me." He carried me down the hall.

"I d-didn't, didn't want to t-trouble you. I'm fine, r-really."

Robert set me down on my bed, his face all creased with worry. He clamped a big hand on my little forehead. Too rough for a nursemaid. I was sweating like a plow-horse, my body playing the role of fever with operatic aplomb.

"Good God, you're burning up. I'm calling the doctor."

"No! I just want some t-tea. Could you please put the k-kettle on?"

"Fine, I'll make tea while we wait for the doctor. Get into your night things."

The moment Robert was out of the room I stowed the baby automatic. Then I tore off my clothes—another set in need of burning, damn it—and put on the most innocent lily-white nightgown I could lay hands on. Once I was in bed, I felt as if I would stay there for all eternity.

Two hours later, the doctor had been and gone. No fooling, I really did have the chills and a burning fever. I'd taken some vile-tasting medicine, and the doctor was to come back in the morning.

"Maxine," I heard Robert say, somewhere in the fog. "I can't stay. My wife. I'll be back tomorrow."

And then he was gone.

I didn't stay in bed for all eternity. I stayed in bed for the next two weeks. After I got well, I missed that influenza something terrible. Hell's bells, it was the only time after Vance and Benny croaked I was able to sleep till morning.

When I was strong enough to get out of bed for more than a pocketful of minutes, Robert was on hand with roses. The flowers reminded me of the mirror in Vance's room.

Robert brought me newspapers while I was indisposed. I read all about the Vance Campbell investigation, the grief of his friends and colleagues, the tributes pouring out of Hollywood and Broadway. I didn't want to read a lick of it, but I had to be sure his croaking remained a big fat whopping mystery. The police were flummoxed, a robbery gone bad, they were pursuing all leads—I knew in my bones they had a zaftig zero. Benny got a tiny mention, billed as a dockworker shot by unknown assailant in Bedford. They got his surname wrong. Perhaps a stickup gone a step too far, the reporter speculated, the city rife with crime and unsavoury characters. I was skilled, it seemed, in theft run amok.

Robert remained in a hovering mode which had become

progressively more irritating over the course of my illness. "My love, I have just the thing to make you feel better in a jiff. And I don't mean these." He gestured to the flowers.

I was on the sofa under a fur rug despite the resurgence of summer heat. Robert kept wiping sweat from his brow. He looked old. I wondered what I had ever seen in him. The marquee seemed nothing but the faint edge of a fever-dream.

"I have a part for you. You're perfect for it. It's a featured role, a real plum. The kind of part you've been dreaming of."

It occurred to me that Robert may not think I'm talented in the least. Maybe he only ever took a shine to my chocolate-box face. I might have known that all along. Honesty, though, is wrongly celebrated. Perhaps this was a pity part, offered up because he'd thought I was going to croak. Why the hell had I ever wanted to be an actress at all?

"We start rehearsals in two weeks. Do you think you'll be well enough?" He seemed almost anxious, as though afraid I might turn him down. The look I'd wanted him to have since the day we locked peepers in this godforsaken town. It didn't move me in the slightest.

For lack of anywhere else to go, I nodded. "Yes, I'll be just fine. Fit as a fiddle."

"Splendid. Now I must dash to a meeting. Just wanted to bring you roses to celebrate your return to the land of the living. I'll call on you later, darling."

The moment he was gone I staggered up and poured a glass of gin. Skinny and weak as I was, it instantly set my head aswim. I countered with coffee and headache powder. I'm nothing if not a fighter.

My Follies days were over, and I was on to being a featured player. What a dream come true. I turned and coughed my cookies in the kitchen sink.

The following weeks were a blur. Staring at the ceiling deep in the night. Descending into nightmares of coppers pounding on the door and dragging me off to the chair. Gasping awake and staring at the ceiling once more. Sleeping tablets became my favourite postprandial sweet. Still are.

One night in the kitchen, sleepless as ever, I picked up a knife and playacted stabbing myself in the chest. I wanted to. Oh, I wanted to. But I didn't have the nerve. So I settled for carving an X over my—

PLAYWRIGHT

—heart.

In the kitchen I pick up a knife and stare at it. It's shiny, newly polished by Cosette, ready for use.

I call out for Henry, listen for his violin. New York is silent.

The knife is weightless in my hand, just like Maxine said.

I watch it move through the air, this knife, this hand.

I'm breathing hard.

I cut—

MAXINE

—deep.

I paid in blood.

If you want me to say I feel sorry for killing them, I won't. They were loathsome creatures. I did what I had to do. "Sorry" isn't the right word for what I feel. The right word doesn't exist.

I received good notices for my performance. I was offered another part, and then another. The doctor said I had ulcers. I added stomach powder to my medicine chest.

Critics continued to be kind, commenting on my chocolate-box features, my first-rate command of character. I should've felt like the cat's pyjamas. I didn't.

A year later Robert and I took a driving holiday upstate, one weekend when his wife was visiting a dying aunt. Like I said, he was a man I no longer loved nor liked, but some beds, once made, are mighty hard to stop lying in.

Robert was a fast driver, taking corners at breakneck speed, revelling in rotten delight at scaring the wits out of yours truly. He was driving even faster than usual that day on account of him casting a kitten about my immoderate—in Robert's estimation—fondness for gin.

"Maxine, you want to throw your career on the ash heap just when the critics are taking notice? You're ruining all I've created! No wonder you're sick all the time—"

"I don't drink any more than you do!"

"I'm not the one on the fucking stage!"

We flew 'round a corner and then—

And that's when I found you, my dear Playwright. Or sometime after that, I am a bit fuzzy on that front. I don't know where Robert is. I don't know where any of the people I once knew have gone.

So now I have you to write my play, and for that I am truly thankful, though I probably don't say so often enough. It is a privilege to have you tell my story. But first, it has been a privilege to put it in my own tongue. Perhaps all people are the same in this: all people have a story to tell, and they need someone to tell it to.

I shall sign off this missive now, hoping and trusting—oh, dear God, how I hope!—you still have tenderness for me after all I've told (and done to) you. (I ankled to the druggist and fetched a wad of sturdy bandages, should you have need.)

I am a girl from nowhere, and I came to New York City, and the city had its way with me. For a moment, happiness: the warmth of the limelight, the feel of the stage beneath my feet. There is no drug like applause.

Love, Maxine

ACT III
SCENE 3

Lights up. The DOCTOR *picks up a glass and throws it against a wall. Glass shatters. The* PLAYWRIGHT *doesn't move. Long beat.*

DOCTOR

After...after she died, I didn't know what to do. I left a note, unsigned of course. Nobody in Greece ever knew my real name. Nobody here knows my real name. The note explained what had happened. I didn't want people to be left not knowing. I wanted her brothers to know. I never wanted anyone to suffer.

(Beat)

Didn't have a clue where to go. So I came back to this country. And waited for the knock on my door, the cops standing there ready to lock me up. It never happened. Obviously. In a way I hoped it would. I decided respectability was a good place to hide, a way to forget. Met up with my old friend Marie. She forged my medical degree.

PLAYWRIGHT

You trust her?

DOCTOR

Doesn't matter. She died years ago.

(off the PLAYWRIGHT'S *look)*

No, I didn't kill her. She overdosed.

PLAYWRIGHT

So you decided to inflict yourself on crazy people.

DOCTOR

I wasn't that many courses short when I dropped out. I know how to medicate patients. It isn't hard. Don't you want to turn me in?

PLAYWRIGHT

Told you, not my scene to write. Besides, I think psychiatry is kinda bullshit anyway. I just play along to keep my sweet suffering agent from having a nervous breakdown. And occasionally I need meds. Only occasionally.

DOCTOR

I'm sorry.

PLAYWRIGHT

I'm not. Except when I wake up in hospital with an X on my chest. I'm just alone, like you.

DOCTOR

You have Henry.

PLAYWRIGHT

I don't *have* Henry. He doesn't remember me, for Chrissake. And he has a girlfriend.

DOCTOR

He's alive.

PLAYWRIGHT

Next time I cut myself, I may be less so.

DOCTOR

You won't cut yourself.

PLAYWRIGHT

Sure I will. It's how it goes on the stage of wonders. The muses get their way. *Dramatis musae*—they hold the knives.

(Beat)

I don't want to die without love. I want someone on this side of the curtain. I want Henry.

DOCTOR

So tell him. You have a chance. I would give anything for that.

PLAYWRIGHT

You have a chance too. Because Anais still loves you.

(Beat)

DOCTOR

That is the most wondrous thing I've ever heard.

PLAYWRIGHT

Life's a world of wonders.

DOCTOR

I don't know what to say.

PLAYWRIGHT

Ask the muses. You have a number of options. Anais would say, moussaka is love. Maxine would say, you gotta know your onions.

DOCTOR

Will Maxine ever come back?

PLAYWRIGHT

Her play's nearly done. She'll be a star. Broadway or bust, that's Maxine.

(Beat)

She left a note for you.

DOCTOR

For me? Why me?

PLAYWRIGHT

She kinda likes you. Don't know why.

DOCTOR

What did she say?

PLAYWRIGHT

(to an imaginary stage manager)

Lights, please.

(as MAXINE)

"Dear Doc, If you're wondering where I am right now, don't you worry none, there's a Cotton Club on every corner and I'm happy as happy can be. So's your sweetie pie. I've been teaching Anais the Charleston. She loves it. A born hoofer, that one. She loves feeding me her eggplant jazz too. Us gals are real copacetic, that's for sure.

(Beat)

Now, here's what I want to put between your ears: never ever go dark. Find your stage. Look for some way to be glad. If we dim our lights, we're doomed, damn it. So write her a letter already. Anais, I mean. She wants to hear from you. You've got a lot to tell her, and she's got a lot to tell you too. And you make sure my playwright doesn't give up on Henry, that sweet soul. Love is meant for the stage. It's time for her second act.

(Beat)

Make something. Love someone. Tell the truth. Pay the price, be the show. That's the ticket. 'Cause we'll all meet again on the other side of the curtain one day.

(Beat)

Well, I've got to be runnin' along now. But, sure as sugar, I've got a good feelin'. A real good feelin' for us all, the whole cast. So let's make our entrance. This is the beginning of a beautiful story."

Blackout

ACKNOWLEDGEMENTS

My gratitude to Radiant Press; in particular, special thanks to my editor, Kelley Jo Burke, for her brilliance, wit, support, and dedication.

A heartfelt hat-tip to Cathie Borrie, Samantha Beiko, and Kenneth Mark Hoover.

Thank you to Leila Younsi and Claire Iselin of the Lugdunum Museum in Lyon, France for their kind welcome.

And, as always, I am grateful for beloved family and friends near and far, on this stage of wonders and beyond.

FSC
www.fsc.org
MIX
Paper from
responsible sources
FSC® C016245

MELIA McCLURE is the author of the novel *The Delphi Room* and continues to delve into the eccentric as a writer, editor, and actor. As an actor, she has traversed a range of realms, from a turn as Juliet in an abridged collage of Shakespeare's classic to the sci-fi universe of *Stargate Atlantis*. Melia studied writing at The Writer's Studio at Simon Fraser University, and her fiction was shortlisted for a CBC Literary Award. Born in Vancouver, she now divides her time between Canada and France, wandering the streets of Paris in search of the ever-shapeshifting muse, and returning to her actor roots in an indie film about the death of Dante.